Praise for Linda Barnes

The Perfect Ghost

"Linda Barnes's psychological thriller *The Perfect Ghost* blew me away . . . A twisty tale of distorted family rivalries and deep-seated revenge . . . Many readers know Barnes for her tall, red-headed PI Carlotta Carlyle, and as much as I love that series, this stand-alone has to be Barnes's best book yet." —*Milwaukee Journal-Sentinel*

"An eerie, suspenseful stand-alone." —*Kirkus Reviews*

Lie Down with the Devil

"Carlotta Carlyle was one of the first female private detectives . . . and her twelfth outing shows why she's still one of the standards against which subsequent female PIs measure themselves." —*The Baltimore Sun*

"Utterly compelling . . . The story moves unhesitatingly from point to point, and each character encountered holds his or her space on the page with confidence and distinctiveness. The reader can just sit back and enjoy the ride." —*Publishers Weekly* (starred review, one of *PW*'s best mysteries of 2008)

"All the action and suspense you expect from a Linda Barnes book are here in spades, with an emotional denouement you probably won't see coming." —*BookPage*

ALSO BY
LINDA BARNES

LINDA BARNES

THE PERFECT *ghost*

Minotaur Books New York

For Alison

THE PERFECT GHOST. Copyright © 2013 by Linda Barnes. All rights reserved. Printed in the United States of America. For information, address St. Martin's Press, 175 Fifth Avenue, New York, N.Y. 10010.

www.minotaurbooks.com

Designed by Anna Gorovoy

The Library of Congress has cataloged the hardcover edition as follows:
Barnes, Linda.
   The perfect ghost / Linda Barnes. — First Edition.
     p. cm.
   ISBN 978-1-250-02363-6 (hardcover)
   ISBN 978-1-250-02364-3 (e-book)
 I. Title.
   PS3552.A682P47 2013
   813'.54—dc23

                       2013002519

ISBN 978-1-250-03698-8 (trade paperback)

Minotaur books may be purchased for educational, business, or promotional use. For information on bulk purchases, please contact Macmillan Corporate and Premium Sales Department at 1-800-221-7945, extension 5442, or write specialmarkets@macmillan.com.

First Minotaur Books Paperback Edition: April 2014

10 9 8 7 6 5 4 3 2 1

ACKNOWLEDGMENTS

My thanks to those who have discussed, argued, read, reread, edited, and otherwise contributed to this novel, including Barbara Shapiro, Hallie Ephron, Jan Brogan, Sarah Smith, Hector Gomez, Catherine Cairns, Maxine Aaronson, June McGinnis, Gina Maccoby, Kelley Ragland, Elizabeth Lacks, and always, Richard and Sam.

AUTHOR'S NOTE

I have taken liberties with the geography of Cape Cod. Dennis Port (or Dennisport) is a village bordering Nantucket Sound, a census-designated place within the town of Dennis, Massachusetts. The Dennis Police Department bears no resemblance to the fictional Dennis Port Police Department.

PART
one

Doubt thou the stars are fire;
Doubt that the sun doth move;
Doubt truth to be a liar;
But never doubt I love.

Hamlet, Act II, scene 2

William Shakespeare

911 TRANSCRIPT, 3/22, IN REGARD TO CASE FILE #11-0897
TRANSCRIBED INTO TYPEWRITTEN FORM BY G. HENRY, 3/24.

Dispatch: Nine-one-one.

A: Yeah, look, um, I heard a noise, like a crash, I thought, but then I figure maybe it's just thunder or something, but then I'm looking out the window, and I think somebody musta driven off the road.

Dispatch: What's your address, sir?

A: I'm over on Willow Crest, by the pond.

Dispatch: What number is that, sir?

A: I'm at 8725, but it's not real near the crash, if that's what it is. Could be it was thunder, and lightning struck over near the pond, but you know how the road turns right near there, kinda sharp? Heard there was an accident down there two years back, maybe three, fellow ran his car into the pond, so no fire, but I'm thinking this time maybe the guy wasn't so lucky.

Dispatch: Can I have your name, please?

A: Are you sending somebody out?

Dispatch: Yes, sir, I am.

A: You tell 'em to hurry, okay? I'd go out there myself, but my
            knees aren't so good. I fell last fall, wrenched my back,
            and I don't want to do that again.

Dispatch: No, sir, please just stay on the line. I'll have somebody
            there as soon as possible.

A: Good, because if I go out and fall down again, my
            daughter will hand me my head in a bucket, but I hate to
            just sit here thinking maybe somebody could use my help.

Dispatch: You're helping by calling it in, sir. Can I have your name,
            please?

A: Thought you'd already have it.

Dispatch: You're calling from a cell phone, right?

A: Hey, could be it's nothing at all. I can't see real good from
            here, not down that far.

Dispatch: Sir, are you still there? Sir?

CHAPTER
one

Teddy, you would have been proud of me.

I left home on my own, and not just to pace up and down Bay State Road like a restless feline, either. I made arrangements online, but I physically climbed into a puke-stinking cab, pinched my nose during the ride to South Station, and raced onboard the 9:50 Acela. I almost bailed at New Haven because I was terrified, because my Old Haven no longer existed, because it sounded so damned hopeful: "Five minutes to New Haven, exit on your right." I squeezed my eyelids shut and resisted the impulse to flee. Instead, I thought about you. I conjured you. I imagined talking to you, telling you about the strangers on the train.

There was a snooty woman, tall, imperious, cradling a full-length fur, patting her mink absentmindedly, as if it were a friendly dog. Two teen lovers, a Celtic cross tattooed on her neck, a too-big-to-be-a-diamond stud in his right ear, entertained their fellow passengers by crawling into each other's laps. A bald man with a hawk nose trumpeted his importance into his iPhone.

Something makes people want to confide in me, no matter how hard I stare at my book. I wish I knew what it was so I could change it. When the businessman abandoned his cell and adjusted the knot in his tie, I had the feeling he was going to start complaining at me, like I was his secretary or his wife, and then just in time I remembered the quiet car. Really, Teddy, it was like you whispered in my ear, *Em, go sit in the quiet car.* I shot to my feet as though the engineer had electrified my seat, lurched down the aisle, and found a place among the blessed book-readers and stretched-out sleepers where I collapsed and breathed until the pulse stopped throbbing in my ears.

I considered swallowing a Xanax, but as I stared out the gray-tinted window at the passing shoreline, I got a better idea: I could pretend there were thick glass windows between me and the crowds, a bulletproof tunnel running straight to Henniman's. I could keep myself mentally separate, isolated and alone. I could figuratively stay on the train and lock everyone else outside, and I wouldn't open the door for anyone but Jonathan.

When an elderly woman peered at me over her rimless reading glasses and smiled encouragingly, I let my face go blank, willing her to turn away, to not mistake me for some friend's college-bound daughter in need of a comforting pat. I must have looked desperate, stricken, agonized in spite of my careful preparation. You can't imagine how much time I spent modeling outfits in the mirror, changing my mind about this scarf, that pocketbook, these pants, this sweater, before winding up in a sophisticated version of what you called my uniform: ink-black jeans and a wheat-colored edition of my usual V-necked T-shirt. At the last minute I added a black suit jacket because everyone in Manhattan wears one. Simple gold jewelry: a necklace and a ring. All those wasted hours and I still screwed up the shoes. I made a mistake and chose the heels you once jokingly termed my "power shoes."

At the time, I figured I'd take a cab from Penn Station to Henniman's. But I was early. When have I not been early? I roamed the station for eighteen minutes, but they kept making scary announcements over the PA. Watch for suspicious persons, abandoned parcels, don't leave your luggage unattended. The lights were bright and hot, and the air reeked of rotting pizza with a hint of urine underneath. A seedy-looking man focused hollow eyes on my pocketbook, sizing me up for a mugging, so I made the snap decision to walk. I visualized a dot on a map: me. The dot would slide smoothly from Penn Station to the meeting with Jonathan.

I erected my imaginary tunnel and under its protective shell sped crosstown to Fifth Avenue, silently reciting sonnets to counter the boom-and-thud construction noise, the screeching traffic. Shakespearean iambs moved my feet, and the map-dot made steady progress until I reached the corner of Fifth. There, despite the simplicity of the directions, I halted, confused. Right or left? Shaken, I almost panicked. My breathing shifted into second gear, but I knew the numbered cross streets would inform me if I erred. I turned right, which proved correct, and then I simply had to scoot down to the Twenties, which would have been fine except for the shoes.

Never look like you need the money when you go in for a loan. That's what I thought when I tried them on in front of the mirror. New and expensive, practically unworn, they seemed glamorous and carefree, but how can you look carefree if your toes are getting squeezed in a vise?

I was hopelessly early. Twenty-two minutes. So I detoured, backtracking up Fifth, bypassing the library because the stairs seemed too steep a challenge, taking refuge in Saks, pushing through the heavy door, thinking I could stand there motionless without attracting notice, flexing my toes and inhaling the overly perfumed cosmetics-counter air. I checked myself in the mirror over the Guerlain counter, and really, I could have been someone else, any one of the young professional women in their late twenties who milled about the store. I looked unruffled, as serene as a Madonna in a painting.

I didn't want to be early, Teddy. Early is so desperate. And that couch in the glass reception cage? It would have been like trying to relax on the rack while the hooded torturers elbowed one another and rubbed their sweaty palms together in anticipatory glee. I was picturing their evil grins when a frozen-faced saleslady showed her teeth and asked if she could help me.

Jesus, Teddy, the days I waited for someone to say that. The years. Can I help you? And when exactly was it that "Can I help you?" started to mean "Can I sell you something?" When was the last time anyone genuinely wanted to help me? Help as in aid, as in succor, as in give sustenance?

I could have moved into scarves or hats or shoes. Shoes would have been best. I could have sat in a cushy chair, removed those awful blister-makers, and wriggled my achy toes. But I felt forced outside into the cold.

I joined the downtown parade, marching behind a man in a leather blazer chatting loudly into his cell. Each cross street thundered with traffic, pedestrian and automotive. Plunging into intersections, I felt like a chipmunk darting under the carriage of an eighteen-wheeler. I wondered if the leather blazer–clad man was talking to his wife or his lover, if the woman was telling him she loved him or hated him, if he'd continue the rest of the day in lockstep or if something he learned during that particular conversation would shatter and spin him around, alter his life and change his path. Irrevocably, the way mine had changed.

I walked right past the Flatiron Building, herded by the press of pedestrians, afraid to stop for fear of getting trampled. Where were all these purposeful souls headed? Were they late, afraid that if they paused and lifted their eyes to the murky sky, they'd stop, paralyzed by fear and uncertainty, dismount their painted carousel horses, collapse on the bare pavement, and howl?

I worked my way to a corner and turned left onto a calmer cross street. I stepped into an alcove and watched the slow drip of water off an awning. My clothes felt too tight. I needed to pee. I should have used the restroom at Saks. It was time to meet Jonathan. I backtracked and opened the door, signed my name on the list. The guard glanced at my wavering signature with an expressionless face. I added the time in the provided space, and he nodded me toward the elevators.

I was one of twenty waiting in the lobby. I couldn't bring myself to squeeze into the first elevator, and the second took its own sweet time. I pressed my lips together and thought, *Relax, nobody cares if you're a little late,* but my body didn't hear me. I looked for the stairs, but I didn't have time for twelve flights. It would have to be the box.

The elevator stopped at every floor. Pause for the doors to part, wait for strangers to shuffle in and out. Wait, wait, wait for the doors to close again, then hover, hang, while the mechanism debated whether to rise or drop. During the slow-motion endurance test, I ran through the upcoming scene: You'll see Jonathan, you'll shake hands. I wiped a damp palm on the thigh of my pants. You'll see him, you'll shake hands.

The new receptionist looked like a replica of the old receptionist: young, remote, plastic. I gave my name, and she invited me to take a seat on the agony couch. I stood by the bookshelf instead, pretending to read the titles of upcoming releases.

The latest as-told-to T. E. Blakemore, front and center, was well displayed. The cover credit, long sought, was no more than our hard-won due, and it took an effort to keep my hands from paging to the inside back flap and staring at your photograph. You were such a splendid public face for us. So charming and witty, so quick with a clever remark. I didn't need to open the book to see you. Remember? Such a bitterly cold day, and I wanted the frozen Charles River in the background? I wanted that glint in your eye, that devil-may-care smile, tousled hair, craggy face. The wind snatched your hat off.

"Em? Are you okay?"

Jonathan, starched white shirt, navy suit pants belted too high, tie slightly off center, stood in front of me and I had no idea how long he'd been there. He looked exactly like the editor he was, the indoor pallor, the wire-rimmed glasses, the narrow, stooped shoulders. His right arm was extended as though he'd stuck it out for a handshake and gotten no response.

"Bring us some water, please," he ordered the receptionist. "We'll be in my office." He placed a hand between my shoulder blades and propelled me down the hallway. "You're not going to faint, are you?"

I told him I was all right.

"You did faint," he said accusingly. "Once."

I concentrated on the rush of air entering and leaving my nostrils. It started, anyway, the rapid heartbeat, the sudden feeling of suffocation. The mind knows no end of dread, and if it does, the body takes over.

But, Teddy, I didn't faint.

I didn't handle it perfectly. Jonathan asked if I needed a paper bag to breathe into, so I was far from perfect, but I perched on a chair and composed myself and asked Jonathan how he was doing.

He admitted he was fine while gazing at me as though I might detonate my bomb-vest. The door burst open, and the receptionist thrust two bottles of Poland Spring into his outstretched hands.

The water slid down my throat, deliciously icy, while he asked about Marcy, whether she was coming to the meeting. When I told him it would just be me, he said he wasn't disappointed, au contraire, he was delighted. Trying to be gallant, but I could see how uncomfortable he was. And I thought I could use that to my advantage. You know how good I am at staying quiet. He squirmed, then managed a weak smile and asked what he could do for me.

I didn't answer.

"I hope you're not worried about the advance. It's a heartless business, all right, but nobody's going to give you any trouble."

"Jonathan," I said, "listen to me. You can't cancel this book."

The words spoken; the battle joined.

He pushed back his chair, stood, and took three steps to the window, where he fussed with the angle of the blinds. He had a good view; a tiny closet of an office, but a glorious panorama of rooftops.

"I'll finish the book," I said. "I know: Teddy's not here—but I can do it. You can put it out as a Blakemore, or you can use my name alone—whichever works for you."

He kept his focus on the sky, as though waiting for a fireworks display. "I don't know that we can go along with that."

The royal *we*. The evasive, weaseling *we*. As if it weren't Jonathan himself who had stabbed me through the heart. As if he hadn't cast his vote of no confidence.

He returned to his desk and lowered himself into his chair. "I'm sure when you think things over, you'll realize it's for the best. You must be completely overwhelmed. Distraught." If I hadn't frozen him with my eyes, he might have leaned over and patted my hand.

"Teddy and I were colleagues," I said. "Colleagues. Not lovers."

"I thought—"

"A lot of people thought." My throat dried up, and I took a hasty swig of Poland Spring.

"Don't get yourself in a snit about repaying the advance right away. Take your time. We all know that—"

"Time is what I need. Time to finish the book."

"Em, we've been over this—"

"Jonathan, what do you imagine my role was in the partnership?"

"I'm sure you did all—"

"I wrote the last book. Every word in it is mine."

"Teddy's reputation sold this project. You know that. Garrett Malcolm could have had anybody. He asked for Teddy."

"Teddy? Or T. E?"

He glared at me like I was parsing him too closely, nitpicking.

"Jonathan. I'm the E. I'm the Moore."

"You don't handle the interviews."

"I can manage the rest of the interviews," I said, and the minute I said it, Teddy, I knew I could do it. "There aren't that many. I have all Teddy's tapes. He was almost done when . . ." I swallowed. "I have entire chapters of a finished manuscript. The early years are complete."

"But—"

"I have a contract."

Jonathan took some time unscrewing the cap on his bottled water. "The contract is an agreement with the two of you as the single legal entity T. E. Blakemore."

"You could make it happen, Jonathan."

"Malcolm can't delay. He's got other commitments."

"Can't or won't?"

"When you're Garrett Malcolm, it doesn't much matter, does it?"

"It's basically follow-up now. A few meetings."

"He liked Teddy."

"Everyone liked Teddy."

Jonathan wasn't expecting me to agree with him. It threw off his timing. He fidgeted, then addressed himself to his desk blotter. "Malcolm won't like working with a woman."

"Jonathan, that's exactly why I didn't bring Marcy in on this. I didn't want her to threaten you with a discrimination lawsuit." The thought had truly never entered my head; it was like my tongue was talking without me.

12

"It's that he's had bad luck with . . . I didn't mean—" He sputtered to a halt.

I knew I had him worried, that I'd somehow grabbed his attention, made him reconsider. "There would be a great deal of public sympathy for my position."

"The project can't be late."

"Why not? It's not like Malcolm's in the news every day. He's an icon. He'll still be an icon."

"You're serious about this."

"Completely."

He gave me a careful once-over; I tried to look like a woman who'd never fainted in her life.

"What about the other interviews?" he asked. "Not the sessions with Malcolm. The prepublication interviews, the media, the talk shows?"

I gave him my best smile. "What Teddy used to say: 'We'll burn that bridge when we come to it.'"

He tapped his fingers on his desk, swiveled his chair, sipped his drink. "Malcolm won't like it."

"But he'll agree to it. He'll agree if you tell him it will be fine, that the book will be everything it would have been if Teddy were still here. He trusts you, Jonathan."

He stared at his hands. "I don't know."

"I need this book, Jonathan. That's my bottom line. If you go after the advance, I'll fight you every step of the way."

"Em, I have to say I'm surprised." He raised his eyebrows and looked at me as though he were seeing me for the first time.

"I'll fight. I want you to be clear on that." My heart was racing, pounding like it was trying to jump out of my chest.

His tongue edged between his teeth. "I'll have to talk to some people."

"You do that."

"And Malcolm will have to agree to give you access."

"I'm sure you can manage that, Jonathan. He signed the contract, too."

I watched as Jonathan carefully balanced the pluses and minuses, the possibility of another bestseller, the threat of a lawsuit, the difficulty of dealing with a woman who might faint.

"I'll see what I can do," he said finally.

"I won't keep you then." Terrified my knees would buckle at each rapid step, I made it down the corridor, onto the turtle-slow elevator, all the way outside and around the corner before I collapsed on a concrete planter, drawing deep heaving breaths.

It hadn't gone that badly; it hadn't gone terribly wrong. He hadn't refused me. A passing jogger smiled, and I raised my face to the sun.

CHAPTER
two

Garrett Malcolm

From Wikipedia, the free encyclopedia

Garrett Justus Malcolm, born December 4, 1962, is an American actor, producer, screenwriter, and director. He is a member of the renowned Malcolm family of American actors, son of Ralph Malcolm and the British actress Eve Hester, and

Born	December 4, 1962
	Falmouth, Massachusetts, U.S.
Occupation	actor, director, producer, screenwriter
Years active	1966–present

grandson of Harrison Malcolm. He first appeared on stage at the age of four as a page boy in *Henry the Fourth*, a production starring his grandfather. He continued to act throughout his childhood at his father's Cranberry Hill Theater on Cape Cod. His first Broadway role was in his father's production of *Macbeth* (1968).

Spouse	Claire Gregory (m. 1992–1998)
Parents	Ralph Malcolm
	Eve (Hester) Malcolm
Relatives	Harrison Malcolm (grandfather);
	Ella Garrett (aunt)

Following a turbulent childhood marked by drug and alcohol abuse and three stints in rehab, he successfully made the transition from child prodigy to adult actor, appearing in the romantic comedies *French Kiss, Twisted Silk*, and *Bryony Falls Express,* for which he was nominated for a Golden Globe Award as Best Actor in a Supporting Role. In 1986, he formed Cranberry Hill Productions, named for his father's Cape Cod estate and theatrical company, and began writing screenplays.

The first Cranberry Hill production, shot on location in and around the Malcolm estate, was the immediately successful action/adventure film *Blue Flame* (1988), which introduced the actor Brooklyn Pierce in the role of Benjamin Justice. Malcolm's original screenplay was nominated for both a Golden Globe and an Oscar and stunned many critics when it won the Academy Award. *Green Gem* (1990), the sequel to *Blue Flame,* won nominations for Best Director as well as Best Original Screenplay, while Pierce was recognized with a Golden Globe win as Best Actor. Claire Gregory costarred with Pierce in *Red Shot* (1992), which was nominated for seven Golden Globes and three Academy Awards. Gregory won the Oscar for Best Actress. She and Malcolm were wed later the same year.

Taking a break from action/adventure, Malcolm cowrote and directed two comedies starring Claire Gregory, *Rip Tide* (1995) and *Still Moon* (1996). *The Savage Place* (1998) won Malcolm his second Academy Award, this one for Best Director. *Heartbeat* (2002) brought another nomination for Best Original Screenplay.

He was recognized as one of *People* magazine's Most Beautiful People in 1998, 1999, and 2000. He has a reputation for publicity avoidance and has clashed with paparazzi on his secluded estate.

In 2007, he won an Emmy Award for his televised version of Eugene O'Neill's *A Moon for the Misbegotten.*

CHAPTER
three

I got the contract, Teddy; I got it.

    I was dredging through the e-mail when Jonathan called. Henniman's forwarded seventy-eight messages, most of them old and originally addressed to you, but others, mainly condolences, for me. There were e-mails from condolers I'd never heard of, famous names I'd never met. They made me blink back tears, although none of them got to me the way Marcy's did, the card she sent; she absolutely adored you, Teddy. Jonathan hadn't weeded out the junk mail, so I read ads for male-enhancement products and online-only prescription drug sales, as well as a cryptic message from <McK> saying he knew you'd be interested and giving a Web site URL. The site was password protected. I tried your usuals, but no luck.

An online dating Web site, Teddy? One of those?

Henniman's also sent information on media events, which made me swallow convulsively. Did Jonathan imagine I'd do the same TV talk shows you handled so splendidly, so nonchalantly? I was pondering the question when the phone shrilled.

As Jonathan spoke the golden words, I relaxed my death grip on the receiver and the scraggy lawn behind the apartment building blazed Technicolor green. Tap dancers and a marching band materialized; a shaft of sunshine pierced the soggy gloom. Alas, Jonathan didn't know when to quit. He kept on talking until a massive wave of thunderclouds gathered on the horizon. Henniman's would stand by the contract, but there would be *no deadline delay*, no delay at all, period. Jonathan had gone ahead and reserved a slot for me to meet with Malcolm *tomorrow,* which I would need to confirm *as soon as possible.* We needed to move with all due haste because the PR campaign was set in concrete, *which was definitely a lie.* The powers that be believed I couldn't possibly make the deadline. They were setting up hoops for me to jump through and the minute I failed, they intended to drop me a page of legalese from the executive suite, stating that I was heretofore in default of contract, which they therefore wished to cancel forthwith, and would I please promptly remit a check in the full amount of the advance?

I scribbled the phone number for Malcolm's personal assistant on a scrap of paper. Jonathan could have fought for me, fought for more time. He could have, but he didn't, the slime-covered beast, the utter bastard. Why would he? No one ever fought for me but you.

What would have become of me without you, Teddy? To say I was scared when I started college is to minimize the boundaries of terror. My vocal cords wither at the memory of my first day at BU, me, the homeschooled hermit who'd chosen lectures held in vast halls where I planned to meld with the seat cushions. I never so much as considered a seminar because if you were one of a dozen, they noticed you. They expected you to engage, and I rarely spoke then; I hardly breathed. Small and drab, I'd become skilled in the art of disappearing, invisible as a stick insect on a branch. Neat, orderly, and mechanically minded, I was easily disregarded; I counted on that. If anything broke, I fixed it. I didn't make trouble and I never looked to others for help. It never occurred to me to seek guidance when I selected classes. Instead, I picked them by their scheduled time. The safest, most studious, least popular grinds attended classes early Monday mornings and late Friday afternoons. I was so nervous my eyelashes trembled, never mind my hands.

I imagine you knew from the way I held myself that I was different. If you'd spoken to me during your introductory Survey of Western Lit, I would have bolted like a frightened foal. You wrote instead, brief notes on graded assignments, and your words dropped like manna from heaven. I read them a hundred times, interpreted them as though they were obscure and meaty hieroglyphics. I decided to be the best student you'd ever had, the best you'd ever have. I inhaled your every adverb.

You challenged me while everyone else ignored me. What did I think about the motif of disguise in the *Odyssey*, the symbolic blindness in *Lear*? You endorsed my ideas about the whiteness of the whale and the double-consciousness of Katherine Anne Porter's heroines. You said I had a thoughtful voice, insight, an original mind. You declared my prose lively when I was only half alive.

I clapped a hand over my mouth, stared at the clock, and stumbled into the bedroom. Who would bring in the snail mail while I was gone? What on earth would I wear out in the real world? I started hauling items from the closet, tossing them helter-skelter on the bed.

You called me the champion chameleon, the adaptable one, the writer who listened with a secret inner ear, who captured the soul of the subject, made him sound exactly like himself but more so. I'd become a master of disguise at the keyboard, but what blouse or skirt would disguise me best, display and proclaim me a qualified interviewer? I knew what you wore for interviews, but as a man, you had it easy. I knew every detail of your wardrobe. Even when you were only my professor, I studied you.

I memorized you while you lectured, your shaggy hair and wide grin, your slightly off-center mustache. There wasn't a posture or a facial tic I didn't know. Model, mentor, connection, you were everything to me then. Of course, you had other acolytes, and it seemed to me that they were the pretty girls, the alluring, brightly dressed, chattering girls. But they couldn't work the way I did. Their devotion was nothing compared to mine.

I owed you. If I knew how to interview, it was because I knew how you interviewed, what kind of questions you asked, the way you inexorably urged your prey toward the water hole.

I stared over a field of beige sweaters and slacks. You'd have dressed casually, neatly pressed jeans, sweaters. Ties, even vests, but no jackets. Or maybe you'd have worn something flashier, more in key with a show-business celebrity. Garrett Malcolm was a movie star, after all, not a business tycoon, although of course, he'd made millions. I refolded a faded cardigan, stood on tiptoe to shove it onto the shelf at the top of the closet.

I was born into the wrong family; simple as that, complicated as that. Oh, Teddy, the inventory of what I didn't know about the world when you first met me could have filled volumes in an encyclopedia. You never realized the extent of my isolation or the depth of my ignorance. You can't imagine what it was like. Commercial jingles were the closest I got to poetry. I never saw a book till I blundered into the public library. Other students learned calculus in college; I learned to brush my hair and teeth, file my fingernails. I want to keep what I have, what you gave me. What I earned. I know it's not art, Teddy. What we did, what I did, has little to do with the whiteness of whales, but it's writing. It's work, a bold answer to the inevitable question *What do you do?* It's a way to support myself beyond mere and meager subsistence. It's a life. It's my life.

God, if you were here, you'd tell me to stop dithering and get on with it. I visualized items on a list. Confirm the appointment, set a schedule, make the deadline. I'd need to make snap decisions, pack quickly. But I hadn't been to the Cape since I was a child; I was getting nervous and damp-palmed just contemplating the journey. It seemed like I'd gotten back from New York only ten minutes ago.

I did twenty minutes of deep-breathing exercises before phoning. Afterward, I made actual lists on lined yellow paper. The first read: bus ticket, rental car, maps. The second: underwear, socks, shoes, pajamas, pants, shirts, jewelry, pills, Maalox, makeup, toothpaste, toothbrush, alarm clock, deodorant. You would have laughed and said it was just like me to make a packing list when everything I owned looked the same, when I could fit most of my wardrobe into a single suitcase. The third list was divided into two parts. A.M.: take pills, shower, put on makeup, get dressed, eat, brush hair, brush teeth. P.M.: charge cell phone, take pills, wash face, set alarm clock. A ridiculous list for a twenty-six-year-old woman, but I was terrified I'd forget to do something.

I eliminated from consideration the shoes I'd worn to New York, got on Weather Underground and reviewed the forecasts for Chatham and Provincetown. I'd need a sweater, a warm jacket, a scarf.

After jamming the duffel tight and wrestling the zipper shut, I reviewed key scenes from Garrett Malcolm's films, made notes, and prepared to squeeze the last drops out of him. I'd use the same outdated recorder you used, carry backup batteries, but I'd think of the recorder as a prop rather than a necessity, as a badge of the profession, use it even though I didn't need it, not with my memory, and I'd behave the way you behaved, relaxed and forthright. You and Malcolm would have gone out on the town, shared a drink, but I didn't think I could manage that; I'd drop the glass or something. Oh, I wished I could do the interviews by phone. I come across better on the phone. I can talk on the phone. People can't see me, can't peer into my eyes.

I know, I know, you'd say I'm not overly clumsy, maybe you'd say I'm not clumsy at all. You'd say, get a grip. But I have this image of myself and it isn't the same as the woman reflected in the mirror. The mirror girl has flat gray eyes in a pale oval of a face, an unlined face, almost a child's face. She's no great beauty, but her soft brown hair is nice enough, chestnut-colored, really. She's young and painfully thin, but not unattractive. When I consider myself, in my mind's eye, it isn't the mirror-woman I see; I see the waif in Salvation Army cast-offs, the girl with dishwater eyes, lank hair, and bad teeth, the chunky, gawky adolescent. That's the true me.

I watched Malcolm's films late into the night, Teddy. You've seen the early action thrillers, the ultra-successful Brooklyn Pierce greats, as often as I have, but the responsibility of painting the small existential comedies, the likes of *Still Moon* and *Rip Tide,* for people who haven't seen them, loomed like a giant hurdle. Then there were the modern noirs, filled with sin and redemption. Most of the people who buy the book will have watched the thrillers, the Academy Award winners, over and over, so making them fresh for Malcolm's fans will be a massive challenge, too.

I never imagined I'd get to meet him: Garrett Malcolm, actor, director, producer, screenwriter. I felt like I knew him from his films, his voice, the word-pictures you sent back, and the photographs.

I recalled the laughter on your tapes and his deep, soft voice. "Director" conjured images of a demagogue who yelled his head off, but Malcolm's films were different, so why wouldn't he be different, too? He must have an amazing mind. And what a colorful life; no wonder the publisher paid so well. And I was going to meet him, share the same room with him, sit and talk with him. The hairs on the back of my neck prickled.

Remember that baggy blue sweater you left here? I stuffed it into the bulging duffel. Since I'd never wear it to an interview, it wouldn't matter how wrinkled it got. Your scent still clung to its woolly fibers; I could pat it the way that lady patted her fur on the train, like it was a lover, a boon companion. I could wear it to bed. If I felt a panic attack coming on, I could press it to my nose and breathe.

CHAPTER
four

Teddy, just as I was bumping my duffel down the stairs, who should appear, like an unholy spirit haunting the vestibule, but Caroline? I'd padded my timetable for every conceivable delay: tardy cab, Storrow Drive traffic, sudden snow, unexpected detour, but I hadn't anticipated Caroline. How could I?

Diva that she is, I'd have pictured her in head-to-toe black, but she wore the kind of jeans that cost hundreds of dollars instead, plus knee-high suede boots and a shearling coat with a hood that framed her face. She carried a brown Bloomingdale's bag and poked impatiently at the doorbell as I flattened myself against the wall.

I could have retreated, rushed upstairs, and locked myself in. The cab would wait five minutes, honk a wistful note, and depart. The bus would leave without me; the opportunity would pass me by; life would pass me by. My breath rasped in my throat as I forced myself away from the sheltering wall and thumped the suitcase resolutely down the remainder of the stairs. Caroline glared at me through the glass till I unlocked the inner door.

She's a force to be reckoned with, your wife, all jangle and nerves. Slim and mean and restless, a predator, ready to pounce.

Shall we go up, or must we do this in the hallway? Can't you just hear her, high-strung and nasal, the icy correctness of that "shall"? Nature should have made her taller so she could stare down her nose to greater effect.

You married her because she was beautiful, you told me. I tried to see her as you might have, as you must have seen her years ago, but it was hard to conceive of any softness or kindness in that steely visage, any alluring curve in that disciplined body. She was beautiful the way a starkly modern statue is beautiful, not a marble sculpture, but a metallic one. Her profile was sharp and precise, an ice-edged cameo.

She demanded to see your room.

"Office," I corrected her.

"Whatever you want to call it."

"Sorry." I indicated the duffel. "I'm on my way out."

"You never go anywhere."

"I am today."

"But I'm already here."

"You can come back some other time." Another time when I wouldn't answer the bell. I tried to push past her, but she feinted left and blocked my way.

"Are you moving out?" she asked.

"No."

She made a show of consulting her wristwatch. "What time will you be back?"

"I don't know."

"You won't say."

"I'm late. I have to go."

Our volume must have risen with my desperation because Melody poked her head out the door of 1C, the apartment directly beneath mine. The prettiest thing about Melody is her name and the second prettiest is her voice, which was deep and authoritative as she asked whether I needed any help. What help she could offer was limited to the cell phone clutched in her claw-like hand; she was poised to dial 911.

Caroline's eyes shifted as she took in the owl-like face that peered out the door at a level slightly higher than my waist and realized that the interrupting woman sat in a motorized wheelchair.

"It's okay," I told Melody.

She regarded my duffel with alarmed and questioning eyes. "You're leaving?"

"Will you take in my mail? If you see anything piling up? Take-out menus and stuff?"

"You're going away?"

"Don't worry. The van's gassed up and ready to go."

Melody and I are not neighborly. It would never occur to either of us to drop by for a chat or go out for a drink. I keep her cantankerous van fueled, tuned, and repaired in exchange for its monthly use when I grocery shop at the Star Market on Commonwealth Avenue, the one that's open 24/7 and never has a wait at the checkout line at one A.M. on Tuesday mornings. On the rare occasions when I purchase milk or juice for Melody, she is scrupulous about prompt repayment down to the last penny, but we rarely encounter each other, preferring to communicate by e-mail and squeeze envelopes containing lists or cash under each other's doors.

"Why not lend me your key? I'll give it to your neighbor when I'm through." Leave it to Caroline, quick on the uptake, to find an advantage in any situation. She smirked and held out her hand as though I were bound to obey her royal command.

Melody, evidently deciding that her interference might do more harm than good, ducked her head back into her shell and left me to soldier on alone. My breath caught in the back of my throat and I thought longingly of the swivel chair in my office, my own narrow bed, my feather pillow, all the comforts I was leaving behind. It didn't seem fair that I had to face those losses and deal with Caroline, too.

"If Teddy had wanted you to have a key, he'd have given you one." I inhaled through my nose, felt my pulse quicken.

"I forgive you."

"Next time, phone before you come and—what did you say?"

"I forgive you."

I stared at her, flummoxed. "*You* forgive *me? For what?*"

"You know what I mean."

How you used to rant about the futility of arguing with Caroline, the utter idiocy of debating a woman who possessed less logic than a two-year-old. Walking away, taking a time-out was the only option, you said, but you rarely took your own advice and inevitably wound up playing the game, embroiled in another round of acrimony and discontent.

Not me. "My cab will be here any second."

"Teddy said you never went anywhere. Some recluse you are."

I stared longingly at the glass-paneled door. Caroline seemed so strong, so well defined, so overpowering. My heart was jumping around my rib cage like a fidgety rabbit.

"How about a trade?" she said.

I wasn't clear what she meant until she brandished the shopping bag.

"I brought you his notes. And a couple of other items you might want."

You never kept any of your work at home. You didn't trust Caroline not to burn it all, notebooks, tapes, whatever, when she got angry.

"He left some things up at that house in Eastham," she continued, noting my puzzled eyes.

"You've been there?" I was so upset my breath started to whistle.

She regarded me as though I were mentally deficient, impaired. "Of course. I had to go, to see where he was when—"

"It's rented through the end of the month. You had no business there. You had no right to—"

"Don't you dare tell me what I can do."

I lunged for the bag. "Give me that."

"Show me Teddy's room."

She thought she had the upper hand, thought she'd made a deal, but the idea of Caroline in my apartment, in my room, sniffing my sheets for evidence of sexual secretions, leaving behind traces of her overpowering perfume, was intolerable.

A Town Taxi pulled up. I waved frantically through the glass at the driver.

Caroline put her hand on my arm. "I'm willing to trade, straight up, the bag for the key."

I hate to be touched. I flinched, drew back, and tried not to show my disgust. "I'll call you when I get back."

"Everything that belonged to Teddy belongs to me now."

"His notes belong to me."

"They're worth something. They're valuable."

"They're valuable *if* they're part of a book. You need me to finish this book or you won't be able to collect Teddy's share of the royalties."

She glanced speculatively up the stairs. "I could break in."

"Go ahead." Anything to get her out of the way.

She took a single step sideways, halted. She was still in my way, but I thought I might be able to squeeze by her. Can you imagine Caroline picking a lock, Teddy? Ohmigod, she might chip one of her blood-red talons.

"I mean it," she said.

"Good. So do I. The alarm is set, and Melody won't need to call 911 because it's a direct connection to the police department. Not the university police, either. The real police."

"There were policemen at the funeral."

"Policemen?" The word tumbled and fell with the weight of a brick. A policeman had called first thing this morning, but I'd tried to block it out, excise it from my memory.

"Good morning. Hello. Uh, yeah, this is Detective Snow, Dennis Port Police Department. Miss Moore, if you could call me back at 508-555-3872, I'd sure appreciate it. That's my cell number and I'm looking into the circumstances of an auto accident down here, a fatality, Theodore Blake, friend of yours, and I'm sorry for your loss. Like to ask you a few questions about Mr. Blake's work here and so on, so please get in touch. Or you can call the station, that's 508-555-3400, and ask for Officer Rimes. No, better call my cell. Detective Snow. I might not be available the rest of today, but you ought to be able to reach me tomorrow."

Caroline kept on speaking, demanding to see your room, while I recalled Detective Snow's exhausted tone and gravelly voice, and regretted that I hadn't picked up, a thing I rarely do, preferring to monitor my calls. I always answered your calls, Teddy, and I should have taken his. I'd intended to, but my hand had stayed frozen above the receiver. I wondered whether Detective Snow had attended your funeral, ill as he sounded.

"Were they in uniform?" I asked. "The policemen?"

I hadn't called him back.

"No, but you could tell. Shiny suits and lace-up shoes. And one introduced himself, a little gray man? Detective Snow?"

"I never met him."

"No, you weren't there."

It's true; I didn't attend your funeral. It's not like Caroline would have welcomed my presence.

If we'd been part of a diorama in a natural history museum, you could have entitled it "The Wronged Wife." We maintained our frozen tableau until the Town Taxi driver sounded his horn. The noise broke the spell; I grabbed my duffel with one hand, snatched the Bloomie's bag with the other, charged through the vestibule and out the door.

I yelled at the cabbie to drive, drive fast, and he did, screeching his brakes at the corner while I fumbled in my bag for a Xanax and choked it down dry.

CHAPTER
five

Tape 022
Sylvie Duchaine
1/28/10

Teddy Blake: *You were Garrett Malcolm's first editor, Ms. Duchaine, weren't you? On* Blue Flame?

Sylvie Duchaine: My claim to fame and fortune, my dear, and do call me Sylvie, please. No matter what else I may do, I will always be associated with Garrett, and *Blue Flame* will certainly be mentioned in the first line of my obituary. Yes, even when he was starting out, he seemed to know exactly, but I mean exactly, what he was doing. I was at the very beginning of my career, too, so I had no idea what a rare talent he was, how lucky I was. I was—I am so spoiled by having had him as one of my very first directors.

TB: *What sets him apart from other directors you've worked with?*

SD: From the beginning, he has a plan, a carefully thought-out plan, but—how can I say this? One that frees him rather than captures him, if you know what I mean. He knows what he wants, and yet he can make changes in the moment to get where he wants to go by a different path. Like when you're walking through a busy neighborhood and you hit a dead end. Some directors, some writers, don't know what to do, but Malcolm always senses his way around the obstacles. He's adaptable, but he's focused. Because Garrett works with the actors before he shoots, because he takes the time to know them, he gets beautiful film. It's so easy to make a film with a director who has vision, who edits through the writing.

TB: *How did your relationship with Malcolm begin?*

SD: Pure luck. He intended to make *Blue Flame* with my friend, George Terry, as editor, but then there was trouble scraping together the money to start filming and George accepted another film, a dream job in Norway. He recommended me before he left. So Malcolm and I went to lunch and talked about what kind of light he wanted, the speed, the spirit of the film, and before we knew it, it was dark, way past dinnertime. We spoke the same language, we listened to the same music, we loved the same films. We didn't finish each other's sentences or anything, but it was like I'd unexpectedly met someone from my hometown, a missing family member. We were both young, filled with enthusiasm.

TB: Blue Flame *was a small-budget baby, wasn't it?*

SD: My God, yes. There was no time and less money. Not a lot of film to leave on the cutting-room floor. But what he got from the actors was extraordinary.

TB: *You never saw the set, did you? I remember reading that you don't like to visit the set.*

SD: It's not my way, no. First of all, I hate locations. I hate traveling. I think of myself as audience, as the audience's representative, in a way, so I don't like to see anything that reminds me that the film isn't real. I want the film, I want only to see the film, and to know where the story's going, and to work with that knowledge.

TB: *And Malcolm was fine with that?*

SD: Malcolm and I learned from each other. We learned together. I'm one of those Murch-trained people. I cut on the fly, twenty-four frames a second, marking the moments where I feel the need to cut to a new shot. Murch always said it was like jazz, like a drummer knowing precisely when to hit the snare, hearing the music in the moment.

TB: *Were you and Malcolm lovers?*

SD: Whoa, whatever gave you that idea?

TB: *You did. What you said. You spoke the same language, listened to the same music, finished each other's sentences—*

SD: No, we didn't. And I'm not going to go there, Teddy. Not about Malcolm, not for a book.

TB: *It would all be off the record, Sylvie. I'm just trying to understand the man.*

SD: I'm not going there.

TB: *Somebody will.*

SD: Not me. I'll talk about film.

TB: *Okay.* Blue Flame *was such a success that there was a lot more money available for* Green Gem.

SD: The money wasn't that significant.

TB: *But by the time you did* Red Shot . . .

SD: It still wasn't big-budget. Mainly the money went to hiring better actors.

TB: *Like Claire Gregory? Can you talk about Claire?*

SD: God, what can you say about Claire that hasn't been said? Cancer, and so fast, such a tragic loss. God, she was beautiful clear through, like an angel. My Catholic grandmother would have said God wanted another angel in heaven, that Claire was too good for this world, but I don't go there, either. Just a damned rotten shame. Pancreatic cancer, and it was before they had all this gene-matching and long-term treatment. It was quick and painful. A wonderful talent, and the sweetest sweet woman, too. Once they married, I'd certainly never—damn. I'm not going there, Teddy.

TB: *She was easy to work with?*

SD: I only worked with her film, and the only other actress who has that kind of range, that kind of luminosity, where you can see what she's thinking, like she's almost transparent, is Meryl Streep. And Claire, when she was young, had the kind of humor Meryl only developed with age. So—I don't know—do you remember Carole Lombard, or is that too long ago for you? I think of her because of her humor and her command, and because she died young, too. The only problem working with Claire was that every scene, you wanted to use every take.

TB: *It's something to be proud of: the Justice trilogy.*

SD: Those films were such a joy. I was disappointed Malcolm didn't keep the series alive. At the time, it was pure selfishness: I thought I'd never work again. It was such a long time ago, and such a short time, if you know what I mean. After the Bond films, they were the ones, the new ones, the bright-tomorrow pictures. People love them even now, they quote them, they have their own fan sites and blogs devoted to Benjamin Justice. They were the films of our innocence, the one-man-can-save-the-world films. No wonder they're still popular. They were funny and clever and they didn't try to be more than they were: entertainment, date-night movies, old-fashioned fun. They weren't dark like the Bourne franchise. They were free and crazy and funny.

TB: *And they moved.*

SD: They soared. They rocked. The film scores were addictive. It pains me to hear them in elevators now. Makes me realize what a relic I am.

TB: *Claire was already a well-known actress when she signed on for the third film, but who'd ever heard of Brooklyn Pierce?*

SD: He was Malcolm's discovery, the quintessential beach boy. Yeah. Bad screen test, but Malcolm took one look at him and knew. Brooklyn had that special quality: He made all the other actors look better than they were. He had those great eyes, too. His love scenes were electric, even in the first film. By the time he got to partner with Claire, the chemistry sizzled. It was chemistry that grounded the films, made them more than what they were on the page.

TB: *Were Malcolm and Claire an item then?*

SD: Oh, Teddy, you keep trying.

TB: *An innocent question. Just trying to keep the time line straight.*

SD: Then you know Malcolm and Claire were just about to be married. She was pregnant with Jenna, but nobody knew it then.

TB: *Do you think that's why he stopped the series at three? Because of Claire?*

SD: You'd have to ask him, Teddy. And tell him if he ever does another Justice sequel, I'm available.

TB: *Any favorite editing moments with Malcolm?*

36

SD: So many. The detail work that man would do! The homework! He loved doing research.

TB: *For instance?*

SD: Remember the arson sequence in *Blue Flame?*

TB: *Of course.*

SD: He spent days with a specialist from the fire department, learning different methods of fire-setting, deciding on the best technique. So that when he finished filming, I had every conceivable shot I needed, twice over. We argued about that sequence. I think he'd had such fun learning about fire that he thought the audience would like an education, a break in the middle of a tight action film for a little schooling on arson methods. He totally obsessed about the fire-starters, the alarm clocks the terrorists rigged to delay ignition. I used a few quick cuts, close-ups, the wooden floorboards, the damaged propane tank, the flaring lighter. He played with the sound, too, the long hiss of the escaping gas, the striking of the lighter. He was a stickler for authenticity.

TB: *Over the years, how would you say Malcolm has changed?*

SD: Like everyone does, he became more himself. After the Justice films, he took a break. Then he did the two comedies, *Rip Tide* and *Still Moon.* The critics didn't like that. They thought he was taking too long a break, like he'd gone on an extended vacation, but I think those films are way undervalued. Underrated. They're worth watching for Claire's performances alone. They're sweet and unassuming, small but intense. They were much more popular in Europe than they ever were in the States. And then after Claire's death, he concentrated on those two incredible noirs. The similarities in his films, the obstacles his heroes face, and overcome or don't overcome, those are his trademarks. The intensity of his characters, the way they experience the world, the way they persevere.

TB: *Do you see Malcolm as being like the heroes in his films?*

SD: It's too glib, too easy, Teddy. He had a hermit-like tendency from the start; but with Claire, he socialized. With her gone, he shut down for a while. But he came back and made some superb films. And then the isolation, the theater group on the Cape, it's like he's gone backward—toward the limitation of theater over the freedom of film, but that's just how I see it, because you can't manipulate live theater in an editing room. Maybe he feels he has more control as a theatrical director, but it makes me sad.

TB: *Why?*

SD: Because he doesn't need me anymore, I guess, although I wouldn't like to read that in your book.

TB: *Off the record, then.*

SD: It's like he's living in the past. Staying on the Cape where the Justice films were shot, where Jenna was born, working in theater like he did when he was a child. It seems like a retreat somehow, and I wish he'd come back to film. It's not like we don't need him. He's one of the great film talents, up there with Scorsese and Coppola, and *that* you can absolutely quote me on.

CHAPTER
six

Rain pelted down on the Southeast Expressway. Windshield wipers clacked like a metronome, and I found myself wondering whether Malcolm and Sylvie had done it. Did you decide one way or the other, Teddy? Malcolm was drop-dead handsome then, dark and brooding, and he had a reputation for that kind of thing. When he acted, they said he slept with any available starlet. When he directed, he moved up to leading ladies. Would he have drawn the line at an editor, or jumped in the sack with her?

A more relevant question: How had Caroline gotten her hands on a tape that should have been safely stowed in the office? Did you make a copy and take it with you to the Cape? I peered into the Bloomie's bag and checked the tape's label. It looked like the original, so consider yourself scolded for lifting it without telling me. God, Caroline could have tossed it in the trash on a whim.

Now that I've scolded you, let me also praise and bless you. The tape made me remember how I loved the sound of your voice, Teddy, that deep bass-baritone with the growl around the edges, and how grateful I was that you'd taped the out-of-towners first. If I'd needed to board an airplane, interview La Duchaine in Paris, track down Malcolm's friends and colleagues in Los Angeles or London, I don't know what I'd have done.

The bus to Hyannis was bad enough.

I sat bolt upright on the padded seat and calmed myself with a silent recitation of facts: Caroline hadn't canceled the lease, so I had a place to stay. I knew my way around the Cape. One of my few fond childhood memories is of a house—a shack, really—near Truro. Not because of the people I was with, one foster family in a long string of them, but because of the wild beauty of the dunes and the surging ocean.

I'm not sure how old I was, but my knowledge of beaches was restricted to TV simulacra, smooth white stretches of sun-warmed sand. The Truro beach proved television wrong. Brown and chilly, its grainy sand lay buried under a sharp layer of pebbles. The swarm of local kids wore hard rubber beach shoes. My foster father yelled and called me a baby when I complained that my feet hurt.

Once I had painfully waded deep enough, it was heaven to lie back, float, and imagine what a wonderful life I could have led as a fish. With my ears underwater, I assumed it would be understood that I couldn't hear anyone calling my name. It was blissful, the quiet fish-world peace. I felt utterly alone, but free and unenclosed. I wanted to stay in that world, dwell there forever. My foster father splashed through the waves to carry me out, which seemed like a reasonable alternative to stepping on sharp pebbles at the time. He wasn't drunk then, not yet. The sharp crack of his slap across my face was still to come.

The Peter Pan Bus Line runs down to the Cape. Maybe that's what made me think of childhood. For years, vacation to me meant stones cutting into my feet, fear of tracking blood on the floor.

The bus lurched and belched alarmingly. With a start, I realized I hadn't finished examining the contents of the Bloomie's bag. I reached into its depths and pulled out a book of matches, two business cards— one from a realty firm, one from a legal office—and two partially chewed pencils.

I'd have noticed the notebook right away if it had been turned right side up, but it lay facedown, its yellow pages obscured, its cardboard backing a close match to the bottom of the brown bag. I jiggled it loose, found the binding ragged with remnants of torn-off pages. At first, I thought the remainder of the book was blank.

A page near the back crawled with letters and numbers, quickly and carelessly written as though you'd been taking notes or doodling during a phone call. One sequence could have said "JULY," or maybe "JFLY." Another looked like "HMB," a third said "2nd BST BD." The numbers were large, with comet trails of zeroes: 11,000,000.00, 48,000,000.00, 118,000,000.00.

Expert as I was in deciphering your handwriting, I struggled with the letters and numbers. July meant nothing to me; it was April. Had you meant to rent property on the Cape in July? Was the Realtor's card connected to the month? I fingered the business cards. Picarian Realty. Not the firm I'd dealt with on the rental and you hadn't said anything to me about July. The lawyer's card read: RUSSELL, AMES, AND HUBER. I quickly folded it and jammed it in my pocket.

"HMB" rang no chimes, nor did the astronomical numbers. I was stumped and puzzled by the figures. They couldn't be dollars, but what about lira? Had you gotten a foreign offer for the book? Accepted the "second-best bid"? Why didn't I know about the first one, about either of them? One worry led to others, spreading, deepening. Yes, Caroline hadn't canceled the lease, but what if she'd persuaded the neighbors not to let me in? What if no snug picket-fenced house awaited, no bedroom where you'd slept, no couch with the indentation of your body, no desk where I might sit, knowing you'd sat there, too? The prospect drained the heat from my body, and not till we'd crossed the icy ribbon of the Cape Cod Canal, passing over the metal span of the Sagamore Bridge, did I convince myself that my plans remained solid.

Caroline had expensive tastes. Caroline needed the next installment of the advance almost as much as I did. Caroline wouldn't jeopardize the book. She wouldn't interfere.

CHAPTER
seven

The bus was bad enough, the car only marginally better. A cobalt
blue Ford Focus with barely enough trunk space for my duffel,
a midget compared to your Explorer, waited in Hyannis at a rental
dealership near the bus stop. I drove it quickly off the lot, pulled over
at a level spot two blocks away to adjust the seat and the mirrors. The
rain had slackened, so I paced the exterior to make sure they hadn't
tried to pawn off a vehicle with a dinged fender or a hissing tire. When
I popped the hood, the engine looked clean, but I pulled the dipstick
anyway, then opened the engine oil cap and peered inside through the
oil-filler hole. Everything looked shiny, so I got back inside, flipped on

the engine, and walked around back to examine the exhaust, which was fine, just white water steam. Consulting the rental company's map, I reaffirmed the straight shot up Route 6. The map was small, but reassuringly detailed.

I felt powerful driving, even though I stuck to the right lane while faster cars passed at high speed. The Cape's skeletal structure was simple. Route 6, the spine, charged up the middle of the narrow ridge of land, with Route 28, intermittently called Main Street, reliably to one side, and Route 6A, the old King's Highway, on the other, till they converged near the Orleans Rotary and Route 6 rolled on alone all the way to Herring Cove and the Province Lands.

After a stretch of multilane highway, the road narrowed abruptly to a scant lane in each direction, the only improvement over the old "Suicide Alley," a strip of yellow warning markers that barricaded the median. Signs said to turn on your headlights even in daytime. The Land Rover behind me crept up my tailpipe, and my hands clenched the wheel.

The character of the road changed again, multilane, but stop-and-go, with traffic lights, cross streets, and drivers no longer in such a hurry. Art galleries and ice-cream shops prevailed over infrequent chain stores. I passed seafood stands, a chiropractor's office, a billboard advertising a women's clinic, and swept around the Orleans Rotary into Eastham, where all the streets seemed to be called Seacrest or Seaview. Some of the small shops sported colorful flags to show they were open, but more seemed deserted. Ladders leaned against windows. Workmen painted and repaired wind-scoured façades. This far up the Cape, past the bent elbow of the peninsula and nearing its clenched fist, fewer and fewer guest accommodations were open. Signs read CLOSED FOR THE SEASON.

I passed a gas station coupled to a garage that advertised a mechanic on duty. Maybe it was the same garage that housed the twisted remains of your car. That's what usually happened, wasn't it? They towed the car to a local garage. I wondered whether Caroline had viewed the wreckage during her brief pilgrimage. Maybe she'd encountered the cops who'd attended your funeral there. Maybe that's why they'd seemed familiar. I remembered Detective Snow's telephoned request for a callback. I should have taken his number with me, but I hadn't. I glued my eyes to the road.

Eastham was gone in a flash. Wellfleet followed; Truro beckoned. I crept along, searching for Goshen Street. There it was, just up the street from the Dairy Bee. I turned left at the traffic light, right at the third intersection, left again. Willis Road, a tiny gravel turnoff, opened on the right, and the house was exactly as you'd described: a shingle-sided, dormered cottage with a steeply slanted roof, a doll's house, a summer place barely winterized.

The blue-trimmed brick house next door was larger by half. Two fierce women, you'd proclaimed, and one elderly shaggy dog. Guardians of the key. One chatty, one terse, one incontinent. I prayed for the terse one.

At first glimpse I thought she was a man. I kept my eyes down and requested the key. I could hear the dog snuffling behind the door.

"His wife already cleared out the place." The woman was huge and bearlike in a chenille bathrobe. A cigarette dangled from one corner of her mouth.

"I'm his business partner," I said. "We have the rental till the end of the month. I called and spoke to someone named Ruthie?"

Her voice was nothing like Ruthie's. No one would have dared call this woman by any name that ended in a cute diminutive.

She took a drag on her cigarette, and the ash glowed briefly. "Just a minute." The door closed and the dog barked. When the woman reopened the door, I caught a glimpse of a standard poodle's graying muzzle.

"You know that guy in the blue van?" the nameless woman asked.

I denied it with a shake of my head.

"Keeps driving by the house. Stopped a couple times, looked in the window. You gonna be there alone, you be sure and lock up. Windows, too. Ran the van smack over the ice crocuses, didn't bother to stop."

Sturdy blue flowers lined her side of the narrow driveway. I assured her I'd be careful and thanked her for the key.

"He comes back, I'll call the police." She slammed the door. Fierce, indeed.

I tucked the key in a pocket, grabbed the duffel in one hand, my laptop and the Bloomingdale's bag in the other. Oh, the relief of flipping the lock after carting my belongings inside.

The foyer was cramped, the kitchen an alarming shade of yellow, the bathroom tiny. Exhausted, too tired to eat, I shoved clothes onto hangers in the smaller of the bedrooms. It was narrow, but the view was lovely, a small pond, a stand of oak and maple. You'd have chosen it over the drab larger room. I was sure it was the room in which you'd slept.

My mind skittered to the penciled notes on the yellow pad. "2nd BST BD," could be the second-best bedroom, in which case you'd have been talking to the owner of the house or the rental agency that handled the property. I envisioned the numbers and shook my head. You hadn't paid any of those enormous sums for a one-month, out-of-season rental. You probably could have purchased every house on the street for money like that.

I went to bed early, but even with the grace of Ambien, couldn't sleep. Such a long time since I'd left the nest and flown away, yet here I was, perched in a strange aerie. I tried breathing exercises. I tried counting. The plumbing gurgled, and a clock hissed and ticked. I missed the familiar noises of the apartment, the ping of the heating unit, the rain on the windowpane. It rained on the cottage roof at two in the morning, but there was no one to share the sound with, Teddy.

I padded around the cottage twice, checking doors and windows, staring out the peephole.

I replayed your interview with Sylvie Duchaine in my head, recalling that old Hollywood credo about how films are made three times. Once by the writer, once by the director, and once by the editor. Our books were made three times, too, once by the subject who lived the life, once by you with your probing questions, and once by me in the written word. How would I ever manage it, handling your job as well as mine? Meeting, interviewing, a man as famous as Garrett Malcolm?

I heard the poodle bark around four thirty. It made me remember that girl, Barbara what's-her-name, the French lit major with the dangly earrings who used to walk Pogo for you during your Tuesday office hours. I wondered whether you'd ever slept with her, an echo of my thoughts earlier in the day when I'd wondered whether Malcolm bedded Sylvie. Maybe you were right, Teddy, maybe I do brood too much about sex.

CHAPTER
eight

RE: Accident Report
SENT BY: rsnow@dennisportpd.org
SENT ON: March 30
SENT TO: Paul Jericho, Chief of Police

Paul,

Thanks for sending the AR. I'll look it over. IMHO, Lennie did a fine job managing the scene. No way he knows the guy's some big shot, and with so much going on, I would have done the same thing, started things in motion without waiting for the accident crew. The regional guys know that. It happens. You can't keep the roads shut down forever. Things get screwed up, usually in tourist season, granted, but it happens. Sorry I was out of the loop that night, because I know you could have used all hands on deck.

I'm pretty much back on my feet. Had Lennie drive me to Blake's funeral, which was quite a big do. Thought it might smooth Mrs. Blake's feathers, but no guarantee on that. Lennie started the ball rolling on the vic's cell phone records. Guy might have been texting. Old for that, not a kid, but if he was some kind of writer, he might have been texting, or even talking, and that could be why he lost control. Also, sent Lennie back to do a grid search, check for animal tracks. Maybe a deer ran out of the woods. Or a dog. It's fine that he sent the wreck off to D'Arcy Brothers. They've got a good lockup garage, and damage-based analysis isn't time-sensitive. You can leave it and come back to it years later. On trajectory analysis, it's just measurements and formulas. Lennie filled in all the diagrams, so no sweat.

Next is BAC and toxicology. Tricky reconstructing a one-car fatal, but the tox will tell if he was drunk or doped. If this one's going high-profile, you can try to expedite, but they'll push back. No authorization for overtime.

I guess what troubles me most is Lennie didn't bang doors right away to check wits and their memories ought to be fresh. I listened to the 911. I know you think I can ID everybody in town by voice, but this one's got me stumped. It's a bad stretch of road up there. Lennie says streetlights were operational and the vic had his headlights on, but if the guy was unfamiliar with the road, or speeding, and didn't see the switchback-curve sign, even if the weather wasn't bad, he wouldn't stand much chance on that curve.

Shirley says thank you for the plant. If she hadn't made me go to the hospital, I might have made it to the accident scene, but the docs say I wouldn't have got much farther. This way, all I needed was a couple stents. Timing is never good for a thing like this, but the docs patched me up good. I'm home now, making phone calls from the couch, but I'll be back at work before you know it.

E-mail with anything you've got. I'm happy to have something to do, but don't let Shirley know, okay? She'll take away my laptop.

Russell Snow, Detective Grade One
Dennis Port Police Department
One Arrow Point Way
Dennis Port, MA 02639

CHAPTER
nine

Let me set the stage for you, Teddy. Appropriate, right? Since Malcolm seems to be taking a break from movies to do a stretch of live theater.

Time: The present. Act One: The Old Barn at Cranberry Hill.

Malcolm's personal assistant set the venue for the encounter, demanding we meet at the barn since the great director would already be present, reviewing production schedules, inspecting set designs, checking lighting plots. What a busy, busy calendar Malcolm kept! The PA hoped I appreciated that a person in Malcolm's august position, with his many commitments, couldn't take time to concentrate solely on a petty item like a scheduled interview. Whether Malcolm himself had urged him to put me off or whether it was the PA's own snide initiative, I wasn't sure.

The size and grandeur of the estate numbed my hands on the wheel and made me wish I'd rented a better vehicle to blend with the yew hedges and stone fences, the subtle glow of understated and plentiful old New England money. The driveway stretched for miles, crushed shells murmuring under my wheels, before dividing into a web of roadways. It came to me that those huge figures on the yellow pad could be estimates of the value of Malcolm's property. Would you have checked that with a real estate agent? Such huge numbers, if they signified dollars, were likely to be associated with the director.

I followed the PA's directions, weaving between four major structures: the Big House, the Red House, the Amphitheater, and the Old Barn. Distinguishing the Red House from the barn made for a bit of suspense, but I got there, and I got there early because I had the feeling Malcolm wouldn't bother waiting if I were two minutes late.

No one was there, Teddy. How's that for dismissive? I knocked, paced the perimeter, called a tentative, then a louder, hello, and finally entered through immense unlocked double doors. The barn's interior was high and peaked like a church's, but filled with the smell of sawn wood rather than incense. Instead of pews, there were sawhorses, stacked lumber, and several bright red fire extinguishers. Shelves sliced horizontally across one long wall: hand and power tools; coiled rope; buckets; boxes, cardboard and wooden, labeled and unlabeled, covered, open, bristling with electrical cords. The opposite wall was a vast open closet, topped by a shelf of wigs on blank-faced fiberglass heads. Ballerina tutus, monkish robes, scarlet satin gowns, and floor-sweeping togas hung from sturdy rods.

The costumes, colorful as they were, didn't attract me the way the tools did. I fingered the edge of a jigsaw blade and inhaled the sharp aroma of oil and steel. I change a mean flat tire, tinker with balky toilets, fuses, and circuit breakers. One foster dad was an auto mechanic, but I basically taught myself, a good thing since I'd probably have more panic attacks than I do now if I were at the mercy of garage mechanics, plumbers, and electricians. I paced the width of the room twice, listening to my footsteps echo on the floorboards, and came to a halt facing a blackboard covered with overlapping drawings, designs for a stage set. A few sketches were drawn in chalk, more inked on paper, taped to the blackboard or thumbtacked along the wooden frame. Watercolor renderings suggested a variety of lighting schemes, some dreamlike, some strikingly vivid and real.

I jumped about three feet when a door slammed.

"Don't ever smoke in here." The PA, Darren Kalver, thin, thirtyish, with a straw-colored flap of hair and pale eyelashes, was alone, and his narrow mouth looked as unwelcoming as he sounded.

"I wasn't. I wouldn't." I had no reason to sound as guilty as I did. The smell of the bearlike neighbor's cigarette had brought on a faint urge, but I hadn't succumbed.

"There was a fire when Mr. Malcolm was a child. He keeps extinguishers in all the buildings."

"I'm not from the fire department."

"I know that."

I'd hated his haughty voice, even over the phone. You never mentioned him; you probably didn't deal with underlings. He glared at me as though I were a particularly loathsome bug, explained in a pinched tone that Malcolm's tight schedule had changed unexpectedly, but that we might manage to catch up with him at the Big House. He insisted on driving me to the new rendezvous; his way would be faster. I agreed, assuming he had some secret shortcut. What he had was a golf cart so he could crisscross the estate without benefit of roads.

More than once I thought the cart would careen out of control and overturn on the hilly, uneven ground. I clutched my handbag to my chest while the salty wind blew my hair in my face. Kalver chose a path that rolled steeply down to the shore where the Amphitheater sat beside the ice blue Atlantic. In other circumstances, the perfection of the setting might have touched me, but his erratic driving made me so queasy I could barely admire the view.

The Big House was larger than I'd imagined, a traditional Cape that seemed to have grown via various additions into a rambling hotel with a steep-pitched, cross-gabled roof and enough bay windows to keep a cleaning staff permanently spraying and polishing. Kalver ushered me inside, nodded curtly toward a chair in the foyer, and disappeared. I waited for Act Two to begin, trying not to take the long intermission as a deliberate insult, but feeling that someone definitely wanted to put me in my place.

A formal living room opened on the right; framed and forbidding ancestors confronted well-worn Oriental rugs and prim blue velvet sofas. Closed doors, papered with old theatrical posters, studded the remaining foyer walls. I fiddled with the tape recorder and tried to regulate my heartbeat. *Breathe,* I ordered myself. In through the nose, out through the mouth. As the rasp of my inhalations diminished, I gradually became aware of a vocal rumbling behind one of the doors, recognized the timbre and tone as Garrett Malcolm's, increasing in volume, reaching a crescendo of anger.

"I don't know what the hell you were thinking."

There was an abrupt click, then silence, during which I considered escape. My legs were tensed to run when Kalver reappeared and ordered me to go right in.

Act Two: Time: Forty-eight minutes after our scheduled appointment was slated to begin. Place: The Great Room. I don't know what else to call it. You didn't mention that room, Teddy, not its intimidating size or *Architectural Digest* grandeur, not the wall of windows opening over the ocean, or the wide veranda, or the tall Chinese vases filled with forsythia, tulips, and daffodils. I felt awed and diminished, undersized, unprepared. Like I'd come to apply for the position of governess.

"So you're Teddy's girl." The voice came from a desk near a monumental stone fireplace, a calibrated voice, a trained instrument. No effort behind it, but you could have heard it in the second balcony.

Teddy, the tapes fail to convey the impact of Garrett Malcolm.

High cheekbones, a bit of hawk to the nose, a prominent forehead, a big, flexible mouth. Those were the key parts, but the whole was more impressive, like a painting of a Cardinal done by an Old Master. I'd seen photographs that narrowed his eyes to slits, but they were wide now, blue and piercingly intelligent.

I gave my name since the PA hadn't bothered, and added a muttered, "Pleased to meet you."

He lowered his gaze to a scrapbook centered on his desk. "Look, I'm sorry, but I can't manage this today."

"Teddy's girl," and now this curt rejection. My eyes stung. I made them focus on the desk, an elegant cherry writing table, scrapbook dead center, a stack of bound manuscripts at one end, a decanter and glasses at the other. Behind the table, the fireplace and stone chimney. To the left, a portrait of Claire Gregory, a heavily framed, museum-quality oil, gleamed softly under a spotlight. You didn't mention that, either.

I swallowed. "We have an appointment."

"Excuse me for asking, but how old are you?"

I should have worn a dark suit and high heels. I could feel my cheeks color.

The famed director tapped the fingers of his right hand impatiently on the desktop. "I suppose I can spare five minutes."

"That won't be enough."

"Young lady—"

I could have melted under his dismissive gaze, Teddy. I could have seeped into a marshmallow puddle and oozed under the closed door, but by that time I'd done too much, risked too much. I was so far from my comfort zone, such a stranger to myself, that I heard my own voice as though it came from a distance.

"You can give me exactly what you'd have given my partner, the same time, the same thoughtful answers, the same respect."

His chin jerked as though I'd yanked it by a string. "Teddy earned it."

"You and Teddy had three sessions left, three two-hour slots. I'm ready to go."

"And I'm not." He stood, tall and whip-thin. Deep gray fabric hugged his chest, a cross between a sweater and a tee, spun from yarn too fine to have anything to do with sheep.

"Jonathan told you to brush me off."

"Why would you assume that?"

Heat flooded my face. It wasn't Jonathan he'd yelled at on the phone and now he'd suspect I'd listened at the door, eavesdropped like a housemaid gathering crumbs for a gossip column. I was searching my mind frantically, scrabbling for anything I could offer that might change his mind about working with me, when he slammed the scrapbook shut and said, "Christ, they all want to play Hamlet."

"'They have not exactly seen their fathers killed,'" I responded automatically. "'Nor their mothers in a frame-up to kill, . . .'"

"'Nor an Ophelia dying with a dust gagging the heart, . . .'"

"'. . . because it is sad like all actors are sad . . . .'"

"You skipped some lines."

"I know. That's because I wanted to ask if you agreed with Sandburg. That all actors are sad?"

"Do you know your *Hamlet,* too? In addition to your modern verse?" He seemed, if not impressed, amused.

"I can give you a soliloquy or two. But you've already played Hamlet. Successfully, too. A Broadway triumph, a Tony nod."

"I didn't win."

"No."

"Well, then, in my case, you might say they all want to direct *Hamlet.*" He moved closer to the windows and stared out at the gray-green sea. "It's stuck in the back of my brain, a kind of obsession, a kind of itch.

I've already waited too long to scratch it. If I'd done it when I was younger, I could have mounted a production with some kind of integrity. Now it's turning into a freak show. I just got off the phone with an ass of an agent who wants me to cast Gina Paris Graham as Ophelia. Can you imagine? Straight from showing her boobs on the cover of *Maxim* to the classic stage? My God, it was different when I started. It makes me feel old."

At forty-three, he looked ten years younger, vital, not in any way old.

"They want me to do a hip-hop *Hamlet,* too cool for words. Add a musical score. Cast rappers and movie stars and throw away the script. Gina Paris Graham!"

He went on in that vein, working himself up to a fine rant, pacing to and fro, waving his hands, and I watched him the way an audience ogles a star, because he demanded it, not with his words but with his presence, his magnetism. Even if I hadn't studied his parentage or noticed the posters on the walls, it was clear that he'd been born to theatrical royalty. His father, the famous Ralph, had paced the same way, flinging his arms high and low; probably the great Harrison, his storied grandfather, had flaunted similar mannerisms.

"I'm interested in the undercurrents, the subtext. The gossip, the courtiers, scurrying around, currying favor. The liars. Hamlet is surrounded by people he can't trust."

He paused and regarded me as though it were high time for me to speak my line.

"Rosencrantz and Guildenstern," I said.

"Gertrude and Claudius."

"The Ghost."

"Yes, exactly, the whole procrastination foolishness. A ghost, a walking shadow, and it instructs you to do murder, to avenge your father's death. So why the hell doesn't he leap into his mother's bedchamber and kill the usurper then and there, skipping all those soliloquies?"

The long pause demanded an answer, and I gave the best one I could summon. "Because of evil. Because of hell."

He looked at me then, focused on me, acknowledged me, his blue eyes alight. "Yes. Yes, it's a damn serious step, murder, especially if you believe in your immortal soul, if you believe in justice before the final judge, the way Hamlet does."

He lapsed into silence, and this time I didn't speak, so captivated was I by the intensity of the performance. I considered applauding, but it wasn't a show. He was an outsized personality, one of nature's focal points.

"If I didn't think I'd be compromising a minor, I'd offer you a shot of bourbon," he said.

"I'm of age."

"Bullshit you are."

Filled with star-power charisma, he had self-deprecating charm as well. His level gaze flustered me. I found it hard to meet his eyes.

He poured himself a drink from the tray on the desk. "Didn't Teddy get enough? I really don't have time for this."

"What's important is not so much what's in the book as what's not," I said. "The interviewer gathers hours and hours of tape, from you, your colleagues, your friends, but the writer makes the choices, shapes the cut. Think of me as your editor."

"You seem a clever enough child."

"I'm not a child. Teddy trusted me completely. You won't need to repeat anything or bring me up to speed."

He sipped his drink. "I promised Darren I'd get rid of you."

"Why?"

"He schedules me. He's filled all Teddy's slots with board meetings and legal business. So dreary, and now he says I have no available time."

"I won't be a nuisance. I'll work around your schedule." I smiled to show him I wouldn't be dreary.

"So I promised to send you away and pull up the drawbridge. Already rehearsed the scene."

Oh, God, I'd rented the car, moved into the house, hung my clothes in the closet. Big as it was, the room didn't hold enough air to fill my lungs. The lights seemed to dim, and I thought I was going to faint. Then I realized he'd said "promised" and "rehearsed." In the past tense. As though he'd changed his mind.

"Was it a good one?" I said evenly.

He shrugged. "The words 'when hell freezes over' were in there somewhere."

"You were playing it from memory."

"What do you mean?"

"Remembering all those studio hotshots who told you to come back when hell freezes over. When you wanted funding for the Justice films." I would not faint. I wouldn't.

"I was almost as young as you are." He regarded me speculatively. "Which hotshots?"

I ticked the names off on my fingers. "Hugo Esterhaz, Javier Blanco, Gregory Albert Smith."

"You've done your homework."

"I've listened to every tape."

He passed his hand over his upper lip like he was checking to see whether he'd sprouted a mustache. "I suppose you'd have to be tougher than you look. Three sessions left?"

"Possibly four."

"Three. You've heard all the tapes?"

"Teddy sent everything straight to me."

"You seem determined."

"No more than you were when you got the funding for *Rip Tide*."

"From?" It was a direct challenge, a gauntlet hurled.

"Byron Applebee. Twentieth Century-Fox. April 4, 1995."

He stood still for a heartbeat. Then his eyes crinkled into tiny folds and he lifted his glass in a silent toast. He laughed, Teddy.

He laughed, and I fell in love.

CHAPTER
ten

The golf cart wasn't waiting like my personal chariot at the front door of the Big House, and I had no desire to hunt for the disapproving PA. Afraid Malcolm might change his mind, I took off walking, almost running, ignoring the chilly wind, trusting the map in my head to lead me in the general direction of the barn.

Pretty good, don't you think, Teddy? Rattling off the Carl Sandburg poem like that? Pretty good for me, anyway. You probably had him eating from your hand in two minutes. You were such an empathetic man; compassion seeped from your pores. People talked to you the way they'd speak to a trusted family doctor, an old friend, a psychiatrist. You inspired confession like the sight of an upturned collar. You had the gift of ease, of gentle persuasion. My skill is in disappearing, losing myself, clarifying famous people's thoughts in their own authentic voices. I know I have a long way to go before I'm as good as you were.

Soon the peaked barn roof was visible, but it appeared and disappeared with the gradations of the hills, seeming closer one minute, then farther away, like a mirage. The grass was soft and muddy from the early April rains. My boot heels sank into mush.

I felt like a battered rag doll by the time I collapsed behind the wheel, legs shaking, cheeks crinkled from smiling idiotically to myself. I slammed the door, grateful to be alone, surrounded by a precious bubble of silence. Malcolm and I had set a new time: tomorrow at three o'clock.

I was unsettled by the director in person. No matter how well I knew his voice, his actual physical presence was intoxicating, overwhelming. Query: Can the writer ever stay out of the story, keep her opinion of the subject wholly secret? I didn't exactly venerate one of the musicians we ghosted. I won't give her name, but you know who I mean, Teddy, the alto with the ego. I scrupulously used her exact words, but I left in a lot of grandiose statements I might have eliminated if I'd liked her better and wanted her to appear more sympathetic. She, of course, didn't seem to mind; I doubt she noticed.

Garrett Malcolm seemed like a man who'd notice.

He wore the subtlest cologne I've ever smelled, a faint fragrance of fresh pine needles; either that or he had a natural scent that ought to be bottled.

I think he admired my persistence, Teddy. Once I got his attention, well, it was complete and total focus, like a searchlight. As though we had plenty of time, as though all his other work had screeched to a halt. I could still feel his eyes on my face.

I'm not used to such attention. Thinking about it gave me a pleasant shiver. He was magnetic. He was sexy. That's what you didn't get across. Maybe it only feels that way to a woman.

I am a woman, Teddy.

Oh, God, right there in the car, I gave myself a lecture. He's handsome, he's well-off, he's famous, he works with actresses, for Christ's sake. I shifted till I could see my colorless face reflected in the rearview mirror. I wasn't good-looking or famous or rich. I forced myself to remember the painting of his ex-wife to the left of the stone chimney.

Claire Gregory. That would be some competition, me versus she, even with her dead. I can almost hear you laughing, Teddy. She'd been a hot leading lady, box-office gold, when the cancer took her, and even though she and Malcolm had divorced, he'd never remarried and he kept her portrait on the wall. Talk about glamour, she had it; she owned it. Talk about contrast; take a look in the mirror.

My heart started racing and my breath burned down my windpipe. I opened the window because the enclosed space of the car's tight interior was a weight pressing on my chest. *Breathe,* I ordered myself. What would I do if this happened during tomorrow's interview? How would I manage?

Forgive me, Teddy, but I couldn't help feeling that you covered the easy stuff. I'm not disparaging the great travel interviews, and I know you were warming Malcolm up for deeper revelations. That's how you worked, general to specific, grabbing the money quotes near the end. You got great quotes about his work, his stage and film triumphs, but I still needed to get the goods about his bad-boy days on Mulholland Drive. I needed fresh personal details about his marriage to Claire, the divorce, the custody battle over their only child. How on earth could I ask? What should I say? I hated to pry, but I needed to, if the book was to be a success. A small group would fork over their cash to learn about his films, but the big audience, the bestseller audience, would buy the book only if he revealed intimate secrets.

I didn't want him to think me petty; I wanted him to like me. I didn't want to pry, but I needed to know. For the book, of course. It's not like I would normally press for answers to private questions.

You would have framed the questions skillfully, tactfully. If you could do it, I could do it. I could do it and I would do it. The rhythmic mantra soothed me, but it took half an hour before I felt competent to pilot the rental Ford. If it hadn't taken so long, I wouldn't have seen Brooklyn Pierce come walking over the hill.

At first I wasn't sure, but that walk, that tiger prowl, was unmistakable. The one crucial interview we'd all but given up on was a session with Brooklyn Pierce, the actor who'd starred in Malcolm's most successful films. Remember the relentless evasions his agent spouted? Pierce was in Europe, unavailable, making a film; no, he was in a monastery in Nepal, devoting himself to meditation. And yet, there he was, coming over the hill, looking as though he belonged nowhere else but in this landscape, nowhere else but on Cape Cod.

He didn't seem quite real, not that I could see through him or any of that *Hamlet*'s Ghost nonsense. It was mainly that he was dressed for a different day, for warmer weather, a summer idyll. His khakis rode low on his hips, pant legs rolled to the knee. His shirt hung open, displaying wind-driven glimpses of torso. If not a Greek god, he was a blond Abercrombie ad, down to the flip-flops and the sand on his ankles.

Ben Justice had been his first big role, and he'd been more than a hit. He'd become an instant icon. Actor and character met and melded in the public eye the way they do once in a decade. Pierce had played other parts since, but none with that level of impact. Seventeen when filming started on the first Justice film, he would always be identified as Ben Justice.

He looked the same age now, as though time had granted him a suspended sentence. My God, maybe he was here to talk about rekindling the Justice franchise. If I could get that quote, Teddy. I had a brief vision of myself on some TV talk show, me but not me, me confident in the kind of reed-slim suit a TV anchorwoman wears, me breaking the news that Brooklyn Pierce was back as Ben Justice.

I knew what I ought to do: Leave the car, seize the moment, interview the man on the spot or, if that was impossible, make a firm appointment to interview him later in the day. My heart rate, which had slowed, took off like a late train speeding from the station. My hand made it as far as the door handle and stalled. I'd steeled myself for the session with Malcolm, but an impromptu interview? Unprepared? I couldn't move.

Brooklyn Pierce, hero of three of Malcolm's finest films, marched over the hill and disappeared. He seemed headed for the shore rather than the Big House, but he might have been going the long way round.

CHAPTER
eleven

Tape 038
James G. Foley
2/12/10

Teddy Blake: *It's great to talk to someone who's known Garrett Malcolm from the beginning.*

James Foley: Right, that would be me. But I'm surprised Cousin Garrett gave the okay to get in touch.

TB: *I guess you're sort of the black sheep? Mind if I open a window?*

JB: Kinda thick in here, huh? I tried to quit, I do try. I do quit—about every weekend. That better? You ever see me act?

TB: *I don't think so.*

JF: That's very polite, but hey, even if you had seen me, likely you wouldn't recall. Second grave-digger, man in the crowd, spear-holder number two. If I'd used the name Malcolm, might have been a different story from the get-go, but Foley was good enough for my dad, and it's good enough for me.

TB: *Your father married Garrett Malcolm's aunt?*

JF: Yep. His dad's darling sister, Ella, another superb Malcolm-family actress. Never took the name Foley. A Malcolm forever, my mom. You've heard of her, I bet?

TB: *She died young.*

JF: Not the luckiest family in the world, but close-knit, loyal. Played together, ate together, acted together. Lived together at the old place, Cranberry Hill, but it didn't have a fancy name then, just called it "Old Place"—Shakespearean pun, you know, reference to "New Place," Shakespeare's house—and believe me, it was nothing like what it is now. It wasn't dirt poor, don't get me wrong, but it was shabby. Every penny was reinvested in the theater. We wore discards from the costume shop.

TB: *You and Malcolm are the same age?*

JF: You won't believe it, but I'm younger than he is. Year apart, traded childhood diseases back and forth like tennis balls. When I got chicken pox, he only got two freckles. Mumps, I got easy. He didn't get it till way later, and then he got it bad, but nobody ever put us to bed or babied us if there was a show that night. We were child actors, soldiers of the eternal theater in the sky. We joined all the crowd scenes, yelled "rhubarb" and "garbage" when the action called for general hubbub. Did you know "rhubarb" and "garbage," repeated over and over, sounds like crowd noise? That's the sort of education we got. We were taught never to peer through the curtain, make faces, freeze up, or break character. Garrett learned to direct the same time he learned to walk.

TB: *Sounds like a fairly happy childhood.*

JF: We had some terrific times, I'll say that. We didn't know we were poor. And we weren't, really, old Ralph wasn't, not sitting on all that lovely land. If we had sandwiches for breakfast, lunch, and dinner, it was because they were the fastest thing to make. Baloney and white bread sustained us, but we fed on hot and cold running Shakespeare. I learned to read with the soliloquies; they're my ABCs, and I can give you chapter and verse for the whole of the canon. The money went for props and costumes, not bicycles or private schools. And there was more pride than money, a sense that we were on a mission to save the Legitimate Theater. I wonder what Garrett's parents would think if they could see the place today.

TB: *It's beautiful.*

JF: Yeah, but . . .

TB: *But?*

JF: They weren't fond of movies and they hated TV. Legitimate stage was the be-all and end-all to them, especially Shakespeare, and it's not exactly a secret that all the money that went into rebuilding the place, expanding it, came from film and TV work. I mean, Garrett didn't do any legit stage work for ten years. His father thought TV was demeaning, the lowest of the low, opiate of the masses. I felt that way, too, I'm sorry to say. Had my opportunities to do TV, but I was too high and mighty. Mistook myself for a Malcolm. Something Garrett Malcolm never does.

TB: *How so?*

JF: I just meant Ralph and Eve, and old Harrison, too, were ultra-conscious of their status on the American stage. They talked about it like that: The American Stage, Seventeen-Seventy-Six and Onward: We Were There. Joseph Jefferson, the big name of his time, was a direct descendant. That bad Booth boy who shot President Lincoln? Practically ruined dear Laura's comeback in *Our American Cousin*. And Gene O'Neill. Always Gene, never Eugene. And of course, Shakespeare, glorious Will. They made him an honorary American on the grounds that he would have emigrated to the States if he'd only had the chance. And the rivalry with the Barrymores. Oh, the Malcolms told this great story. They were the chosen ones. Garrett's a terrific guy, don't get me wrong. He's better than any of them. More talented. His dad was a harsh taskmaster, a tyrant. He wanted a whole slew of kids, a whole theatrical troupe. There was a time when—

TB: *When?*

JF: The old man wanted to adopt me so he could leave more sons. Can you believe it? He had a thing about it, probably from playing so many

British kings. The only way the dynasty would be secure would be to leave behind plenty of sons. As if my dad would stand for that. Aunt Eve always said she'd make sure I got my share, but the old man went all Shakespearean on her, blood of my blood, and that was that. You'd think old Ralph would have been happy with me, forgiven me, his own sister's son, but no, I wasn't of the pure Malcolm blood. My dad wasn't an actor, and my mom had to be punished for marrying outside the theatrical gene pool.

TB: *Forgiven you?*

JF: Forget that. We're a dwindling family, the great Malcolms, and now there's only the one child in this generation.

TB: *Jenna.*

JF: The brilliant Jenna. Although Cousin Garrett could marry again, I suppose.

TB: *Any prospects?*

JF: Garrett's very close with personal stuff. I got the impression that this book was a high-minded effort about his cinematic genius, that you were gonna ask questions about his directorial POV and what kind of camera angles he uses.

TB: *I'm interested in that, too.*

JF: But you'd rather get the dirt. Like why he and Claire got divorced? Well, no way I'm talking about Claire. Garrett foams at the mouth if I even ask about her family, her mother, for chrissake, her sister. Matter of fact, old Cousin Garrett's the least likely subject for one of those in-his-own-words autobiographies I ever came across. He must be up to something, maybe got a screenplay in the works, something he wants publicity for. Don't even put that in your notes. I don't want him knowing I said that, okay?

TB: *Off the record.*

JF: Off the record, Garrett and Claire were perfect until they suddenly weren't perfect anymore. It was a storybook thing at the start. He was her perfect director, and she was his perfect actress. He could squeeze a performance out of her that would trump anything anybody else could get because he knew how to push her, and when to back off. And she inspired him, especially when it came to comedy. Such a shame.

TB: *The divorce?*

JF: Ugly, very ugly, and probably why Garrett won't speak to Claire's parents to this day. But I meant what a shame about her death. Jenna's the silver lining, but I'll bet she's off-limits for the book.

TB: *I haven't met her or talked to her.*

JF: So Garrett hasn't said anything about her coming back? Not to sign any papers? Not for an upcoming board meeting or anything?

TB: *Board?*

JF: The theater has a Board of Trustees. Largely ornamental.

TB: *I haven't heard anything.*

JF: Well, like I said, there's a kid got it all going for her, heiress and talented thoroughbred. Old Ralph melted when she entered the picture and he was as tough a bastard as they come. I will say on the record that Jenna will be one of the great actresses of our time.

TB: *Where is she now?*

JF: England, Australia, playing the provinces. She's still a kid, what, sixteen? Wow, wouldn't it be something if Daddy's directorial comeback was Jenna's film debut? Hey, don't say that I said that. Pure speculation, but a Malcolm touch for sure.

TB: *Does she go by Jenna Malcolm?*

JF: Who knows what name an actress will choose? But when she makes it, everyone will know. They'll realize right off. She looks like Claire, moves like Claire, speaks like Claire. Garrett sent her away, wanted her well away from the craziness here, taking her falls out of the country, where nobody would recognize her, where nobody gives a good goddamn about the Malcolm name. Didn't want to read about her in Hollywood gossip columns, who she's screwing, which celebrity hangout she's gracing with her presence. You give one good performance here and then everybody wants to get the goods on you, partying with the wrong pervert or doing drugs, and then you're in rehab or jail and welcome to a career as a coulda-been, which is a level down even from a career as a has-been like me.

TB: *Do you still act?*

JF: Kind of you to ask. I dabble in a few things. Investments, real estate, and I do voice-overs, read for books on tape, which still qualifies as acting, I suppose. If I wanted to, Cousin Garrett would employ me as the third spear-holder, but I don't want his charity and he knows it. I don't want his bit parts, either, to tell the truth. I'm a traditionalist and I don't like the way he does Shakespeare up there now. I go by the book, and I don't want any modern interpretations. The old stuff is good enough for me, but Cousin Garrett is always reanalyzing, doing the plays in ways Will never dreamed of. I can't abide that showy garbage, and so we go our own ways artistically. And you can see who has trod the most successful path.

TB: *Wait a minute. You were in one of the Justice movies. I recognize you now. The third one, the one Claire Gregory was in? You had blond hair?*

JF: Almost white. Yep. I was a minor bad guy, Sal, one of the few parts I ever played who had a real name. Brookie shot me on the bridge over the Bass River?

TB: *God, yes. You were terrific.*

JF: Thanks. I only had two lines, but it got me my SAG card— Screen Actors Guild. God, we had fun. That night was so cold, when I got shot, and we did that bit so many times, at the end we were screaming loonies. I thought that role would lead to something else, that's what you think when you're young. You do one role and it'll lead to another role, and so on and so on, up the mountain range, each peak bigger than the next. You don't realize you're at the top of the hill until you're down in the valley. At least I wasn't in the valley alone.

TB: *You're talking about Brooklyn Pierce? You call him Brookie?*

JF: Brooklyn was a blast to work with, but Garrett didn't like sharing the spotlight, didn't want anybody to outshine the director. People talked about the Justice movies like they sprang out of Brookie's head, didn't give Garrett proper credit or respect. Jesus, cut all that shit, that's all off the record, okay? Brookie had a swelled head, too. I mean, how could you not, with the reviews he got, the attention he got. He was young, too, hell, we were all young.

TB: *Are you still in touch with him? With Pierce?*

JF: Yeah, we're old buds. I've been talking to him about collaborating on a screenplay. You might mention that to my dear cousin Garrett, if he asks how I'm doing.

TB: *Sure. And if you talk to Pierce, can you tell him I'd like an interview? I've been trying to get in touch through his agent, but—*

JF: Brookie can be hard to reach. Look, if there's anything else you want, let's do it another day, okay? My head's pounding. That's enough for now, okay? I need another cigarette. Maybe a drink?

CHAPTER
twelve

I congratulated myself: The scrawl on the yellow pad was most likely JFLY, not JULY, and it probably referred to your interview with Garrett Malcolm's cousin, James Foley. You often took notes in a consonant-only shorthand. JFLY = J. FOLEY.

Teddy, as I listened I realized it wasn't your questions but your silences that made your technique so devastating, those long, unspooling voids during which the interviewee waited for the next question, waited, but heard nothing, and so rambled on almost in desperation, answering the question he heard in his head as the logical follow-up. You got not only what he deemed important in the subject's life, but what was vital in his own. You got insight.

Your silences worked their magic in your classes and in your office hours as well. How many times, when you were a professor, did you wait your faithful students out, luring them to volunteer? Remember that girl, Doris, the one who was so eager to get an A? She served as your unpaid teaching assistant; she'd volunteer for anything, even chauffeur you around the city. All you had to do was give her the eye. And wait.

If JFLY was shorthand for James Foley and 2nd BST BD meant you'd slept in the second-best bedroom here in the rental house, the one I'm sleeping in now, then what did HMB stand for? I did a quick tally of interviewees and failed to locate a match. Why had you been thinking about the Foley interview, a background piece we'd considered relatively unimportant? He'd mentioned Brooklyn Pierce; maybe that was the reason for your interest.

I called Pierce's agent and left a detailed message. I tried to keep my tone mild and unaccusatory, but I'm not sure I succeeded. While waiting for a callback, I paced the living room of the rented house and skimmed every other transcript that so much as mentioned Brooklyn Pierce. I Googled him, viewed his fan Web site, checked Wikipedia and the major magazine sites. Not a single gossip site placed him on the Cape; one swore he was filming in Australia, another put him in an L.A. rehab spa.

How essential was it that I get an interview? His star had flickered since the Justice trilogy, but he was still a player. Even if there was currently more speculation about his bedmates than his upcoming movies, a few revelations from Brooklyn Pierce could mean an additional hundred thousand book sales. Hardly as large as the figures you'd scribbled on the yellow pad. I put my cell on the bedside table. It was three hours earlier in Los Angeles; his agent might return my call.

I tried to sleep, but I kept pondering the identity of the man in the blue van who'd peered in the windows and crushed the neighbor's crocuses. Inured as I was to ambulances wailing along Storrow Drive, the beep-beep of backing trucks, the shuffle of the elderly man in the overhead apartment, the strange and unexpected noises of the isolated Cape house alarmed me. A low hum issued from the heating system, punctuated by an occasional bang.

I got up and rechecked the doors; front and rear were locked and chained. I shoved the backs of kitchen chairs under the handles for good measure, found my purse where I'd left it on the counter, and scrabbled in its depths for my bastard file.

How you used to laugh about the bastard file; when I first mentioned it, you thought I meant "file" as in manila file folder, or possibly computer file. You never considered a metal file, a tool, till I held it under your nose. Clutching the file, admiring its heft in my hand, I climbed the creaky stairs. The wind whistled through the pines, a droning accompaniment to the faint pounding of waves on the shoreline. The ocean felt like a looming presence even though it was out of sight. I placed the file beside the silent cell phone on the bedside table.

"Bastard" in conjunction with "file" refers to the fineness of the teeth, between middle and second cut. My file is technically a smooth knife-edge file, but the mechanically minded foster father who gave it to me termed it "bastard" as a joke, with the recommendation I use it only on its namesakes, of which he certainly counted as one. I drew the thin blanket close and huddled into a cocoon near the edge of the bed, well within reach of the file so I'd be able to grab it in case of emergency. The sheets felt rough and icy against my skin. Someone must have changed them. There was no smell of you on my pillow, but I was comforted by the thought that you'd slept here. The wind rattled as though it wanted to knock out the window glass and invade the room. Irritated by each ping and bump, I finally set the radio in between stations so the white noise would overwhelm the rest of the water torture.

I must have doubled my Ambien by mistake because I woke late and groggy. Ashamed of my midnight fears in the piercing sun, I removed chains and chair backs and restored the metal file to my purse. Wrapped in my bathrobe, I spread peanut butter on toast, using sparse provisions brought from Boston. I made a grocery list that included coffee and orange juice, then worked through a tricky transition in a section about Garrett's youth, keeping in mind the positive spin he wanted to place on his childhood.

Today's interview was scheduled for three o'clock. I tried on my sophisticated Manhattan outfit, but it looked all wrong for the Cape. I sniffed the crotch of my jeans. They were ostensibly clean, but when I put them on, they looked unexpectedly grungy, and my all-purpose V-necks seemed worn and drab. Confronting Garrett Malcolm was challenge enough, but when I thought about the additional possibility of facing a heartthrob like Brooklyn Pierce, my heart quailed.

One of my foster mothers wore so much makeup it looked like she pasted a mask over her real face every morning. She wore what she called "foundation garments" that completely altered her actual shape. Another so-called mom regarded makeup and push-up bras as cheating, not only ungodly but a fraud perpetrated on men by girls who lacked character and natural beauty, which came from deep inside or the grace of God, depending. Any man would recognize and disapprove of such fakery, she maintained. That she was dead wrong about men did not deter her one iota.

I patted faint pink gloss on my lips and considered phoning the Dennis Port Police Department, returning Detective Snow's call. They must have an online presence, a screen displaying a phone number other than 911. I could call the general number and ask for Detective Snow. But if I used my cell, they'd keep a record of the number. I hated the idea of strangers knowing my cell number.

Damn. My list of necessities cried out for more than coffee and orange juice. Hadn't Malcolm challenged my professionalism with his query about my age? I felt wounded by the encounter, in need of something akin to battle armor, a mail shirt, a corselet of polished bronze. My chances of finding such a powerful garment prior to our afternoon session seemed remote, but once the thought entered my mind, there was no remedy but a quest.

Detective Snow could wait.

CHAPTER
thirteen

In jeans and faded olive tee, I made the half-hour drive to the Cape Cod Mall. If all else failed, I would wear them for the interview and Garrett Malcolm would look right through me.

The salesladies at Macy's gazed through me as well, and even though I'd chosen the mall for its size and anonymity, at the deciding moment I spurned the big anchor store. Too many choices, a kaleidoscope of solids and prints; too many colors, clashing oranges and purples; too many departments, catering to teens and young adults and working moms; too much stuff. I blundered on, hardly noticing where I was going, eliminating stores based on the merchandise in the display windows. Had I panted after running shoes or kitchen accessories, my quest would have been easier. I wanted to look professional, but I also wanted something more. . . .

Glamorous? The saleslady attempted to finish my halting query when I stammered a request for help. I decided she was making fun of me and started to leave, but she put a restraining hand on my arm. I usually hate that, but she was gentle and apologetic. A plump woman in her thirties, she smiled and said she'd be happy to help me find an attractive outfit. Her right cheek dimpled when she inquired what sort of work I did. When I nervously babbled that I was a writer, she assumed I was the one who was going to be interviewed, maybe on television. She asked my name, so I made one up. She dimpled again and said she thought she'd heard of me.

She seemed to understand how flustered I was, how overwhelmed and confused by the racks and shelves of garments. She guessed my size, just by looking, and insisted I'd have plenty of choices because I was so small. She led me to a curtained dressing room so I could be by myself. The flowered curtain billowed, blown by a fan. I didn't mind the tiny room; it was cozy, like a dollhouse.

She asked what I had in mind. I didn't really know, but I had a guide to Malcolm's preferences: all his movies, all his leading ladies. He liked slim, which I am. He liked demure, which I can be. He liked classic lines.

Maybe a simple sweater. A skirt. Neutrals.

The saleslady balked and said I needed color. Not red; it would overpower me. She said I had interesting coloring, and I thought "interesting" is what you say when you don't know what else to call it. Neither here nor there, that's what another so-called mother said. Your eyes aren't blue and they aren't green, either. Your hair's not blond and it's not brown. The saleswoman, Laura, brought me colors that weren't one thing or another, either. Medium hues and saturations, neither green nor blue, neither blue nor gray.

I hid behind the flowered curtain that served as the dressing room door, ashamed of my underwear. I hadn't bothered with it much since we stopped. I should have bought new underwear first. Laura would think I was some sort of religious fanatic. A former nun. Or a prude.

Pretty underwear equals sheer vanity, that's what the "neither here nor there" mother told me, and totally unnecessary in the young. Men sniff around young stuff like dogs in heat, but wait till you get some age on you, she'd say. When you're young, you think you're gonna fly first class, then life races by, and you're lucky if you get to travel coach.

I slipped on a sweater that was somewhere between blue and purple. Laura dimpled when she saw my reflection and said periwinkle was exactly the shade for me. Said I could wear it with jeans or gray or even black. And she said the neckline was perfect, too, but I wasn't sure what she meant by that. It was sort of a scoopy thing. She asked if I had a scarf that would coordinate, then took pity and brought me a few. One caught my eye; it was like a field of wildflowers. She tied it so it poufed where I'd have cleavage, if I had any. The scarf made me look like I might, and I could almost hear my ex–foster mother hissing about girls out to fool men with their wicked ways.

When I asked Laura if she didn't think it was too much, she seemed surprised and slightly alarmed. She said as thin as I was, I could get away with anything. I decided to wear the new clothes and take my old ones in a bag because I wasn't sure whether I was going to head back to the house or not. While I was paying, Laura asked if I might be planning to get my hair cut before the interview. When I said I didn't know anyplace around there, she gave me directions to a nearby salon, scribbling them on the back of her card.

On the way out, I noticed a store with bras and panties in the window, so I stopped and bought a new bra with more shape to it. Not padding, really, just a little bit of shape to the cups. I tried it on in white, but at the last moment I changed my mind and bought it in a deep shade of rose. The color didn't show under my new sweater, and its secret boldness made me feel brave, almost reckless. I shoved my shapeless bra in the bag and donned the new one, a corselet of lace and color, but a corselet nonetheless.

During the drive to the salon, I noticed color as though I'd never seen it before, as though I'd bought new contact lenses instead of new clothes. The whole business of color—bold, indeterminate, pale—seemed strange and different, a spicy foreign taste on my tongue. Maybe it was because spring was beginning or maybe it was the contrast with brick-and-steel Boston, but the colors seemed overwhelming, the sky, washed clean, meeting the frothy sea, and the first green shoots dotting the gray-brown marshes. My usual world was black and white, bound by words and texts, but now I felt filled with color, as though I'd trapped some of the sea and sky in my new sweater and scarf.

Had Laura said to take a right turn at the second intersection or the third? The relaxation I'd felt in the curtained changing room evaporated, and my hands tightened on the steering wheel. I passed an ice-cream shop with a flagpole, a firehouse. The landmarks were right: I must have taken the correct turn. There: the women's clinic I'd seen advertised on the road; and across the street, the recommended parking lot with a single space, like a missing tooth, right in the first row. I filled the gap with the Focus, cut the engine, and made my exit boldly. Like a woman wearing a rose-colored bra.

CHAPTER
fourteen

RE: 911 follow-up
SENT BY: rsnow@dennisportpd.org
SENT ON: April 2
SENT TO: Paul Jericho, Chief of Police

Paul,

Damnedest thing. Lennie went door to door up on Willow Crest,
because there's no address like the 8725 in the 911 call. Woman

named Daisy Hillerman lives at 872, widow of Ernest Hillerman, must be in her late seventies. So her brother was spending the night and the next morning he told her he called the police. They had a big argument about it. She burned Lennie's ear off how her brother never minds his own business and thinks he's a big shot. He can't live alone anymore because he keeps falling down—Lennie says she made him sound like an alcoholic—and his daughter wants him to move in with Mrs. H., but she can't stand him for more than a night. Lennie finally got a word in, asked to speak to him, and guess where he is? Italy on a cruise ship, while his daughter checks out a place for him to live, one of those independent-living places with food, because, according to his sister, he never learned to boil water. He'll be back in ten days or two weeks, she's not sure which. Lennie got the name of the ship; it's a sister ship of that *Concordia* that went down off Giglio.

Lennie knocked doors all down the street, but only one other guy heard the crash although a couple got waked up by the sirens. One house was totally empty. Lennie went back to Mrs. H., who seemed like she'd know everybody's business, and she told him the man lives there just went off to his grandson's wedding somewhere in Oregon. You'd think people would stay where they're supposed to be.

Told Lennie to put something out for the press.

Feeling better. Dropped by the office. Autopsy says Blake died from injuries sustained in the crash. No precipating factors, no heart attack or stroke. Still waiting on the tox.

Russell Snow, Detective Grade One
Dennis Port Police Department
One Arrow Point Way
Dennis Port, MA 02639

CHAPTER
fifteen

The salon was a small, homey place, but the girls were alarming, some with dyed black hair, and studs through their nostrils. It was hard to associate the heavy metal sound track with plump, dimpled Laura, but I mentioned her name as she'd told me to, and the receptionist said Donna would squeeze me in if I could wait twenty minutes and would I like a cup of coffee or else she could manage tea, and somehow I was perched on a high-backed couch, skimming through a pile of newpapers and fashion magazines until a small but emphatic headline in *The Cape Cod Times* sucked me in:

Police Seek Witness in Fatal Crash

DENNIS PORT—Theodore (Teddy) Blake, the well-known biographer who wrote under the name T. E. Blakemore, died late Saturday night after the car he was driving struck a tree off Cypress Street near the Harwich border. He was pronounced dead at the scene. There were no other passengers in the car, according to a police department spokesman.

Dennis Port police received a 911 call at 1:33 A.M. reporting the single-car accident. They urge any witnesses to come forward.

Arnold Kellman, resident at 414 Cypress Street, said he was awoken by the sound of the crash. "I thought I heard something, but by the time I got outside, there was nothing I could do and the sirens were already wailing," Mr. Kellman said. The road near Kellman's home curves to the left before banking right in an S-turn between Swan Pond in Dennis Port and the West Reservoir in West Harwich. Black and yellow signs indicate the curves in the road. These signs had been recently repainted.

According to accident reconstruction investigators, Mr. Blake's Ford Explorer careened over the center line after the first turn before crashing down an embankment about 65 feet later and into several pine trees on the opposite side of the road.

Patricia Gerson, who lives near the property where the vehicle came to rest, said drivers frequently exceed the 30 mph posted speed limit. "Everybody drives way too fast along that stretch," she said. In the twelve years she's lived nearby, she recalls two or three nonfatal accidents. The road near the crash site was closed for three hours.

The cause of the accident is under investigation by Detective Russell Snow of the Dennis Port Police Department, who requests that anyone who met with Mr. Blake directly prior to the accident as well as anyone who witnessed the crash contact him at 508-555-3400. The Cape Cod Regional Law Enforcement Council Accident Reconstruction Unit is also investigating, with assistance from the Barnstable County Sheriff's Office Bureau of Criminal Investigation. Police had no further updates on the accident.

I rested my index finger on the type that spelled out your name and reread the line that termed you a well-known biographer. You would have been pleased to be designated a "biographer" rather than a "ghost-writer," but you'd have preferred "renowned" or "famous," to "well-known." Detective Snow was now Russell Snow, possessed of a first name that on consideration I found vaguely sinister, the hissing possibility of all those esses. Why was Snow searching for a witness? If the road was such a frequent crash site, why were so many entities investigating? Snow's phone number glared at me reproachfully.

Donna seemed just as frightening as any of the stylists at first, as apt as not to dye my hair black and send me forth as a Goth, but she chatted amiably through her pierced lip about her kids and her dog as well as her aspirations for my hair, slowly building my confidence through conversation. And I, who am usually so good with silence, found myself confessing to the upcoming interview with Garrett Malcolm.

"The movie star? The director?"

I nodded, already sorry I'd spoken.

"Owns a big hunk of waterfront, right? Smart guy, hanging on to it. Most of the owners sold early, before the prices shot up. Between Camp Edwards and Otis Air Force Base and with the Biddle property going over to the National Seashore, there's hardly any private land left around here."

She took a quick snip. I tried to scrutinize the length of the severed hair she deposited on the shiny floor while obeying her order to hold still.

"I heard he's setting up some kind of special trust, a land trust, I think they call it, something to do with conservation, to lower his property taxes. Plenty of people in town are against it, say we need all the taxes we can get for the schools and the roads. You'd think he'd just sell the whole shebang and move to Hollywood. I sure would. Who'd stay here in the snow and cold, when he could live anywhere? Malibu Beach, that's where I'd go."

Launched into a monologue, she didn't seem to mind that I didn't respond.

"As long as he doesn't build a hotel, I could care less about his taxes." She squinted into the mirror and tugged at my hair. "Damn property developers, turn the whole Cape into high-priced condos and fancy hotels, parcel it up, and sell it off. Kids can't afford to live near their families anymore. Things don't pick up around here, I'm gonna have to rent out my place this summer, bunk with a friend, earn enough to tide me over the rest of the year."

I wondered guiltily if that was what I was doing, renting a place a townie couldn't afford to keep.

"Anyway, I'll get you looking hot, but then you better watch yourself. Theater's got a worse reputation than baseball." She gave a loud snort that turned into a chuckle. "And that Cape Cod League? If they kept track of local pregnancies, they'd have themselves a brand-new statistic. Exact same thing with the theater dudes, in spite of how they're all supposed to be gay as ballet dancers. One girl told me they keep a list, like a directory, who's available, who'll do what. Slice a path through the homecoming queens every year. We get 'em all in here, weepy after they visit the clinic."

I was glad I'd kept Brooklyn Pierce's name to myself.

"You see the protesters out there?"

I shrugged to indicate I hadn't noticed, but I had. I'd seen the stalwarts marching with their signs. PREGNANT, NEED HELP? and LIFE, CHOOSE IT! as if life was simple enough to fit on a placard.

"Hurts business, Steffi says, pictures of dead babies and cars honking all the time. Not that they don't do checkups and all, but to those protest guys, it's all about baby killing. Hey, you want me to do your makeup, too?"

I hastily refused, and she concentrated on my hair. No dye, I told her again.

She bit her lip. Sulked a little, said how about highlights?

"That's dye, right?"

"I guess."

"Just a trim," I said.

"I'm shaping it."

More hair hit the floor.

"If I had a teenage girl, I wouldn't let her work at that theater, no way, but some people want their kids to get famous, no matter what."

She veered back to real estate prices then, and how she hated and loved the tourists, couldn't live with 'em, couldn't live without 'em. And which celebrities she thought she saw last summer and how they were all over the place, bad as New York City, and how Lady Gaga bought some mansion over on Martha's Vineyard, and if you could get a photo of her, how she really looked under all that makeup, it would be worth a fortune. I was nervous the entire time she wielded the scissors. If I could make Garrett sound like a fool when I wrote, she could make me look like a fool, and I hadn't even done due diligence, simply trusted a random saleswoman.

Garrett. I was shocked that I'd thought of him as Garrett, not

Malcolm, not Mr. Malcolm. This interviewing in person changes everything, bombards the senses. Color instead of black-and-white, the faint tang of piney scent, the whispery touch of strange upholstery, the ocean leaping and falling in the background. Donna handed me a mirror and swiveled my chair full circle.

Just an inch shorter, but my hair was different, soft and feathery. I barely recognized myself. With the new clothes and the haircut, it was as though I'd flipped a page and discovered an unfamiliar chapter in a well-worn book. I felt reborn, new as a spearmint-colored shoot poking its head out of the hard ground.

CHAPTER
sixteen

H ey. Hi. Miss Moore, isn't it?"

Kalver, the previously hostile PA, hesitated a beat too long, a puzzled furrow cutting his brow. Pre-shopping, pre-haircut, my single status must have been an intuitive finger snap.

I nodded curtly. "Where should I set up?"

"Well, Teddy would . . ."

You would have been Teddy from the get-go, friendly Teddy, with a slap on the back. "Yes? Teddy would what?"

"Teddy would have arranged the location with Mr. Malcolm."

"The big room with the view of the ocean, is that available?"

"Whatever."

I didn't warm to Darren, Mr. Kalver, the PA, whatever. Couple the wild golf-cart ride with his slacker demeanor and general nastiness and I could only wonder why Malcolm tolerated him. But even he couldn't dim the pleasure I felt at reentering that spectacular room. The sun sparkled off the glass, refracting the shoreline. Yesterday's ocean had been green and dramatic, wild waves and a glowering horizon. Today's was azure, peaceful, flat and soothing as a warm bath. The arc of windows was a visual magnet, a constantly changing exquisite oil painting, better than the portrait of Claire Gregory.

I set the recorder on a low table near a comfortable leather chair and asked Kalver what Mr. Malcolm liked to drink during interviews. He gaped as though I'd put the query in Albanian. Perhaps, given the large whiskey Malcolm had downed at our first meeting, the idiot thought I was inquiring whether his boss had a drinking problem. I cleared my throat and requested water in case Mr. Malcolm got thirsty. That got him out of the room, which was my goal. I wanted to test the recorder without a witness; my fingers felt awkward as thumbs and I was thankful you never bothered with a special microphone. I settled into a smaller leather chair, nervously readied my notebook and pen. Kalver returned to place two bottles of Perrier on the table, an unexpected courtesy, glasses and ice as well.

"I'll try to minimize the interruptions," he said.

"Interruptions? There shouldn't be any."

"Look, Teddy would have had a clear slot two weeks ago, but it's different now. I canceled a board meeting to fit you in. Opening night is opening night, and Mister Malcolm's doing you a favor squeezing you in."

I ignored him and reviewed my lessons: Look Malcolm in the eye, have questions ready, let him talk, but be ready to steer . . . and then there he was, wearing dark jeans and a black T-shirt. A beaded leather band wrapped his right wrist.

I stood, almost stumbling in my eagerness, and in a flash felt like an awkward teen, a starstruck fan about to gush some unforgiveable platitude. Oooh, can I have your autograph? He put out his hand and, as I took it, he gave me the once-over.

I felt like some cliché ingénue in a made-for-TV-movie: remove glasses, loosen hair from tight bun, swell the corny orchestration in the background. God, what did I think I was I doing? Malcolm nodded Kelver out of the room, sank into the chair, and summoned a smile that crinkled his eyes.

"You don't mind if I tape?" The question sounded simple-minded as I said it. I clicked the recorder and tried to clear my head, to focus. "You gave Teddy great stuff. It's going to make a terrific book."

"How's it going?" His eyes were a shade paler than the ocean.

"Fine. I'm polishing the beginning. You'll see it soon."

"It's going to run chronologically?"

"I'll open with a dramatic sequence, then backtrack."

"A hook?"

"Exactly."

"Have you picked it yet?"

"Your first Academy Award. Or your battle with Twentieth Century-Fox; I haven't decided. It could be something you say today."

"Today? I doubt it. I've got a stage manager who's up in arms, carpenters pounding sets at the barn, the board breathing down my neck, casting decisions to make, and here I sit."

"I'll try to wrap up as soon as I can." Why, why had I ever thought myself capable of handling an interview?

"Sorry. I didn't mean to be harsh."

I tried to smile. "You must have settled on most of your cast."

"Most, but it's not set in stone. I can't talk about it yet."

"Will you take this *Hamlet* to Broadway? Are you planning to film it?" God, these weren't questions I'd written down.

"We'll film, but I don't know if it will be for theatrical release or British TV. Now, what is it you need? Teddy covered my whole life."

I settled back into my chair, and so did he. "You've been wonderfully open. About yourself. But readers will want to know about the actors you've worked with."

"And the actresses." He raised his eyebrows, and his mouth tightened as though he'd tasted something spoiled. "I told Teddy; I don't tell tales out of school."

"I'm not digging for gossip; I'm interested in character sketches. In funny stories, nothing you wouldn't want anyone to hear, nothing salacious."

"You make it seem okay." He sounded doubtful.

"So much has already been written about you. Publishers are as bad as movie critics. They want new material all the time, a constant stream of information, fresh insight."

"You've never done this before, have you?"

I almost choked on a sip of water. "I know how." Even to my ears, I sounded defensive. "Mr. Malcolm, I want to ask you if—"

"Garrett, remember? Or Mal. Friends call me Mal." He gazed at me expectantly.

"Em," I said. It kind of stuck in my throat.

"Emily?"

"Em.

"Like in James Bond? Why don't you tell me a bit about yourself, Em? Since you know all about me."

I could feel the smile freeze on my lips. "There's nothing to tell."

"Come on. I knew Teddy like the back of my hand."

"Everyone felt like that."

"He didn't talk about you. Were you his guilty secret? I'm sorry, am I upsetting you? Damn, I am sorry. You must miss him terribly."

"I do." Longing rose like a bubble in my throat, a crazy desire to see you again, Teddy, all mixed up with the need to be sitting quietly at my desk in my den, by myself. I could feel my breathing start to quicken. "I'm sorry."

"You don't need to apologize. And by the way, you don't need to dress up for me, either. Not that I don't appreciate the effort, but you looked quite sweet yesterday. Demure, like a schoolgirl."

I must have gone beet red. I felt like I had to say something, anything, but nothing came. I don't know how to react to compliments, Teddy. I have so little experience with them.

"Well, Em, which targets do you want me to shoot first?"

"I don't want you to shoot anyone. How's this? When I say the name of one of your movies, you tell me about the people in it, whatever comes into your head. Stories, colorful incidents. Auditions, a day on location, a difficult scene, an improv that clicked or didn't click. Whatever you remember."

"Okay," he said suspiciously. "If that's what you want."

"Let's go way back. *French Kiss*."

"Okay. At the audition with Anselm, they brought in twelve guys to read for the same role, big names. Going in, I thought I was one of two in contention, so I froze, forgot every line, but Audra, Audra Anthony, was so gorgeous she saved me. My character—God, I've forgotten his name—was supposed to be knocked out by meeting her, so the fact that I screwed my lines didn't matter, because I was hopelessly, totally blown away by Audra. It was like I couldn't shape words with my mouth, but it played funny, so I got the part."

"*Twisted Silk*."

"A lot of mind games on that one. Mace Harvey, the director, he wanted me pissed off at Swayze, so he treated me like shit. Everything Swayze did was wonderful; everything I did stank. Swayze, one take; it was perfect. I'd do twelve takes and get nothing but browbeating. It seeped into my performance, this hatred for the guy. Smart director. I hated him at the time, but I've used the same trick myself."

It worked, Teddy. I'd throw out a title and he'd close his eyes for a minute, and then he'd paint it like a picture so I could see the actors and hear them. It went better than I could have hoped. He's quite a mimic. Did he tell you about the night Laurel Henders got so pissed at Brooklyn Pierce she sent the cameraman off to follow him while he and Mattie Clark and a lot of other guys went skinny-dipping at Cahoon Hollow? They added that film to the dailies, which would have been fine except some Hollywood big shot came out unannounced to sneak a peek at them? Did he tell you about the Airheads, the inflatable extras in the first Justice film? How they started to hiss and shrink during a take? No, of course he didn't, or I would have heard it. God, Teddy, I laughed until my ribs ached. His timing was magnificent. I had him on a roll. He was barely conscious of my presence.

The stupid PA stuck his head in the door before Malcolm even acknowledged his knock. "Sorry. There's a call on one."

"Dammit, I have to take this." Malcolm nodded in my direction. "Do you mind waiting on the patio? If it's too cold—"

"It's fine."

The air was bracing, invigorating. I didn't mind the cold. What I minded was the interruption, the timing. I was edging up on *Red Shot*, on Claire Gregory. I'd moistened and fertilized, prepared the ground, and now the PA had yanked it out from under me. With half the patio in shadow, half in sunlight. I walked blindly toward the far end, toward the sunlight and the sea, and leaned far over the wooden railing. The wind ruffled my hair. Did Malcolm take this incredible blue panorama for granted?

Eight minutes later, he slid the patio door open. "Sorry about that. You must be frozen."

I pointed. "Are those seals basking on the rocks?"

"Dammit, I thought they'd gone."

"You don't like them?"

"When I was a kid, my father shot one with a BB gun." He motioned me indoors. "Three seals showed up during run-throughs for

Macbeth. We called them the three witches, and they kept mum during rehearsals, but opening night, they let loose. No Macbeth wants to compete with seals barking. I'll never be able to do *Macbeth* because of those damned seals. Whenever I hear 'Tomorrow and tomorrow and tomorrow—'"

"Did the audience laugh?"

"The audience? Christ, the actors laughed. They roared. You had to hear it: 'Tomorrow and tomorrow' and *eeerk, eeerk, eeerk*. That night, Dad got drunk and winged one of them. Got in heaps of trouble with Fish and Wildlife." He settled back into his chair and pulled a serious face. "Where were we?"

"You were telling me how you met Claire when she was doing *Set Piece*."

"No, I wasn't."

I waited, but he didn't add another syllable.

"People say you wrote the part of Audrey in *Red Shot* specifically for her." Silence worked beautifully for you, Teddy. Why wasn't it working for me? "That's a wonderful likeness of her. Who painted it?"

"I'm not going to talk about Claire."

"Why not?"

"That's a nice trick, but no. Look, I once read an autobiography of George Lucas. Good book. And it never said a word about his wife, other than they got a divorce. Just about his films."

"Was it a bestseller?"

"Claire is off-limits. Teddy agreed."

"No, he didn't. Why did you and Claire break up?" I tried the direct assault out of sheer desperation. Given the long interruption for the phone call, I didn't have time for subtle flanking maneuvers.

God knows, there were enough answers out there. According to *People* magazine, Claire caught Garrett with the nanny. *The National Enquirer* painted Claire as the unfaithful one, screwing not only her yoga instructor but a variety of costars. Every gossip columnist in

America and a few in England and Australia had written the supposed inside scoop. Malcolm had stayed silent then and he stayed silent now. The stillness grew.

"Sometimes you do things, it's like madness, a rage that blinds you. Doesn't everyone wish they could go back, do another take, rewrite a chapter of their life? That's what I love about live theater, the constant replay, the repetition, the perfectibility, the possibility of perfection, not that it's ever perfect. Did you know there are four different scripts for *Hamlet*—four completely different scripts? Two of them are two thousand lines or so, and the other two clock in at four thousand."

"You're changing the subject," I said.

"I'm not going to answer your question. I know you had to ask, I know Teddy was planning to ask, but I won't answer except to say this: I will never say anything against the mother of my child."

"I understand Jenna's an actress." He hadn't said he wouldn't speak about the child.

" 'The line is extended.' "

"The line?"

"My father used to say that, whenever I did the right thing onstage, came in promptly on a cue, spoke a line properly. It was his special benediction. He kept count of all the generations of actors in the family, and he was determined that my generation would not be the last. When Claire got pregnant—" He stopped, mouth open, paused, then shut his eyes. "I'm sorry. We keep apologizing to each other. Why is that?"

"When Claire got pregnant—?"

"I'll finish the thought. If you promise not to press."

"Okay."

"When she was pregnant, my father would recite Shakespeare to the potential actor within. He was certain she would be a he, the chosen child, the ultimate Malcolm star. I'm glad he lived long enough to know he was right."

I remembered what James Foley had said on tape, about the old man wanting more sons. "He wasn't upset when she turned out to be a girl?"

"Tremendously upset. Had to alter his will, and he hated lawyers almost as much as he hated taxes. 'First thing we do, let's kill all the lawyers.' Thought Shakespeare had it exactly right. He was a Shakespearean through and through, my father, and he'd modeled his will after Will Shakespeare's, with all the "first sonne of my body lawfully issuing" garbage. Had to modify it to "heirs of my body," which sounded suspiciously modern to him. He passed away when Jenna was only seven, but he died believing the family business was in good hands. There would be another theatrical generation. He knew Jenna was an actress the first moment she walked onstage. Everyone knew."

"Even at that age?"

"Even at that age," he repeated gravely. "She was the love of my father's life, Cordelia to his Lear. As she is the love of my life."

"When was the last time you saw her?"

He blinked his eyes and gave a shake of his head. "That's enough about Jenna."

"Are the two of you estranged?"

"You're not going to rake that up, are you? Those rumors were nothing but drivel, stuff that started leaking to the press with the divorce. I had—and have—absolutely no problem with the terms of my father's will, with him leaving the land to Jenna. It was simply a way to avoid federal estate taxes, and more to the point, it doesn't matter in the least, because both of us want the same thing: to keep the land for the theater, to keep the theater running. And that is off the record. Understand?"

"But this is your chance to set the record straight, to give your viewpoint, your side of the story. To write history the right way."

"I'm her legal guardian. I act for her till she turns twenty-one. Then she'll take over. And I am not a government official. I don't owe people an explanation of my private life."

"You and Claire reconciled during her illness."

"Briefly."

"That must be a comfort to Jenna."

"Do you think so?"

"Of course."

"Look, that's it about Jenna. No more."

"It would be a big help if I could talk to her. Is she coming here? For a board meeting?"

"Where did you get that from? Of course not. She's still a minor. There wouldn't be any point. She's not coming here, and even if she were, I'm sorry, but I won't have her bothered."

"What about your next film project?"

"I don't have one."

"There are rumors." I glanced meaningfully at the pile of manuscripts on the corner of his desk.

"Always rumors," he said lightly.

"Teddy thought you agreed to do the book because you wanted to be in the public eye before the box office opened."

A rap at the door punctuated my remark. The PA stuck his head in again.

"I agreed to this book because Teddy talked me into it," Malcolm said before focusing on the intruder. "What, Darren?"

"I'm sorry. Someone to see—"

Before the PA could finish, Brooklyn Pierce was in the room, saying, "Hey, sorry, Mal, gotta talk to you, okay?"

If I hadn't been watching Malcolm's face closely, I wouldn't have seen the mixture of distaste and despair that crossed it.

At close quarters, I could see how wrong I'd been about Pierce not aging like the rest of us. He wore a wrinkled suit instead of rolled-up khakis, and the skin around his eyes looked puffy and dark.

"Sorry, sorry, thought you were alone."

"Mr. Pierce," I said boldly. "I've been trying to reach you through your agent."

Malcolm stood. "We'll have to stop."

I jumped to my feet as well, determined not to let the movie star escape again. Quickly, I introduced myself and started stammering out an interview request.

"Hey, yeah, sorry about Teddy," Pierce interrupted. "Great guy, great interviewer. Hey, since she's leaving, I'll walk her out, Mal. Be right back. Don't go anywhere." The movie star's arm was under my elbow and I found myself hustled from the room, practically jogging to stay on my feet. As soon as we were outdoors, the star spun me around to face him.

"Listen, sorry and all that, but I've gotta have that tape back. Hell, just destroy it, if that's easier, but forget about using it."

I didn't deny possessing the tape, only because he didn't give me the chance.

His hand clamped down on my shoulder. "No, never mind destroying it. I want the original. And no copies. Understand?"

"That hurts."

Kalver, the PA, slammed the door, stomped down the walk, and glowered at Pierce, who, having heard him, immediately turned on the charm, smiling and shifting his hand so it looked like he was giving me a gentle farewell pat.

"Great meeting you." Pierce's grin was boyish and sincere, just like in the movies, and he waved as he headed up the path to the house. "Catch you later."

CHAPTER
seventeen

As I keyed the ignition it came to me: Pierce wasn't here to rekindle the Justice franchise; he was here for *Hamlet*, to play the madman, his wrinkled suit a stand-in for Hamlet's "doublet all unbrac'd" and "stockings foul'd." The thought evaporated like mist, dwindled along with my delight in my haircut and Malcolm's compliments. Panic hardened slowly, like gelatin in cold water, and took its place. If Pierce had meant the scene as part of some bizarre audition, he'd have played it for Malcolm's benefit, in Malcolm's view. I was no casting agent. An iron band tightened across my chest.

The sun flamed on the horizon and made my eyes water. I veered into the breakdown lane, determined to compose myself, dabbed my streaming eyes with a tissue, rested my head against the steering wheel, counted the rapid pulse beating in my temples. My sunglasses were nowhere to be found. I twisted and grabbed my laptop off the backseat, booted it, and searched my junk-mail file to make sure my computer hadn't relegated one of your communications to the electronic trash heap. I checked my deleted e-mail file, then reviewed all my e-mail, hunting for any mention of Brooklyn Pierce. The only hits occurred in old messages sent near the beginning of the project when his name turned up on a list of obligatory interviews or in correspondence with his agent and his manager.

How could I return a tape I'd never heard of? That was a valid question, but the question that really intrigued me concerned content. What could the tape reveal that would make Pierce demand its return so urgently? When did you tape it? Did you spot the elusive star marching over a rise like I did, grab notebook and recorder, pop your questions there and then? Even if it were a serendipitous meeting, a spontaneous interview, what could have kept you from phoning me, e-mailing, boasting? You were supposed to tell me everything.

I sucked in a breath, checked the mirrors, and pulled back onto the road. The dunes, the ocean, the quaint Cape scenery made no more impact on my senses than the speed limit signs.

At a red light I tapped my hand impatiently against the wheel. The Pierce tape might be piggy-backed onto the Sylvie Duchaine interview, stuck onto the end of the tape Caroline had held hostage, the same tape I'd recovered from the Bloomie's bag. Yes, that could work, that made sense, if you'd been running low on blank tapes. The Duchaine interview was a short one.

I felt light-headed, faint, my stomach queasy with relief. I'd eaten nothing since breakfast. For a moment, hunger reassured me. Far from heading for a panic attack, I was merely starving. Deliberately relaxing my hands on the wheel, I indulged in a pep talk. The session with

Malcolm hadn't gone badly. He'd spoken about Jenna, confided the story of his father reciting Shakespeare to the pregnant Claire. I'd definitely include that. Teddy, I never realized how much the interviewer relied on constant, quick revision, on what seemed to me almost a mystical process, like mind-reading, the interpretation of pauses, gestures, the shift of tiny muscles beneath the skin.

I smiled in anticipation of hearing the Duchaine tape again, listening to Sylvie sing Malcolm's praises now that I knew him so much better, so much more intimately. I wished you'd flat-out asked whether or not she'd slept with him, Teddy. Warmth crept up my neck as I recalled Malcolm telling me I didn't need to dress up on his account. *Sweet,* he'd said, *like a schoolgirl.*

The minute I got in the house, I gulped sufficient peanut butter to quiet my stomach and fast-forwarded my way through the Duchaine tape, listening carefully to Sylvie's brief response to your final question, then silence, silence, more silence, nothing but silence till the end. Nothing, nothing, no hint of where the missing tape might be.

I breathed deeply and began the search methodically. I delved into the corners of every drawer and cupboard you might have opened. The Pierce tape might have tumbled to the floor from the bedside table, somehow concealed itself under the bed. It could have fallen off the desk. I searched the shag carpet on hands and knees, combed the rough fibers with my fingers, sneezed at the disturbed dust.

I checked the list of tapes and transcripts. You were methodical, Teddy. Each tape bore a label; each was numbered. We were over a hundred and thirty tapes deep on Garrett Malcolm; I'd packed the most recent thirty in my duffel, along with a few of the early tapes, in case I had a question on transcription or needed to check a key quote. When I lined the tapes up in order, Number 128 was absent.

I could tell Pierce I didn't have it. He might believe me, he might not. He might tell Malcolm, and "ay, there's the rub," for I'd assured Malcolm I had all your tapes, that I'd listened to each and every one.

Was this one of your surprises, Teddy, one of your little games? A pop quiz, as it were? I called your house, waited through four long rings before your voice, alive on the answering machine, shocked me so thoroughly I pressed "end call" without leaving any message. Oh, Teddy, your voice with its faint burr on the deepest notes. Heard un-expectedly, it killed me with sadness.

I sucked another deep breath and phoned Henniman's, punching Jonathan's extension as soon as the automated message started bleating.

"Did Teddy send you a tape?"

"Em? Are you okay?"

It was like waking in the middle of a dream. I carefully adjusted my tone from desperate to curious. "Oh, Jonathan, sure, I'm fine. I just wondered whether Teddy sent anything in the mail."

"Is everything all right?"

"It's fine, Jonathan, it's going so well. Malcolm is absolutely coop-erating."

"So you're on schedule? You're ready to send the manuscript?"

"I will be. Soon."

"I didn't get any mail from Teddy, but do you know somebody named McKay, McCann, something like that? He left a couple of mes-sages, mentioned Teddy? No?" He rushed on briskly. "Well, now that I've got you, why don't I transfer you over to Ellie? I know she wants to set up some publicity dates."

"No, Jonathan, I really don't have time now."

I ended the call, punched your home number again, listened stone-faced through your greeting, and left a message for Caroline. Please, could she call as soon as possible?

I reconsidered Brooklyn Pierce's mad scene: *No, don't destroy it, give it back, no copies.* He hadn't ordered me not to listen to the tape before returning it. He hadn't said I couldn't use the material.

What could he have told you? What could have slipped out? Was Caroline devious enough to bait the Bloomie's bag with the Duchaine tape, hide the Pierce tape? Did you talk to her, give her a hint that the tape contained potential dynamite? Talk to her, not to me? The more I considered the scenario, the more likely it seemed. How she must have laughed. How she must be laughing now.

There was nothing for it. I'd have to see her, make some kind of deal for the missing interview. I'd have to disrupt the schedule I'd painstakingly set with Malcolm, plod the bus back to Boston, find transportation to suburban Lexington, confront her. The idea of all that travel made the peanut butter churn in my gut.

I roamed room to room through the unfamiliar house, tried to focus my restless energy on the book, conjure the blinders I needed to work at anything near full capacity. I kept imagining the summoning trill of the phone, the ensuing argument with Caroline. At the apartment, in my tiny kitchen, I'd have brewed chamomile tea and sweetened it with honey; I'd have sipped from my flowered china mug while I turned out finished pages, adding them to the tidy pile on the right-hand corner of my desk. Here, I spooned peanut butter from the jar, licking the utensil slowly while I stared out the kitchen window into darkness. The silent phone seemed to shout Caroline's triumph. She must have played the tape. God knew what she'd do with it, what she'd done with it already.

I could leave for Lexington now, drive myself, brave the terror of crowded highways. I had a car; I could drive. I checked the clock. Too late to make Lexington before Caroline went to sleep, but I could break the journey in Boston, spend the night in my own bed, surrounded by my own possessions, untouched in their orderly ranks, waiting like good children for their mother to return.

The thought of sleeping in my own bed decided me. Determination hardened into action. I folded my new periwinkle sweater, tucked it into an unfamiliar closet, changed into my uniform, and crept out of the darkened house, negotiating the porch steps by the light of my cell phone, wary of the neighbor's prying eyes.

The whoosh of wheels on pavement soothed my ears. Route 6 was a ribbon of straight moonlit road with surprisingly little traffic. Driving felt good, purposeful, a task to complete in a discrete chunk of time, a solace and a comfort. Given reasonable luck, I could deal with your precious wife first thing in the morning and return in plenty of time to keep my appointment with Malcolm.

CHAPTER
eighteen

Massachusetts isn't California; it's not prone to earthquakes, but when thumping jarred me awake, "earthquake" was the word that shrieked though my brain. The thumping continued, mild and rhythmical, while I peered quizzically at the familiar face of the round clock on the bedside table. I'd set the alarm for six thirty, I was certain of it, but six thirty was past and the floorboards shuddered with thuds that came in clumps, three, then a pause, then three more. Melody downstairs. My sleep-drenched brain made the leap and I successfully connected the noise to Melody downstairs, who'd once declared she'd tap on her ceiling with a long-handled broom if she needed me. She'd said it years ago; I'd considered it a remote possibility, almost a comic one. If Melody needed help, she'd ring 911.

I dragged myself out of bed, feeling disoriented and disgruntled. The alarm had failed. It was almost half past seven. I threw on last night's jeans and tee and plunged down the steps.

You always called her Melody Downstairs, as though that were her name, as though it never occurred to you that she might have a proper last name that you might learn by checking the listing in the foyer. Not that I knew much more about her than you did. She never volunteered information and I never asked; she had a right to a private life.

How you'd have laughed at that, I thought, fingers skimming the handrail. You'd have called it an antiquated concept. But the people we wrote about weren't private souls. They were different; they'd entered into a public space via their special accomplishments. Our subjects were volunteers and they set their own limits, revealed what they chose to reveal. Yes, you urged them to tell more; that was your job, our job, and some did and later regretted it. But to a large extent, they painted and framed their own canvases, got to shield awkward or intimate doodles from the public gaze.

"I thought I heard you last night. Hope I didn't wake you." Melody's musical voice heralded her unlovely presence. Frizzled hair, parted in the middle, yanked into a tight bun, a dun-colored shift billowing over a shapeless body. When she didn't invite me in, I felt relieved rather than offended. I'd never entered her domain, had no desire to witness pulleys or bars or whatever arrangements she'd installed to cope with her condition.

"The police were here." She lowered her voice to a confidential murmur, seeming delighted to break the news and eager to gauge its effect on me. "Two of them. Plain clothes. From the Cape, about that man you worked with, the one who died?"

I found myself suddenly obsessed, wondering whether she'd always lived in a wheelchair, if she suffered a disastrous accident or had some dire progressive illness, how she'd come to live in that apartment, how she survived. Why was her life unworthy of a book? A film?

"They were looking for you." Her words dripped portent, as though she imagined herself the oracular figure in some Greek tragedy. "They wanted to interview you about the car crash. Ask you questions? Like on a TV cop show, where you're a witness?" Her eyes, rounder than usual behind their heavy frames, peered up at me.

I should have returned Snow's call immediately. Policemen didn't understand, didn't care about shyness or panic attacks or the need to meet deadlines. They needed answers to their questions so they could fill out their forms. I could sympathize with that, but why they would imagine there were answers to an accident eluded me. An accident was an accident, sui generis, inexplicable.

It would be a matter of forms, filling in boxes, ticking off items on an official list.

"I suppose you told them I'd be back?" I had a vision of Melody savoring and sharing every word Caroline and I had shouted at each other, detailing the nights you'd spent at the apartment as well as the days.

"I didn't tell them *when* you'd be back."

"Because you didn't know."

Her round eyes gleamed through her thick lenses. "I wouldn't tell them, anyway. What right do they have to ask? They wanted to know if I had a key. To your apartment. I mean, suppose I did? They could have grabbed it, used it, poked through all your belongings, pawed through your underwear drawer. And then they could have said I'd given it to them, offered it. There were two of them, big, loud men. They'd lie for each other, no problem, back each other up, their word against mine. Nobody would believe me."

Surely some story lurked behind her anger and paranoia.

"Good thing you don't have a key," I said.

"I'd never tell them anything. You don't have to worry about me."

I had a sudden sense, almost a vision, of Melody's living room: a huge TV for viewing crime-scene investigation shows and late-night film noirs, mismatched shelves packed with vintage murder mysteries. I saw her huddled under a shawl on icy evenings, flipping channels, turning dog-eared pages. The policemen's visit was most likely the highlight of her month.

"I won't," I said gravely. "Are you still good on milk and juice?"

CHAPTER
nineteen

The drive to Lexington took longer than the entire journey from the Cape, jangling my nerves from the moment I crossed the BU Bridge onto Memorial Drive, a nightmare of honking anger that roiled and oozed with barely suppressed rage onto the Fresh Pond Parkway. I stopped at the rotary near Fresh Pond for gasoline I didn't need, just to slide out of the car, stretch, and ease the tendons in my neck. Traffic was less congested on Route 2, but cars whizzed by at high speed on either side till I pulled into the right-hand lane and crept along doing fifty-five.

The missing tape haunted me. What could you have learned from

Brooklyn Pierce that you would have withheld from me, your scribe, your amanuensis? A delicious tidbit of gossip, a tale you wanted to confirm before sharing? Did you have reason to distrust Pierce, discount his information? Had the two of you been drinking heavily, sharing a blunt? Jonathan hadn't gotten the tape in the mail, but he'd mentioned the name of a man who'd been trying to reach you. McKay. I wracked my brain. Did you work with a McKay? Teach with him? Could you have given the tape to McKay?

Your house took me by surprise, Teddy. How odd that I never visited, that you never held a dinner party to which I was invited. I parked in front and checked the street number twice. The place was unexpectedly large, the light gray paint tasteful and fresh. Blue shutters contrasted nicely with the gray, the sheltered entryway was attractive, but it was a standard-issue Colonial, a blip of conformity, with little to distinguish itself from its neighbors. I'd assumed something stark and modern in keeping with Caroline's coldness.

That you would choose to live behind that bland front door seemed odd, if not impossible. You were the rebel; you'd always be the rebel, but it came to me in a rush that I hadn't truly known you, Teddy. I mean, I knew you biblically, of course, in that "Abraham knew his wife" sense. I knew you as a teacher and a mentor and an interviewer, but this house was the home of a suburban paterfamilias.

I inhaled courage and abandoned the car. While you may have been husband to Caroline, you were not the father of her children, not the father of any children. The house was a lie, the same way the marriage was a lie. Halfway up the walk, I found myself wondering which you had envied more: Garrett Malcolm's splendid, rambling house or his beautiful and talented daughter.

I rang the bell twice in quick succession. I wanted to get this over with quickly, return to the driver's seat, speed back to the Cape, return to Malcolm and my chance at life. I thought I'd catch Caroline with her guard down, in jeans or sweats or gardening clothes. I thought

I'd catch her unaware. There was a moment as she opened the door during which her features readjusted, like a Polaroid snapshot coming into focus, but she was blurred only for an instant. Then she was cool and organized again, in total command. Does she sleep in makeup, Teddy? Is she always perfectly dressed and groomed?

She wore a chocolate brown slim skirt, with sweater to match. The scarf at her neck had a touch of crimson. Her face was pale and perfect, a cool mask I couldn't help but envy. What a strength it must be to never show what you feel. I wondered whether she experienced it as strength or burden, whether she seethed under her perfectly arched eyebrows.

She nodded curtly and stepped aside, taking my wish to enter for granted. It didn't occur to me until later that she might not want the neighbors to witness a confrontation. It didn't occur to me until later that she might have been waiting for someone else. Indoors, the high-ceilinged foyer was pure Caroline, cool white walls, veined marble tile, harsh abstract art.

"I came for the other tape."

"And you never travel. Why Teddy believed your bullshit, I'll never know. You've got a nerve, throwing me out of his place, then demanding anything."

I tried to smile. "It's important that I have all Teddy's notes, all his tapes, so I can finish on time. You don't want to repay the advance. Really, you don't need that on top of everything else."

"How thoughtful of you." Her voice was mocking. "I gave you what I found at the Cape house."

That wasn't quite true; I'd grabbed it and run. Instead of pointing out the lie, I said, "There's another tape. Number 128."

Her lips stretched into a no-warmth smile. "Isn't it possible that my precious husband didn't do as much work as you thought he did? Ever think of that?

"No."

"Maybe you should engage your brain. As you leave."

"Once I have the tape I'll be happy to leave." I wanted to rip her eyes out, but I managed to stay calm. "Do you know a friend of Teddy's named McKay? A colleague? A former colleague?"

"I don't know Teddy's friends. That should be obvious, even to you."

"Do you have his laptop, his iPod, his—"

"Is this an endless list?"

"No."

"The police returned his phone."

"Can you check to see if someone named McKay called him?"

She ignored the question. "I imagine they'll give everything back eventually. There are"—she hesitated, searching for a word— "formalities."

"Who told you that? Detective Snow?" My stomach lurched. It occurred to me that I might have made the trip for nothing. Tape 128 could have been in your car when it happened. The police could be holding on to it. They might have listened to it.

"Yes, that's the name. He wanted to talk to you." She turned and her heels clacked up the stairs, four-inch heels in the morning, in the privacy of her own home. I considered following, but the house seemed forbidding and my knees felt weak and unequal to the task. I thought she might have simply deserted me in the foyer, hoping I'd show myself out, but then I heard drawers open and bang shut.

I tried to rub heat into my hands. The bench poised near the foot of the stairs was constructed of metal and glass, and topped with a pristine white cushion. I couldn't imagine having the nerve to dent that icy whiteness, couldn't imagine anyone slumping there to remove dirty boots.

In time the goddess descended, both hands clenched as though she were playing a game, preparing to ask which hand held the treasure. My heart started racing, but I kept my mouth shut.

"Two things," she said. "Then I want you out of here."

"Fine."

She pursed her lips, as though coming to a decision. "First, what do you think about this?" Her left hand opened to reveal a slip of paper, small and folded. She watched as I unfolded it.

"It's a check." I felt stupid even as I said it.

"Of course it's a check. I found it on Teddy's desk, tucked under the printer."

"Unsigned." It wasn't dated, either, but it was your personal check in the amount of one hundred eighty thousand dollars, a washed-out blue rectangle drawn on Bank of America, the address of the Lexington house printed clearly at the upper left. The "Pay to the Order of" line was completely blacked out with heavy lines from a felt-tip pen.

"Did he have that much in his account?" I asked.

"I'll have to see, won't I? Who do you think he was paying?"

I shrugged. "You said two things."

The black microcassette had made a deep mark in her palm. I took air in through my nose and reached for it gratefully.

"Don't get all excited," she said. "It wasn't at the Cape house, so it's probably an old one."

I glanced at the label: 048. Not 128. 048 would be a tape made closer to the beginning of the project. A tape I'd thought safely in the office, like the Sylvie Duchaine tape. "Where did you find it?"

"In a kitchen drawer."

If I hadn't heard you descant on the endless variety of Caroline's lies, I might have believed her. My hand closed over it. "Are you sure there weren't any others? It's important that I have all of them, every one."

"You have no idea what he was like, do you?"

"I knew him better than you did."

That unamused smile again. "You're such a child."

"I'm not."

"Did you think you were the first, the last, the true love of his life? Believe me, he specialized in little mice like you. Or did you think you were the only one he was banging?" She hurled the spiteful words like knives at a target, checking to see which would stick.

I clamped my lips shut and wished I could stop my ears as well. I tried to feel sorry for her, the aging ice queen locked in the ice palace.

"I wasn't really going to divorce him. Did he tell you I was?"

"No."

"Good."

"Don't you miss him?" I said.

"I used to. But that was a long time ago."

CHAPTER
twenty

Tape 048
Mark Barrington

Mark Barrington: If you've read the trial transcripts, you know it all. No reason to look me up.

Teddy Blake: *Just a couple of questions.*

MB: Sure, sure, everybody's got questions.

TB: *You have trouble with that?*

MB: Let's just say I'm uncomfortable speaking on the record.

TB: *Then off the record.*

MB: Off the tape?

TB: *I don't have a problem with that. [Click.]*

MB: Okay, I guess. You know, divorce work, I do so much of it, you asked me about anybody else, I'd have to send my girl for the records, look it up. After a while they're all the same. People lose interest, the guy strays, the woman doesn't want to screw him anymore, the kids are grown. They can't even remember why they wanted to get hitched in the first place. You know the deal.

TB: *But you remember the Gregory-Malcolm split.*

MB: Sure I do. I don't have to look that one up. That's the one that got away. Shoulda put my name out there in lights, that case. I mean, I thought I was the cat's meow, the big-time go-to guy, figured I'd move to L.A., make millions with celebrities for clients, and here I sit on my duff a couple hundred years later. You probably had trouble finding me.

TB: *You wound up settling.*

MB: You do what your client tells you. You can counsel him about what's in his best interest, but in the end you do what he wants.

TB: *The preliminary hearings, the depositions, they seem to go in a very different direction than the final disposition.*

MB: Yeah, you might say so.

TB: *Garrett Malcolm called the shots?*

MB: I was ready, more than ready, I was amped, gonna fight tooth and nail, hungry and mean as a cougar. Garrett wanted the girl with him, he wanted her with her grandparents, he wanted her with that theater group so she could grow up the same way he did, and I thought we had a damn good chance for full custody, given always the hazards of a trial, the decision of the judge. It's always a crapshoot, but things had gotten better for fathers in Massachusetts, and the two of them, their lifestyles would be a giant factor. He, for all the craziness, had a solid home base. Claire Gregory was all over the damn map. Her house was a hotel room in Rome one day, a friend's mansion in Brentwood the next. She might be on location for this film or that film. Malcolm offered comparative stability.

TB: *Sounds promising.*

MB: It was. I coulda won that baby.

TB: *And?*

MB: You're not taping this, right? And then one day he walks in and says it's all off, give Claire whatever the hell she wants.

TB: *And what did you think?*

MB: Strictly off the record? I thought she got the goods on him.

TB: *The goods?*

MB: You know. I figure she's got photos of him screwing other women or men or monkeys, whatever. Shooting dope, doing drugs, doing something that would not only ruin his career but land him in the clink.

TB: *You don't think he just changed his mind, decided a girl's place was with her mother?*

MB: He swung a hundred and eighty degrees overnight, like somebody was holding a gun to his head. I've seen that kinda thing before, and I waited for the explosion. I even started reading the Hollywood gossip rags because that kinda stuff always leaks.

TB: *But in this case, it didn't?*

MB: Look, that's enough. I'm an old fart who talks too much. I see any of this in print, I'll deny you were here. My wife'll back me up, too. Believe me, she will, 'cause she's my fourth wife and she really wants to be the last one.

CHAPTER
twenty-one

What the hell, Teddy?

None of my hopes for this nerve-wrenching journey were bearing fruit. I'd anticipated Brooklyn Pierce's tenor, trained and supple, as the triumphant sound track for my return to the Cape, but this taped growl was slurred and halting. It wasn't Pierce, and worse, it was unfamiliar. I vaguely recollected the name Barrington; no doubt I'd noted at some moment in time that a Mark Barrington had served as Malcolm's divorce attorney, but I'd never scheduled an interview with the man.

Maybe you'd approached him on other business—say, to instigate divorce proceedings against Caroline—and taped him on impulse, the way you must have taped Pierce. But you'd always claimed divorce was out of the question: Caroline would never divorce you. I listened long after the canned voices died, then punched rewind and listened again. Every one of our tapes was numbered. Each tape started with the same identifying information. I already had a tape marked 048 in my registry, and this wasn't it. My 048 was dated like all the other tapes. This one wasn't. And that early clicking noise, that sharp snap where you evidently shut off the machine and descended to the brief-case trick, the one where the interviewer hides a second recorder, a gambit you railed against in class? What in hell were you thinking, Teddy? What were you planning?

I couldn't wrap my mind around the idea of another new tape any more than I couldn't fathom the figure on that unsigned check: one hundred eighty thousand dollars. Given, it wasn't the millions scribbled on that notepad, but it wasn't lira, either. A hundred and eighty thousand dollars.

Route 2 to Storrow Drive on autopilot. I zipped past the BU exit with a brief and yearning glance in the direction of Bay State Road, kept my foot pressed hard on the accelerator. Approaching Leverett Circle, traffic slowed as red cones blocked access to two lanes. I inched toward the rotary and stopped at the yellow light, provoking the en-raged driver behind me to issue three long blasts on his horn.

An unauthorized biographer might have pursued Malcolm's di-vorce attorney, might even have paid him for his tittle-tattle. But there was no chance anything like that would end up in our book. In my book.

The old Southeast Expressway used to be a dreaded stretch of el-evated road that divided downtown Boston from the North End, de-priving both neighborhoods of sunlight and asphyxiating them with exhaust. Now sunken underground, cemented beneath the Rose Ken-nedy Greenway, it's even worse, a tomblike marble-run where frantic drivers cope with inadequate signage, desperate to merge or exit before getting shunted to the wrong destination. Staying tucked in the right-hand lane was not an option unless I craved a forced detour into East Boston.

I knew how you worked, Teddy. You were methodical, not impulsive. Orderly. Focused.

By the time I got as far as Braintree I was sweating and wishing I'd stuck to Route 128, the long way around. The shorter option should have taken less time, but traffic was stop and go, one lane knocked out by construction, another jammed with trucks. I consulted my watch and edged into the fast lane. Traffic loosened and I drove like a woman pursued by banshees, shoulder muscles tightening by the quarter mile.

So much could go wrong at high speed, so quickly and irrevocably. The rental had no dashboard gauges, just a single light marked "engine," an idiot light that might or might not flash prior to disaster. Oil could leak, steering belts fray. Each engine part was vulnerable. Moving parts wear on each other, abrade each other. You have to oil them, coddle them, watch over them. And even if you trusted the engine, there were errant drivers, brake-riders who veered from lane to lane, seeking a momentary rush, a brief advantage, and always, always, humans too stupid and selfish to control their alcohol intake before venturing onto the highways.

A cloud of birds launched itself from an overpass and swooped into vee formation, heading north. Sparrows, perhaps, common grayish-brown birds, but they, too, filled me with dread. Weeks ago, thousands of red-winged blackbirds had fallen from the skies over Arkansas, plummeting onto houses and roadways. Grackles and starlings, struck by lightning in Louisiana, rained down on a small bayou town. Even if the mechanical parts of the engine kept turning, even if no driver intent on mayhem strayed into my lane, falling birds could crack my windshield like an eggshell. I glanced nervously at the clock, flicked the turn signal, and evacuated the high-speed lane.

The Sagamore Bridge was visible in the rearview mirror when my cell rang the first time. It's not yet illegal to answer a cell phone while driving in Massachusetts, but I wasn't tempted because steering took all my effort and concentration. The third time the phone rang I exited Route 6 and made three aimless right turns onto progressively less crowded roads till I was able to pull over on a residential lane.

You have three missed phone calls. You have one voice mail.

The three numbers were identical. I felt a twist in my gut as I pressed keys and entered my password. When Darren Kalver informed me that my three o'clock meeting with Garrett Malcolm would need to be rescheduled, I gulped a deep shuddering breath and thought, *I could have spent another night at the apartment; I could have slept in my own bed.*

Anger, at Caroline, construction delays, carelessly weaving drivers, and now Kalver swelled like a cancerous growth in my throat. I plunged my hand into my purse, seeking Xanax, then withdrew it as though I'd been stung by a scorpion. I couldn't drive drugged. Did Malcolm know Kalver had canceled? Of course he knew; Malcolm would have ordered Kalver's action. Postponed, not canceled. Postponed. I grabbed at that straw. Rescheduled, not canceled.

I blamed Kalver. *You don't have time for her. She's unimportant. She's nobody. Let's put her off. Let's cancel her.* I crossed my arms over the steering wheel, lowered my head till it rested in their cradle, and closed my eyes. All the rush and fury, all the miles yet to drive before I got to Eastham, all the useless miles to Boston and back again.

The tap, tap, tap on the window made me start. Tap, tap, tap, like Melody's broom hitting the ceiling, smacking the floor. Disoriented, I checked my surroundings as I lowered the window. Was I in Lexington? The houses were too small. Had I slept?

"You all right?" The khaki-clad policeman stood between sun and shadow, so I had to squint to make out the features beneath the bill of his cap. I peeked at the rearview mirror. His pale gray cruiser, blue lights flashing, crowded my rear fender.

"I'm fine," I said. "There's nothing wrong."

"Sorry. I didn't mean to scare you. I thought you might be lost or—"

"Yes." I leaped at his suggestion.

"Are you looking for someplace? Someone?"

The name flashed into my mind as though it were written in flaring neon across the windshield. At first I wasn't sure I'd spoken it out loud.

"Detective Snow?" the policeman said. "Russell Snow, up in Dennis?"

"Yes," I said. "I'm supposed to go see him."

"You still got maybe twenty minutes' drive," he said. "Take Exit Nine off of Route Six. You know how to find Carrier Street?"

"No."

"Wait a minute."

The chill from the open window made me shudder, or maybe it was the release of tension when he no longer blocked the window. I was certain he was typing my license plate number into a laptop, making sure I wasn't piloting a stolen vehicle or fleeing a liquor store stickup. I felt the wild desire to escape, race off, even though I'd rented the car legally. I sat statue-like till he returned and unfolded a large-scale map. He was patience itself explaining the route, asking if I wanted him to write down the details.

"It's okay. I'll find it."

"You're sure there's nothing else I can do? You want me to call Detective Snow, let him know you're on the way?"

"Please, I'm fine. I might stop and have lunch or something."

"Good idea."

I thanked him, smiling, trying to radiate confidence and competence until the cruiser pulled out and drove away. I waited till it vanished, making a right turn at a stop sign. I knew I needed to move, drive. The officer might take another right, circle the block, come up behind me again.

I breathed deeply, in through the nose, out through the mouth. It was all right; nothing terrible had happened. The tightly bunched afternoon had unexpectedly opened like a late-blooming rose. I had free time. I would do it, drive to Dennis Port, find Detective Russell Snow, speak to the man at a time of my own choosing. He'd hand over Brooklyn Pierce's tape, safe and secure in a sealed brown envelope.

He wanted to talk to me; I wanted to talk to him. Feigning confidence made me feel confident. I could handle it.

CHAPTER
twenty-two

My idea of a police department was based on the movies. Malcolm's own *Red Shot* provided an iconic image, an urban ghetto outpost, a grim structure that might have been a run-down elementary school or an abandoned factory, with a tattered flag sagging on a rusted pole over a row of barred windows.

The Dennis Port Police Department was a cheerful building that could have doubled as an old-time general store, with a broad front porch, wooden railings, and shutters that framed windows that looked like they ought to be filled with merchandise. Inside, the space was awkwardly partitioned into small alcoves and offices, but the old rafters still gave a sense of what it used to be, a massive single room where people came to buy and share necessities, corn and grain and gossip. The creaking floorboards announced my arrival to a plump man at the front desk, who lifted a phone, barked a few short interrogatory sentences, and buzzed me through a locking gate with the admonition to enter the third door on the left.

The door was wide open, the interior small. The man behind the metal desk rose as I came in, but not without difficulty, and I read illness in his pinched features, gray skin, and labored movement. He had deep-set, light-colored eyes, a sharp nose, and a thin mouth balanced in a narrow, bony face. His dark hair was disheveled, as though he'd just run his hands through it, and lightly streaked with gray. He looked in his late forties, but he might have been younger. His blue shirt and wrinkled gray trousers probably fit better when he weighed an additional twenty pounds.

He didn't hold out his hand. I wondered whether policemen didn't offer to shake hands as a rule, if they didn't want to risk contamination, discover at some later date that they'd shaken hands with a criminal.

A calendar featuring photographs of lighthouses was pushpinned to one white plasterboard wall. Another wall was covered with maps. A round schoolhouse clock ticked as the sick man recited his name, Detective Snow, and stared at me expectantly.

"Em Moore. Teddy Blake's colleague, his partner. He died in a car accident?"

"Speak up, please." Snow subsided into his chair.

I blushed and repeated myself.

"I left you a message." His response wasn't accusatory; it sounded as though he himself had only just remembered.

"Yes, but I forgot. And then I was told you wanted to speak to me." "By?"

"His wife. Teddy's wife, Caroline."

He jerked his chin to indicate that I should take the chair facing his desk, a metal upright with a green padded seat, scarred and saggy with use. The policeman's chair, a wooden swivel, looked considerably more comfortable.

"You weren't at the funeral," he said.

"No. I couldn't make it."

"And Caroline Blake went out of her way to help me?"

"She didn't. Go out of her way."

The room, bright as a laboratory, seemed too small, the walls too close, every detail overly clear, hallucinatory: the dark circles under his eyes, their red-veined whites, the washed-out grayness of his skin, the sweat stains under his arms. The room was too hot; no wonder he was sweating. I thought about Jonathan's office, how pleasant it was by contrast, how Jonathan had feared I might faint. Here, I thought, I might fulfill his nightmare and actually pass out. The air was motionless and oppressively thin, robbed of oxygen.

Detective Snow swiveled his chair; it squawked like a protesting parrot. He used both of his big, capable-looking hands to type on a keyboard. He stared at a computer screen, then focused on me as though memorizing my features for a wanted poster. The computer screen was angled so I couldn't see the display. I felt the urge to rearrange my hair, cross my arms. I twined my fingers around the strap of my purse, then wondered whether he'd think that meant I was nervous. This was worse than seeing a therapist about my anxiety. I did that once.

I said, "Mrs. Blake thought you might give me Teddy's computer, if you've finished with it. I mean, I don't know whether or not it was in the car, or whether it got damaged or anything, but Caroline doesn't have it and I thought—" I let the sentence go. There was no way to salvage it.

He checked with the computer screen. "We gave the widow his effects."

"All of them?"

"I can check, but I think so."

I kept my voice casual. "There would have been a small tape as well. A microcassette, like this one." I held up the tape Caroline had relinquished. My palm felt damp.

He tapped an index finger on his lips and regarded the tape with a level stare. "Little thing like that, anybody coulda missed it."

I wanted to ask whether *he* had missed it, whether he was the one who'd seen you lying broken behind the wheel, tried to help, called the ambulance. "Could you find out?" I asked instead.

"Now?"

"It's something I need. For my work, to finish Teddy's work."

"Vehicle's still in the garage. I can run by, take a look, but I wouldn't count on anything."

"You'll let me know if you find it?"

"You leave your number, I will."

I considered telling him I'd call later to inquire. I didn't like the idea of giving a policeman my cell phone number, which was foolish. Even if I didn't reveal the number, he could find it easily enough. He was a policeman, after all. He could ask Caroline; she'd delight in telling him. I recited it, he wrote it down, and I stood, ready to leave.

"Since you're here, you mind if I ask a couple questions? If that's okay?"

I sat again, mildly puzzled. In the movies, cops demanded answers. This man didn't fit my vision of a cop any better than this converted general store fit my image of a station house. He moved too slowly, talked too softly, like a clerk in an insurance office. I wondered suddenly, abruptly, wildly, if he carried a gun, if he was armed and dangerous. I hadn't noticed a holster when he stood.

"Was your boss a careful driver?"

"He wasn't my boss."

"Sorry. Your partner, was he a careful driver?"

"He had a fender bender last year."

"Did you drive with him often?"

"I didn't really notice his driving one way or the other." I waited for another question, but he didn't say anything, so I asked whether your car was badly damaged. I'm not sure why. I was wondering if he'd actually bother to search for the tape. That was better than envisioning the twisted metal that had once been the Explorer. I didn't know if there'd been a fire, and I didn't want to ask.

"Badly damaged?" He shrugged wearily. "It was damaged, all right. If he'd been wearing a seat belt, who knows? He might have walked away."

"He wasn't wearing his seat belt?"

"He usually buckle up?"

"I don't know. I assumed so. I thought he did. Most people do."

"A lot don't. More than you think." He looked at me as though we were finished, as though he expected me to stand again, say good-bye, and leave.

"But he wasn't driving—uh, he wasn't impaired?"

"Why do you ask?"

"You were seeking a witness."

"The newspaper said we were."

"He didn't drink and drive."

He swiveled his squeaky chair and consulted the computer screen again. "Would you say Mister Blake was a happily married man?"

The question caught me off guard, so much so that I felt giddy, like I might retch or burp or giggle, emit some entirely inappropriate noise. There was no air in the office, none at all.

"Was he?"

"You met Caroline. You should have asked her."

"I did."

I was imagining Caroline's haughty response when it occurred to me that Snow was seriously pondering the possibility that you'd deliberately smashed into a tree as a preferred alternative to life with the ice queen. Had he never heard of divorce?

Caroline had mentioned divorce earlier in the day, in Lexington: *I wasn't about to divorce him,* she'd said. I knew you'd never leave her. Because of the money. But what if she'd issued an ultimatum, ordered you to get out?

I stood, clinging to the back of the chair, glad of its upright sturdiness. Maybe Snow wasn't as dull and unimaginative as he seemed. Maybe any single-car fatality caused the police to wonder whether the driver had impulsively tried to end it all. I considered sinking back into the uncomfortable embrace of the chair and requesting a glass of cold water.

"Are you okay?"

"Fine. You'll call if you find anything?"

"I will."

"Don't get up." I couldn't bear watching him try to rise, no longer wanted to shake hands even if he offered.

I sat in the car, breathing in and out—in through the nose, out through the mouth—till I'd composed myself, till I felt strong enough to brave the highway again. I fastened my seat belt carefully, tugging at the strap to make sure.

CHAPTER
twenty-three

No seat belt, Teddy.

I merged onto 6, got wedged behind a black SUV, and the minute I took note of it, a fleet of black SUVs, speeding like a herd of giant cattle, seemed to surround my undersized car. So many people chose huge vehicles, few with Melody's need for one. You, for example, liked to sit high above the road; it made you feel safe, invincible. I considered the dark blue crocus-killing van the neighbor lady had mentioned. Not the sort of rental I'd associate with a movie star, but if you had recorded the missing tape at the house, Brooklyn Pierce, desperate to retrieve it, might have dropped by and peered in the window, hoped someone might let him in to search for it. I accelerated, hedged in by Lincoln MKZs bristling with bike racks, Honda CRVs topped by ski racks, unadorned Toyota Sequoias, and Fords like yours. If the van's driver had been Brooklyn Pierce, movie star, it was likely the neighbor lady would have recognized him.

If you'd buckled your seat belt you might have survived. How tirelessly I'd have sat by your hospital bed, read to you, nursed you back to health. Lips pressed into a flat line, I kept up with the press of traffic while straining to listen to a faint intermittent thump, the first symptom of engine failure. Miles and minutes later, I realized I was hearing the wheels hit the highway seams.

By the time I pulled into the driveway, carefully avoiding the neighbor's crushed flowers, each muscle that controlled my arms, neck to shoulder to fingertip, was paralyzed with tension. As I opened the car door, my tingling hand brushed the seat and the microcassette leaped into the air as though propelled by a slingshot. It took ages of groping to locate the tiny square against the dark carpet.

Anyone might have missed such a thing if they hadn't known it was there. I would tell Brooklyn Pierce his interview had been lost in the accident. I'd need to make it sound convincing so that he'd believe me and agree to sit for a second taping.

I was so eager to lock myself indoors that I didn't notice the slip of paper on the floor until I'd walked over it. When I unfolded it, the print as well as the words seemed strange and unfamiliar.

First Encounter, it said. *Sunset.* The stiff paper was bent into tiny folds at one corner. I reopened the front door and studied the casing. A folded note stuck in the crack could have fallen to the floor when I opened the door.

First Encounter? I plunked tape recorder and laptop on the desk, marched into the kitchen, and ran the tap water. While it chilled and cleared, I studied the scrap. Underneath the three printed words was a scrawl, low and to the right, like a signature on a painting. I filled a glass and drank thirstily. The first letter was a *W*. No, an *M*. Once I deciphered the *M*, the rest was apparent: Capital *M*, lowercase *C*, capital *K*.

Jonathan had asked about McKay. And hadn't you gotten an e-mail from <McK>?

First Encounter? Sunset? Outside the kitchen window the sun hung low in the sky. As if on cue, the doorbell rang and even though I'd half-expected it, I flinched and grabbed my purse, sure receptacle of the pointed and ready bastard file.

A glance through the peephole and I relaxed my grip on the sharp-edged tool. The bearlike lady who lived with sweet-voiced Ruthie rocked back and forth in heavy boots on the stoop

"Leona, from next door," she affirmed as I edged the door ajar.

"Yes?"

"Ruthie said to tell you: He was here again, hanging around, peeping in the windows."

"The man in the van?"

She nodded curtly. "Ruthie stares out the window a lot, now she's out of work. She's nervous as a cat, says you better call the cops. Woman got murdered up in Truro not long ago, and she keeps nattering on about it. I'd call them myself, but she doesn't want any cops ringing our doorbell."

"He came by today?"

"Soon as your car pulled up, Ruthie shooed me over to tell you."

"Well, thank you. And thank her." I started to shut the door.

"Don't you want the license number? To tell the cops?"

"Ruthie got it?"

"I did." She tapped her head to indicate that she'd memorized it.

I hesitated, overcome by an aversion to hospitality. If I let the woman through the front door, it seemed to me I'd need to offer coffee or tea, answer questions, make small talk. A face-saving thought intruded:

the folded note sat on the small table in the entryway. I could write the digits beneath the cryptic message and keep the screen door shut.

Leona recited the plate number, peering through the screen, watching as I took it down, then surprised me by saying, "First Encounter? You heading to the beach?"

At first I thought she might be talking to herself, but she was smiling, expectant. "Great sundowns over there. Seen some beauts there, me and Ruthie."

"I'm sorry?" I said.

"Didn't mean to pry, couldn't help seeing what you wrote. You'll enjoy it."

"What?"

"The sunset. First Encounter Beach, half mile or so from here? Off Samoset Road."

CHAPTER
twenty-four

Samoset Road cut a narrow, winding path through scrub grass and low furrowed hills, and I drove along in spurts and starts, hurrying, slowing abruptly, alternating between hope and anxiety. In a kind of waking fantasy, the man in the blue van, the mysterious McK, with a courtly bow and a gentle smile, handed over the Brooklyn Pierce tape. He looked a little like you, Teddy. I shook myself out of the rose-colored fog. In the real world, he might be trouble, might even be dangerous. A crocus killer.

A public beach on Cape Cod at sunset is not an abandoned urban warehouse at midnight. Beaches were open stretches of level ground, and I'd stay in the car until I figured out the drill. The locked car would serve as a suit of armor.

The road twisted and doubled back. A graveled parking area opened on the right, but the road turned left, continuing, closing in on the shoreline. I followed till the road ended in a narrow, semi-paved rectangle. A blue van sat on its haunches, looming over two smaller cars. Its Massachusetts plate matched Leona's license number.

I parked in a slot that offered a glimpse of ocean waves through high dunes. Along the water's edge, a ponytailed woman walked an elderly golden retriever. I found their presence comforting, reassuring. I sat for three minutes. When nothing happened and no one approached, I decided to venture onto the sand. I kept the car keys clutched in my right hand as a precaution: homemade brass knuckles.

Sand layered the concrete, grinding beneath my heels. I detoured to peer inside the van. Through tinted side windows I made out stacks of paper, overflowing crates, messy piles of clothing, signs indicating that the van doubled as a domicile. I circled it warily, then headed toward the beach. The path was softer than the parking lot, sand clear through. Flattened by thousands of footsteps, it humped over the dunes and descended in a steep rush to the beach.

The lady dog walker nodded and smiled. A trio of youngsters, engaged in piloting a homemade kite with a multicolored tail, ignored my arrival. A man hovered over them with the anxious concern of a parent. I mentally assigned the dog walker to the azure Subaru, the kite flyers to the silver Volvo. The man standing alone at the high-tide mark, staring out at the ocean, was the only other human in sight.

In his late teens, possibly early twenties, his stooped posture declared his discomfort with his stringy height. His large head rested on a thin stalk of neck, and his skin looked pale in the faltering sunshine. A three-day growth of dark stubble covered his face. He smoked a cigarette in short jerky puffs.

He didn't raise his head till I was twenty feet away. Then he not only looked at me with piercing brown eyes, he darted glances left and right as though he expected I'd brought along a posse who were even now encircling him. He wore a faded gray jacket, cowboy style with patch pockets. The straps of a lumpy backpack cut his shoulders.

I stopped five feet away. *Why are you bothering me?* was the thought foremost in my mind, but I didn't get to say it before he spoke.

"Glenn McKenna," he said. "Em, right? You got ID on you? Lemme see it."

I'd locked my purse in the trunk of the car. I shook my head.

"How'm I supposed to know you're who you say you are?" He cupped a hand around the cigarette, protecting it from the wind, and hunched his shoulders.

"You're the one peeping in my windows. You're the one who wanted to meet." I turned and took a step toward the path.

"Wait up. Hey, c'mon, don't get in a huff."

"I'm not in a huff. What do you want?"

He shifted his eyes, but said nothing.

"I take it you knew Teddy?"

He nodded, almost imperceptibly.

"Do you have a tape for me? A microcassette?"

"Yeah, yeah, well, the thing is, what do you have for me?"

"For you?"

The wind whipped along the beach, and I shielded my eyes from the blowing sand.

"Maybe I got something for you, but I gotta slow it down here. I gotta know the deal's on. I figure any deal I made with him ought to go for you."

A deal, Teddy? *A deal?* I sucked in air and replied carefully, "I'm sorry, but there seems to be something I'm missing."

The retriever barked triumphantly and paddled into the surf, pursuing a stick. The man lowered his voice and gestured me closer.

"Sorry about what happened. You know what went down? He have a heart attack?"

I kept my distance. "A car accident."

"Yeah, but he was alone, no second car or anything, right?"

"Give me the tape. Teddy would want me to have it."

"Tape?" McKenna eyeballed the kids with their kite, measuring the distance between their tight circle and our windswept sand. He pushed the hair off his face and said, "Walk with me."

His secretive hush was making me look over my shoulder, as though anyone would care what we said to each other. The kids were involved with the whipsawing kite, the father with the kids. The woman played fetch-the-stick with her dog. McKenna regarded them as though they might be cleverly disguised foreign agents.

"Not far," I said.

He marched rapidly along the shoreline, in the direction opposite the woman and her retriever. I trailed behind, my short legs a disadvantage, sand squishing in my shoes.

"So you don't know anything about me?" He spoke as though he couldn't quite comprehend the possibility. "Teddy never talked about me?"

"That's right."

"He didn't give you my card?" He sounded aggrieved.

I shook my head and trudged, half a step behind. His legs were long, his stride jerky and hesitant. He tossed his cigarette butt on the sand, ground it out with his heel, yanked a cardboard square from his pocket, and pressed it into my hand.

GLENN MCKENNA, it announced. CCTRUTHTELLER.COM.

"You're a blogger?"

"Citizen journalist," he muttered. "Run a Web site. Lot of celebs on the Cape, more in the summer. I track 'em, let people know where they are and what they're up to. You could call me a gossip merchant.

I don't handle the Islands. Somebody else does those. You get more so-called stars on Martha's Vineyard and Nantucket, but I do fine. I do okay."

I nodded because he seemed to expect a response.

"Teddy asked me to hold off doing a story about him, so it wouldn't impede his access. You and me, we can work out the same kinda deal." His shotgun spew of words was delivered in a flat monotone with a curious lack of emphasis that failed to underscore the urgency in his eyes.

"I suppose you can interview me. When I have time. But you said you had something for me."

His eyes raked the beach, examined the dunes, scrutinized the dwarf shrubs and beach grass, glanced at the kite flyers to ensure they'd left their long-distance listening devices at home. "I had something for Teddy. Tell me, how fast was he going? When it happened? Was he speeding?"

The rapid-fire questions hit me like punches in the gut. I turned away, shook my head, said I didn't know, but my reaction didn't stop McKenna.

"Was he drunk?" he insisted.

"No. I don't know. No one's said anything."

"Exactly. There was hardly anything in the news. You'd think it woulda gotten more press, coverage on the radio, TV."

"I hadn't thought about it."

"You should." His eyes darted out to sea like he was scanning for lurking submarines. "It was over in Dennis Port, right? I can check it out; I know everybody on the force. They know me. I'll ask around."

"I don't want a lot of grim details, okay? So—"

"Think about the timing. Think what it could mean."

"I don't understand."

"You know why this is First Encounter Beach? Right?"

"This is far enough." I planted my feet in the sand, football fields away from the kite flyers. The dog yipped faintly in the distance.

"Pilgrims." The wind parted his hair as he turned to face me. "December 1620, third expedition in the shallop, the boat they carried over in pieces on the *Mayflower*. Twelve men, Winslow, Bradford, Carver, three crewmen, and the captain, too. They'd seen the Indians— Wampanoag, probably—gotten hints of them. Hell, stole their seed corn. Came ashore right here, looking for a decent harbor, fresh water. Ate their dinner, set watchmen while they slept. Disturbance around midnight, yells and noises. Thought it was wolves or foxes, but then, early morning, they heard voices and knew it was Indians: The first encounter."

I crossed my arms over my chest and shivered, imagining the beach in December with the wind cutting like shards of icy glass. Sundown in chilly April was cold enough for me. The light was failing in the sky; the kids reeled in the kite while the father folded his beach chair.

"If you have something that belonged to Teddy, you should give it to me. Okay?" I wanted to get back to the car before they left the parking area.

"You don't like history?"

"It's cold and I have work to do."

"We'll walk back." He suited his actions to the words and we set off into the wind. "I'm coauthor?"

"I'm sorry?"

"I want to make sure you're gonna give me the same kinda deal Teddy promised. I'm not as concerned about the money; that would be gravy. But I want the credit."

"Credit?" I had the impulse to scratch my head, like a cartoon character showing puzzlement. "What kind of credit?"

"On the Malcolm book."

Utterly baffled, I tried not to show my confusion. "I assume you have something in writing?"

"You gotta be kidding. What I've got is information, stuff that will tip the book right over the edge."

"Over the edge?"

"Into bestseller-land."

"What kind of information?"

"Exactly," he said, nodding his head.

"We're not gossipmongers or sensation hunters. We don't do that."

"Right. Teddy said get him proof, get him people willing to talk."

"About?"

"Don't you believe the people have the right to know? Don't you believe in transparency? I'm planning to set up on the Gawker network, with CCtruthtelling or, if I can swing it, with Evan Russell's Gossipnet. You've heard of that, right? But so far I'm small potatoes; they don't want to hear from me." He spoke so quickly I wasn't sure I was following him. "Listen: When the Pilgrims came here, they weren't the first. They dug stuff up. Half a mile from here, corpses: a man with yellow hair attached to his skull, maybe a French trader, and a child. Think of it: December, and they didn't have their harbor yet, no shelters, no place to make a stand against the winter."

"Wait. You were talking about now, about Teddy." For the first time, I wondered whether Glenn McKenna might be slightly deranged. Something rabbit-like and shifty lurked behind those brown eyes.

"Just because a man's famous, he can't walk over everybody else. He can't refuse his duty. A man ought to be held accountable, just like the rest of us. Maybe you don't agree; I didn't think Blake would. I mean, you make your livelihood off these people, these rich creeps. You tell what they want you to tell, one side of the story, right?"

"This is about Garrett Malcolm?"

"Teddy gave me an advance. 'Course, if he didn't, I'd have gone to one of the magazines. *People* would pay for this, but I'd sooner go to a webzine."

"Teddy gave you money? How much? Did he give you a check?"

"But the credit, that's more important. Are you down with this or what?"

The woman whistled and the dog raced out of the foam, stumbling and shivering. I mumbled something about needing to know more.

McKenna's eyes raked the sand for hidden cameras. Then he knelt, removed his backpack, and unzipped the front pouch, shifting his stance to shield his actions. I leaned to the left and watched him finger through the single manila folder, removing sheet after sheet, reviewing the few remaining pages, making quick, penciled marks.

"This'll give you a kind of idea where I'm going. Keep it safe."

He handed me the folder like it was secret-agent stuff. I started to back away.

"Don't you want to know how the first encounter ended? Pilgrims and Indians?"

What I wanted was to be inside the car with the doors locked and the heater blasting before the dog-walking woman left the beach. The wind picked up till it was almost a howl. I wanted to run, but the man's intensity was compelling, a force as implacable as the wind. I nodded as he straightened and shouldered the backpack.

"Nobody knows who fired first. Everybody ran around and hid. Arrows and bullets both. Scared the shit out of each other, but nobody got hurt."

The dog lady hitched the leash to the retriever's collar and started up the dune path. Clutching the folder to my chest, I followed her, moving as quickly as I could in the sand.

"Stay in touch," McKenna called.

I paused. "How can I reach you?"

"Through the site. Or tomorrow night, I'll be over at Coast Guard Beach. Yeah, you can meet me there or e-mail me through the site. You'll want to know what I find out. You know, over in Dennis Port?"

I flew up the path, digging my toes into the sand. To my relief, he didn't follow. In the rearview mirror, the sun quenched its fire in the bay.

CHAPTER
twenty-five

S amoset Road's unmarked curves defied my determination to drive
so rapidly McKenna couldn't follow in the van. When I reached
Route 6, I yanked the steering wheel left instead of right to throw him
off the trail, which was stupid because he knew where I was staying.

My God, Teddy, what were you thinking, associating with that
creepy scarecrow, dealing with him? Thank God, he hadn't asked to
meet in a bar where I might have reaped the full benefit of his body
odor. The thought of a bar, or rather the conjunction of the thought
with the flashing neon of a pizza joint, pulled me almost forcibly off the
highway. Parking spaces were available in front, but I pulled quickly

around the side and hid in the back lot so McKenna wouldn't spot my car if he drove past.

The call of food and drink was strong, but I ignored it and grasped my cell phone. When Darren Kalver picked up on the second ring, I requested his boss.

"He'll be able to see you tomorrow at ten-fifteen."

"That's fine. May I please speak with him?"

"Is it necessary?"

"Yes." I didn't bother adding that I wouldn't have asked otherwise. The phone went silent and I wondered whether the PA had put me on hold or cut me off.

"Em, I'm so sorry I had to cancel. How are you?" Malcolm's baritone soothed me instantly, the way a pacifier mollifies an infant. I remembered how he'd complimented my appearance and my cheeks flushed as though it were happening all over again.

"I was hoping to get in touch with Brooklyn Pierce."

"Half the women in America are hoping the same thing," he said drily.

"I need clarification on a point in his interview."

"I didn't realize you'd interviewed him."

"Teddy did."

"Of course. Well, maybe I can help. Clarify whatever it was."

"It would be better if I spoke directly with Mr. Pierce."

"Can't help you there."

"You don't know where he's staying?"

"I think he already left town, to tell the truth."

"Then he's not your Hamlet?"

"My Hamlet? Are you kidding?"

I thanked him and ended the call. His mention of the truth, that wholly unnecessary "to tell the truth" struck a false note, made me uneasy, made me think he was lying. Flicking on the overhead light, consulting a guidebook, I keyed in the number of the Chatham Bars

Inn, a castle-like hotel surrounded by gray-shingled cottages, the local resort most likely to host celebrities. No one named Pierce was registered. I tried the Wequassett Inn, the Queen Anne, and several other deluxe retreats with no luck. Pierce might have registered under a pseudonym. He could be staying with friends in a private home.

Two loud and jovial men piled into a nearby pick-up truck, faces red with beery afterglow, balancing boxes of pizza on their knees. I inhaled the scent of molten mozzarella as I exited the car.

The counter man carded me when I ordered a beer. I paid in advance and an elderly woman with an apron over her jeans brought reheated slices—one mushroom, one cheese—to my rickety table. I bent and tucked a folded napkin under a table leg, then held both hands over the steaming pizza, absorbing the heat, considering how odd it was to eat in a public place, sit down to a meal surrounded by strangers. The walls were orange and grimy, but the light was cheerful and the sounds of clattering silverware and idle chatter pleasant. The slices looked limp and unappetizing, but I felt a surge of confidence shoot through my veins. I drank beer. I took a bite, felt the cheese squish against my palate as I opened McKenna's folder.

The first two pages were reprints of letters in tiny blurred print, jammed together eight to the page, deploring the immorality of actors, letters that, except for their explicit and modern vocabulary, could have been written at the time of Will Shakespeare or Joseph Jefferson or when Eugene O'Neill lead his dissolute company to the dunes. Each was dated, and the initials C.C.T., added in pencil, indicated they'd all been published in *The Cape Cod Times*. Occasional sentences were heavily underscored. "At Cranberry Hill, the only work girls do is the Devil's work" featured a string of hand-drawn exclamation points. The names of the senders had been carefully obliterated.

I downed half my Budweiser. Teddy, I have to say I didn't see the need to pay some wing nut for the startling revelation that the Cape housed its share of screed-writing cranks.

In addition to excoriating the behavior of actors, there was an underlying drumbeat of financial dissatisfaction, an echo of the kind of stuff Donna, the hairdresser, had mentioned. Letter writers warned that the land surrounding the theater, a valuable town asset, was in grave danger of disappearing from the tax rolls forever. Two recommended closing the theater outright, encouraging commercial development of the site so that more year-round jobs would gravitate to the Cape.

One letter, with even smaller type and an official-looking logo, proved indecipherable. I strained, but the print was so tiny I couldn't make it out. I studied the letterhead, but McKenna had used a Sharpie to mutilate the name and address. When I held the blotchy document to the light, I could make out four letters of the last name. I wrote them down along with the only legible words in the next line of print: "Islands District."

When I flipped to the third page, the letters gave way to rough copies of photographs. I chewed pizza and ran my eyes down the page. Attractive young men and women cavorted in foam-topped waves, faces blurred, bodies hard and lean. Two or three girls were topless and I wondered if they were local girls following the devil's dictates. A photo near the bottom caught my eye. A man who might be Malcolm, a younger Malcolm with no gray in his hair. The background was a street scene, no hint of the ocean, a low-slung building.

I flipped to the fourth page and discovered remnants of a cramped list. Glenn McKenna may have been in your pay, Teddy, but he was nuts. The CIA did less redacting. Line after line had been heavily X'd out. The remaining text seemed to be a record of occasions on which police had been summoned to Cranberry Hill, a list of complaints by neighbors concerning loud parties, or heavy traffic on narrow roads after a performance.

Aha! On July 27, 2004, actors lit a beach bonfire without obtaining the required permit. If this constituted the dark and seamy underside of a great man's life, it was less than compelling. I was tempted to ball the papers up and use them for target practice on the over-the-counter TV screen, blacken the eye of the perky sportscaster previewing the upcoming Red Sox season. I wanted to forget McKenna, declare him a homeless bum who stored squirrel food in his backpack along with whatever current "project" he imagined himself "working" on. But you weren't a fool, Teddy. If you gave him money, you must have had a reason. Surely you hadn't entrusted him with a tape on which Brooklyn Pierce made some game-changing, book-altering revelation?

I finished my beer and imagined Pierce, Ben Justice himself, striding into the pizza parlor, waltzing through the neon-lit doorway. What a stir that would cause. The idea made me reconsider McKenna's usefulness. If Pierce were staying on the Cape, McKenna, the celeb freak, might know where to find him. I left half the pizza, cold and shining with grease, on the table.

The rented house sat quietly on the dark street. Moonlight picked out the skeletal branches of overhanging pines. I pulled into the drive, killed the engine, and listened to the silence, glad I'd left the living room lights on. Their welcoming glow shone through a crack in the curtains.

I dumped my coat in a heap at the door, booted my laptop, consulted McKenna's grimy business card, and entered the URL for CCtruthtelling.com into my browser. If McKenna were any good, he'd have Pierce splashed across his home page. Brooklyn drew eyeballs. His antics, rehab stints, girlfriends, and excesses were the stuff of gossip Web sites. Not till I was staring at the opening screen did I admit my desire to view McKenna's brainchild whether or not it led to Pierce's current whereabouts.

Considering my impression of McKenna, CCtruthtelling.com was a surprisingly professional product—garish, but well-designed—and McKenna, to give him his due, gave the viewer an immediate eyeful of photos and screaming headlines: Unexpurgated tales of debauchery!

Nude sunbathing! Drugs and lechery on luxury yachts! CCtruthtelling invited readers to submit their pix! Tell their stories! Advertise here! By Web standards, the site wasn't a skin show, more an innuendo show, a malice fest. The lawsuit-protection question mark was invoked frequently. Ads for tattoo parlors, escort services, and other celebrity Web sites rimmed the screen.

The Cape area boasted several souls who might qualify as celebrities in any jurisdiction, movie stars like Chris Cooper. Ben Affleck's mother owned a house in Truro. Martin Sheen was occasionally spotted at area beaches. But at CCtruthtelling, anyone who dated a celebrity was a celebrity; a member of a pro sports team was a celebrity; a model was transformed into a celebrity if she appeared on the arm of a sports hero. Anyone who appeared on a reality-based TV show was a celebrity. A Barnstable girl who sang on *American Idol* was fair game for any cell phone photographer or tattletale ex-boyfriend. Any politician or ex-politician or family member of a politician signed up for lifelong harassment. The special "Catch a Kennedy" section was devoted to photos of any member of the famed political clan approaching or leaving their Hyannis Port estate. Since Garrett Malcolm was a superstar and anyone who worked with him was the goods, you, Teddy, would have been a first-class "get."

You called celebrity "fame's shallow second cousin," but I know you felt its lure. You never missed reading the daily "Names" section in *The Boston Globe* and when a publication date approached, you sent advance notice to the gossip mavens. You kept score. How many TV interviews did our book on movie fave Gemma Haley rate? More or fewer than the subject of our previous book? Forgive me, but I sometimes thought you were jealous of the celebs, miffed if not angry that TV hosts chose to interview them instead of you.

Pages of CCtruthtelling, salaciously labeled first base, second base, and so on, were devoted to the Cape Cod Baseball League, picturing athletes embracing females in various stages of undress. If a girl dated a member of a Cape Cod League team, her photo—not a high school graduation shot, either, but a shot of her drunk in a gutter—was duly posted and her entire family publically demeaned. Pages devoted to Cape summer theater were, if anything, worse. Last summer's "superstars" were relentlessly photographed: Kirsten Dunst! Dakota Fanning! Libby Beckwith! Orlando Bloom! Olivia Wilde!

I had no idea so many famous and semifamous souls set foot on Cape Cod, all seemingly unaware that McKenna had them in his sights. I hadn't noticed any photographic equipment through the tinted windows of the van, but McKenna was a wizard with a telephoto lens. Over half the photo credits were G. McKenna, and while the majority of photos weren't obscene, they were lurid and nasty, the kind of shots that celebrated the awkward, drunken encounter, the bathing-suit bra prior to readjustment.

I wondered if McKenna paid waiters in top-flight restaurants and chambermaids at ritzy inns to tip him off, or if he relied exclusively on volunteers. The site didn't seem like much of a revenue source, but the ads must bring in something. I continued scrolling, searching, for mention of Brooklyn Pierce.

I was embarrassed at how often I found myself staring at photos of overexposed flesh. It was like stopping at the side of the road to view debris from a train wreck, but I was unable to look away. I believe in freedom of the press, but I found myself questioning its limits. Glenn McKenna would say he was pushing the boundaries, no doubt. He probably had a dozen lawsuits pending. *The Boston Herald* is a tabloid, but compared to CCtruthtelling, it was *The New York Times* in the golden age of journalism.

Which married actor spent the night with which beautiful actress? Who nuzzled his way-too-young gf at the Nauset Beach Club Thursday night? I slummed my way through CCtruthtelling, amazed by the level of innuendo, the lack of verified fact, the smutty speculation about people who were not celebrities at all, just ordinary folks who ought to enjoy a reasonable expectation of privacy. Some shots must have been deliberately posed. And most of the females must be paid rather than amateur talent. If the girls in the photos were merely dates, earnest if misguided teens, wouldn't at least one of them have grabbed Daddy's shotgun, always supposing Daddy didn't grab it first?

I pictured the blue van with the tinted windows. Not only must McKenna live in it, he must constantly move it. If he had a fixed abode, enraged fathers would line up to shoot him.

I tore my eyes from the site when I realized I was scanning for photos of Malcolm, photos of the director with other women. I fled to the kitchen and gulped a glass of water, berated myself for that indulgent beer. While standing at the sink, just to do something with my left hand, I opened the drawer to the left, a junk drawer, the kind you find in any kitchen. The magnifying glass was the first item I saw.

Relieved I hadn't tossed McKenna's folder in the trash along with the remnants of pizza, I perused it under the glass. The four letters I'd copied from the illegible missive were "oole." "Islands District," the words I'd picked out of the official-looking seal were part of the phrase "Office of the Cape and Islands District Attorney." The letter thanked the sender for his timely warning concerning a local resident, one Garrett Malcolm.

CHAPTER
twenty-six

Tape 132
Patrick Fallon O'Toole
4/2/10

Teddy Blake: *Thanks for making time to see me.*

Patrick Fallon O'Toole: Well, a person could say I've got time to burn now. Pleasure to meet you, read that book you wrote, the one with that actress, what's her name, yeah, Gemma Haley. That was one helluva read, so I'm happy to cooperate. Retired man's got nothing but time. They make any movies outa your books?

TB: *Not yet.*

PFO: Well, they ought to. Really, they should.

TB: *Thank you again. For the compliment as well as your time.*

PFO: Retired, unemployed, same difference. So, you're writing about Garrett Malcolm this time? Let me say right off, I've got nothing but admiration for the man and his work, and I hope he doesn't hold that old business against me. It was the job, and I had to do it.

TB: *I'm gathering background material.*

PFO: Okay, like I said, I've got the time. And probably, I mean if he's in on this, if it's an authorized biography—

TB: *It is. Actually, it's an autobiography. In Malcolm's own words.*

PFO: Bet he'll have a few choice ones for me and not exactly printable, either. I go back a ways here, District Attorney better part of thirty years, knew the old man, Malcolm's dad, Ralph, so I probably saw Garrett on stage before I ever met him, though Shakespeare's not exactly my thing, went to opening nights every summer to keep the wife happy. She liked to get all dolled up. I'm more of a golfer, but my wife, she always wanted to see the shows, and it was a good thing I went, I suppose, got to mix with the people and all. Just not my kind of thing, watching grown-ups prancing around a stage, not that I don't like a good Clint Eastwood movie, you know?

TB: *Can you zero in on your professional contact with Malcolm? When did that begin?*

PFO: I'm not gonna go back to when he was a kid. Statute of limitation, boys will be boys, and all that business. He and that cousin of his, the Foley boy, they got up to their share of high jinks, but if I had to write down every stupid thing I did when I was a teenager, that would be one helluva long list.

TB: *Mine, too.*

PFO: See what I mean?

TB: *Wouldn't boyish pranks be something for the local police department?*

PFO: On the whole, sure, but you know, there are exceptions. Like, when stuff happened down the Kennedy Compound, the locals weren't always the first ones to get the call. Can I freshen your glass?

TB: *As long as I'm not drinking alone.*

PFO: No chance of that. Where were we?

TB: *Your professional relationship with Garrett Malcolm.*

PFO: The Fire Department was the A.H.J., 'scuse me, the Authority Having Jurisdiction, not me, at the beginning. Small potatoes. They wanted a fireman standing by every performance—new rules, but Malcolm figured they were just being pains in the ass because of the fire that happened back when he was a kid, so he says okay, we don't need the fire department all the time, just if the play uses fireworks and stuff. And then they went and did some show with fire and didn't alert the department, and that was right around the time that night-club in Providence, Rhode Island, blew up, and a hundred people died. So folks went nuts. I had a heart-to-heart with Malcolm and we fixed things, made sure he had a regular guy from the fire department there at every performance.

TB: *But that wasn't the extent of the trouble?*

PFO: Not entirely. There was a certain element attracted by some of his shows. Now, let me say I have no trouble with crowds in general. The Cape Cod League, they've been a real asset, very supportive of the community. They hire your off-duty police officers, make sure there's no inconvenience to local property owners. Most of the theater groups do the same. Nobody wants trouble.

TB: *It's hard to associate big crowds of drunks with a summer Shake-speare festival.*

PFO: All I'm saying is they didn't hire enough men to police their grounds. It's not just Shakespeare there, either. They do other stuff, modern stuff. They hire big-time actors, movie stars. Stars draw a dif-ferent kind of crowd, like rock-and-roll bands. And the neighbors—you know, people buy a house here, they're paying up the wazzoo. What do they want? Quiet. They want calm. They want to ride a bike to the beach, have a picnic. They don't want some Hollywood scene. 'Least they didn't. The Cape is different now. I'm glad to be out of the whole thing, glad to be out of politics.

TB: *Would I be right in saying that your dispute with Malcolm was po-litical?*

PFO: Whoa, you're jumping to conclusions. I didn't just pick on the man because I had nothing else to do.

TB: *Sorry.*

PFO: We had a runaway problem, what you might call a rash of runaways, late nineties, early oughts. Local kids, teenagers, mainly girls. It was like a contagious disease and we couldn't locate the source of the infection. Now, most of them were fine, you know? Two weeks' wonder, and then it turned out the kids who ran went to visit Aunt Lizzie in New Orleans and forgot to tell Mom, or got drunk, wrecked the car, and hitchhiked to Vermont.

TB: *How did Malcolm come into it?*

PFO: A few, well, maybe only a couple of the runaway girls auditioned for him, for that theater. I know that sounds pretty skimpy, but we were getting these letters. The real problem started with the letters, and I admit I may have been duped, my office may have been duped.

TB: *Anonymous letters?*

PFO: Right.

TB: *And this was around the same time as Malcolm's divorce?*

PFO: I didn't know that! I don't follow any of that gossip shit. But I suppose I should have known better. Girls these days, they run after the men. But it didn't seem right to me, using high school kids, call them theatrical apprentices, and get unpaid labor, you know? Shit, good thing I'm not running for office anymore, statement like that. I'm sure the kids learn a lotta useful skills. That's the kinda thing I'm supposed to say.

TB: *And the girls who auditioned?*

PFO: I remember one girl, first to run off. Didn't click as an actress, so decides she'll be a model. Entered some online "contest," and one of her friends drove her to New York City to meet some pervert going to put her on the front page soon as he checks out how she looks with no clothes on. She wasn't more than thirteen, still in junior high.

TB: *She came back?*

PFO: I only wish she'd come back earlier, before I went and talked with Malcolm, but her father was pressing me, thought he was a big shot, you know how that is. Malcolm didn't like being accused of anything and the timing was terrible for him, too. Turned out he was in the middle of trying to get some court order so he could visit his little girl.

TB: *And word got out that you interviewed him? That you suspected he had something to do with the girl's disappearance?*

PFO: Yeah, word got out, not that my office put it out. But word leaked. I felt bad about it. And I think word leaked about what that young girl was up to, too, because when she came back her folks moved her to a private school with more rules than Marine boot camp. Things like that happen, and you can't go treating every runaway like some big-time killing.

TB: *Like the Helga Forrester case.*

PFO: That drink need freshening?

TB: *Thanks, that would be great. Do you mind talking about the Forrester case? I understand it was the occasion for another run-in with Malcolm.*

PFO: I certainly never meant for that to happen. It was unfortunate. Especially, as it turned out, for me. But I didn't just pick him out to be a victim of prosecutorial excess, although to read the papers you'd think I was as vindictive an SOB as walked the earth. You gotta understand what was going on then. The pressure I was under. Only had a handful of murders on the Cape, ever. And that one was a three-ring circus. Unmarried woman with a baby, and all the speculation about how the daddy had to be the killer. When I didn't wrap it up in an hour and a half and run the credits, the whole place went nuts. Neighbors accusing neighbors, TV talking heads foaming at the mouth. Hadn't been for that murder, I would still have my job. Terrible thing, to be thinking of your own reelection when that poor woman's dead with her little child looking on, but I probably couldn't have handled things worse if I'd sat down and made a list of ways to lose the election.

TB: *There was no indication that Malcolm knew the deceased, am I right?*

PFO: Just wait a minute. It wasn't about that, it was about the DNA. Why don't you just shut up and let me tell you about it?

TB: *Sorry.*

PFO: You can't go badgering a witness. It was just a terrible time here. There were so many suspects, but nobody saw anything. Nobody heard anything. Folks like to come up with all these theories, even if they won't hold water let alone beans, and there was some guy writing a tell-all book and everybody hinting they knew what was going on. We decided the best thing to do was use technology, use what we had, which was semen found on the body. We knew it wouldn't be popular, but everybody was scared. There was a killer out there. People were buying guns, threatening their neighbors.

TB: *Whose idea was it to collect DNA samples from all the men on the Cape?*

PFO: The FBI. That's right, the sainted FBI, but you woulda thought I'd come up with it in some kinda dream, no, make that some kinda séance I held with the devil himself. It was the FBI's idea. They thought the killer had ties to the area. They suggested it, called it a global genetic canvass. We weren't the first place to do it, or the only place. They solve crimes like that in England, in Germany, too. In 1994, I think it was, Germany, they took DNA samples from 16,000, maybe 17,000 men, and they got their killer, guy raped and murdered an eleven-year-old girl. They tried it in Baton Rouge, too, or someplace in Louisiana. If the Forrester woman had been killed in the summer, we wouldn't have tried it, so many damned tourists on and off Cape, but in the winter this place shrinks down to nothing. Once we ruled out all the women and the kids, it seemed manageable. And not the whole Cape, either, just the three or four closest towns.

TB: *But there was trouble?*

PFO: We tried to keep it real low-key at first, asking people politely to volunteer when they came into town, at the supermarket, the garage, the sub shops, the post office, handing out swabs, taking information: name and address. And I'd like to point out that it worked. We found the guy and he's in prison.

TB: *You brought Garrett Malcolm in for questioning. Did you do that with everybody who refused to give a DNA sample?*

PFO: Are you kidding? We had folks speed-dialing the American Civil Liberties Union.

TB: *But you brought Malcolm in.*

PFO: I do regret that.

TB: *You threatened him with a court order.*

PFO: One of my investigators exceeded his authority. He is no longer with the DA's office. He was removed long before I lost the election.

TB: *Do you wish you'd handled things differently?*

PFO: Of course I do, but at the time there was nothing else I could have done. There was this reporter from some local rag beating the drum, beating the drum. Why don't prominent citizens like Garrett Malcolm have to comply? Why don't they get DNA from Garrett Malcolm? Never mind that the state lab had a backup about a thousand years long. Plus we had other options to go to, lots of areas we hadn't investigated yet, like seasonal workers and stuff. You know, with celebrities, there's no right way to handle it. No matter what you do, you're too lenient or you're coming on too strong, making an example out of them. I came down too hard, I brought Malcolm in, and I got tossed out of office for my trouble.

TB: *You link the two events.*

PFO: They were linked in the press. I was linked with saying something terrible about a great and wonderful man whose wife died of cancer, a man who donated money to political campaigns and local charities, a decent guy who, it turns out, wasn't even on the Cape when Helga Forrester got killed.

TB: *He wasn't here?*

PFO: He had an alibi, a good one.

TB: *So why do you suppose he refused to comply? The procedure wasn't difficult.*

PFO: I'm a former district attorney, not a mind reader. I was trying to eliminate the gossip, that's all. I hope he doesn't still hold it against me. And I hope he reconciles with his daughter, too. Has he, do you know?

TB: *I don't think so.*

PFO: Well, that's too bad. I'd rather lose ten elections than lose contact with my kids. Wouldn't you?

TB: *Haven't got any. Kids.*

PFO: Oh, well. That's okay though, you got books. Send 'em off in the world, see if they sink or swim, just like kids, huh? Think you'll send me a copy of this one when it's done? I'd like that.

TB: *I'll make sure you're on the list.*

CHAPTER
twenty-seven

I felt angry on Malcolm's behalf: unsubstantiated rumors weren't our usual fare. When I'd listened to the tape for the first time, when I'd transcribed and essentially dismissed it, I'd wondered why you'd bothered interviewing a washed-up hack politician. Now, I felt I knew at least part of the answer: McKenna.

You could hardly have believed Malcolm guilty of involvement in the Forrester killing. The case was solved, the killer in jail, serving life with no possibility of parole. McKenna might have sicced O'Toole on Malcolm; a photo of the famous director entering the District Attorney's office, posted online alongside some scurrilous accusation, would have been milk and honey to him. It was possible, even likely, that McKenna invented some of his own gossip. But you'd never pay for that sort of rubbish.

A man like Malcolm, a wealthy landowner, a handsome Hollywood star, might stir neighborhood passions. His cousin probably wasn't the only one jealous of Malcolm's possessions and success. I tried to put myself in your shoes, Teddy, decode the DA's interview from the point of view of a writer in touch with Glenn McKenna. Were you hoping to find some hint that local gossip—or the DA's overreaction to local gossip—changed Malcolm's mind about fighting Claire for Jenna's custody?

I reread each grubby letter, studied each photo. On the fourth page, faint hand-drawn circles appeared around occasional letters and numerals. Someone had scrawled "0=pswd" on the reverse side of the same page, an equation I hadn't previously noticed. I located the e-mails Jonathan had forwarded after your death, quickly isolated the message from <McK> which I now recalled in sharp detail, an e-mail that led to a password-protected site, a dead end at the time.

0=pswd. Circled digits equal password. I printed the circled letters and numerals on a scrap of paper. Hands poised at the keyboard, I felt the manic joy of the puzzle solver, but I hesitated, pondering the choice: To enter or to ignore. Information is a strange and unruly beast. Once you know, you can't unknow, can't unlearn or conveniently forget. Once you leap into the abyss, you can't tread air like a cartoon character with pinwheeling feet, reverse gravity, and regain the cliff.

I closed my eyes as my fingers keyed the password. The screen flickered and changed.

A less polished site than CCtruthtelling.com, this seemed to be McKenna's preview site, the private pages where he stashed materials prior to publication, perhaps while taking time to check their veracity or, more likely, their potential for attracting lawsuits. The printed material McKenna had given me was taken directly from this work space, the photographs far clearer in full color. The carefree sunbathers gamboled in the waves. Were the girls recognizable celebrities? None of the faces seemed familiar.

Several shots featured broad expanses of water in the foreground, figures in the background on a distant beach. I focused on the far background, a small building, a wooden shack, visible behind the laughing people.

I scrolled down. Yes, that was definitely Malcolm, a younger Garrett Malcolm, the shot reframed so that he held hands with a partial woman who disappeared out of the frame. The woman's features were blurred, as though she'd abruptly turned her head. Her dark hair flew outward in a wedge that obscured her profile. Underneath the picture, a caption, no, not a caption, but a string of numbers: 939495?

I wondered whether there ought to be spaces between the numbers, whether they represented years: '93? '94? '95? Malcolm had married the glamorous Claire Gregory in 1992. I studied each screen of McKenna's preview site, hunting for another version of the shot, one in which the woman's face was clear, her identity revealed. I compared the woman with other women on the site, to the frolicking sun worshippers enjoying the crashing waves, but I didn't find a match.

Maybe, I thought, it was nothing more than a shot of Malcolm and a casual acquaintance, someone he'd bumped into on a street in a nearby town. I studied the twined hands in the photo. The pose suggested a certain intimacy, a quality of urgency, almost secrecy.

Malcolm's marriage to Claire had lasted six years. The one characteristic of the woman in the photo that stood out, that was absolutely clear, was the color of her dark hair, brunette, almost black. Claire Gregory, like Harlow and Monroe before her, was a legendary blonde.

CHAPTER
twenty-eight

Yanking shirt over rose-colored bra, I viewed my shadowy reflection in the mirror with a degree of satisfaction. The blue V-neck was pale and worn, but with new underpinnings it felt and looked subtly different. I wished I could have said my new underwear made me feel confident as I drove off to beard the dragon in his den, but it didn't. A friendly dragon, an admired dragon, a dragon who insisted I needn't dress up for him, granted. But a dragon nonetheless.

Once I'd capped last night's obsessive Web site viewing, I'd wrestled sentences into their best order, voicing Malcolm's thoughts about costars and colleagues till well past three in the morning. I'd finished a new chapter and buffed an early section to a polished shine. I'd been lost in his voice, Teddy, possessed by it. Remember what he told you: *The great thing about acting is for ninety minutes I get to be somebody else.* Alone, working, writing, I felt like somebody else, like some exalted species of recording angel privy to Malcolm's innermost thoughts. The prospect of his actual presence, his male scent, his watchful eyes, clouded my mind. What was the best way to get him to open up and really talk to me about his daughter and his relationship with her? If Jenna's portrait were hung alongside her mother's, I could get the ball rolling by admiring it, but I'd seen no photos of Jenna Malcolm. Unless she was one of the girls frolicking on the beach in McKenna's soft-porn candids.

Malcolm awaited me with his assistant nowhere in sight, glory hallelujah. After spending the better part of the night listening to the man's voice, I still found it thrilling, a supple device that made each utterance seem meaningful. Coupled with his sheer physical attractiveness, the wide cheekbones and crinkling good-humored eyes, the effectiveness of his voice doubled. He wore a dark sweater that melted into velvety corduroy trousers.

"How's *Hamlet* shaping up?" It wasn't my first official question, but I wanted to know and the words helped fill an awkward interval as he ushered me down a hallway.

" 'Doubt thou the stars are fire; Doubt thou the sun doth move.' "

" 'Doubt truth to be a liar,' " I said. "Act Two, scene two."

" 'But never doubt I love.' An intriguing poem, isn't it?"

"Hamlet doesn't think so. What does he say? 'I am ill at these numbers.' "

"Meaning my verses suck."

"And then he calls himself a machine, right?"

" 'Thine evermore, most dear lady, whilst this machine is to him.' "

His dazzling smile was like a reward for remembering the lines. As he turned a corner, the hallway narrowed and dipped. He paused, took my hand, and led me down the single step with a courtly move lifted from an Elizabethan dance.

"You'd make a nice Ophelia," he said.

Nice, I thought, in something like despair. Sexy underwear and the best he could do was nice, nice and reliable, like a plain vanilla ice-cream cone.

When he led me to a room less than a quarter the size of the one with the Claire portrait and the window wall, I was disappointed at first. Then he pressed a button near the light switch and with a faint buzz of machinery, wide roman shades began to climb the walls and peel down from the sloped ceiling. I inhaled sharply and stifled a delighted gasp.

It must have been a conservatory once. There were still pots of greenery, ranging from delicate ferns to hardy rubber plants. Three walls and half the roof, now revealed, were tinted glass, and the ocean view was incredible, the water shimmering, close, and of such an intense blue-green that I almost didn't notice the remaining solid wall, which was covered with photos so densely grouped they might have been wallpaper. Wrought-iron chairs and a big rattan sofa piled with flowered pillows made the room feel like a summer porch or a cozy outdoor patio. On a desk, an Oscar statuette, cocktail umbrella perched rakishly on one shoulder, did paperweight duty next to an ornate clock.

"Pick a chair," Malcolm said.

They formed a semicircle near the desk. I chose the one at the right because it had a convenient small table nearby. Instead of sitting behind the desk as I'd assumed he would, Malcolm sank into the chair next to mine, rearranged the cushions, put his feet up on a settee, and gave a satisfied sigh. The chairs were definitely worthy of sighs, big comfortably padded monsters. With the sun beating down and the view of the ocean, it felt magical, as if the room had fast-forwarded the calendar and transformed the chill April day into a late summer holiday. I set the recorder on the table and repositioned my notebook, thinking that when it came time to choose the author photo, I'd recommend a shot of Malcolm at this desk, the Academy Award beside him and the wall of photos in the background.

"Would you care for a drink?"

"No, thanks."

He got up, went to the desk, poured three fingers of decanted amber. "You don't have to drink Scotch. You can have water, my child. Or Coke?"

"I'm fine. I had a beer last night." God, why had I told him that?

He raised an eyebrow. "At a bar?"

I nodded, not trusting myself to speak.

"And you got carded, didn't you?"

"They checked my ID," I admitted.

"I'll bet they did." His tone was light, teasing. "So, the last time you got me to gossip about my colleagues. I hope I didn't say anything too rotten." He brought the drink back to the chair, did the settling business with cushions and footstool again.

"You'll get to review the whole thing when I'm done."

"And you'll take out the objectionable parts?"

"If you object, I'll tell you why I thought it was important to include it in the first place."

"Doesn't the ocean look great? Why don't we go lie on the dunes, play hooky, and to hell with this stuff?"

"If I lived here, I don't think I'd get anything done. I'd lie on the beach every day." I finished checking the levels and flipped on the tape. The click and whirr were tiny sounds, but they effectively shifted the tone.

He was suddenly all business. "Last time, you wanted me to tell you about Claire."

"You talked to Teddy about film, acting, directing, vision and technique, but now we need to get more personal, to balance the book." I nodded encouragement, but I think he'd already decided to talk about her, chosen this particular room as the stage set for his revelations. I wondered if this had been Claire's hideaway, her study.

"No one realized how smart and funny she was, not at first, and that's the daily double in Hollywood, funny and beautiful. If I hadn't lived with her I'd have been as awestruck as anyone, but when you see somebody fall out of bed in the morning and struggle to crack eggs into a pan, you lose that sense of worship pretty quickly. God, she could destroy anything in the kitchen and look so demure and devilish while she was doing it." He paused and pressed his lips together. "I like the way you listen. Claire was a good listener. Actors need to listen."

I flushed. "How did you meet?"

"The real story or the made-up story?"

"Both?"

"We were in the public eye. I was much older than she was. We saw each other on the set, something clicked, and we spent the night screwing ourselves stupid. Then we tried to keep it under wraps."

"That's the made-up story?"

He laughed. "Oh, yes, the real one is much more sordid."

"You were dating Sybilla Jackson."

"God, Sybilla, yes. Dating's a quaint word."

"The supermodel. You were living with her."

"We were fucking, but we weren't exclusive. Syb knew what she was getting into. I didn't fool her, or anybody, with chitchat about orange blossoms and happily-ever-after. I was an old-school bachelor. And don't ask what it was about Claire, because I don't know and I never will. Going into it, I thought it would be another fling, a week, a month, a year, and I didn't care. I needed to be with her. And she needed to be with me."

"You have something of a reputation for sleeping with your leading ladies."

"Only something of a reputation? Anything I tell you, I can take out of the book, right?"

I nodded.

"I like to know everything about the people I work with, and sex is one of the ways I work, or used to work. I was always a little bit sorry I was so determinedly hetero because there were men in the movies and in the plays that I never knew as well as I knew the women, unless, well, sometimes we shared the women. All my films, at the core, are about relationships, and the more relationships I have, the more I understand them, or maybe the less I understand them. But that chemistry, that first time, there's nothing more compelling than the moment when two strangers glance at each other and yearn to be naked in bed together. As a director, as a writer, I specialize in that chemistry."

I stared out the window, pretending to be transfixed by the view. I was probably reading more into the situation than he intended, but he was definitely different today, more casual, more relaxed. Even the room was less formal; the couch, more a daybed than a traditional sofa, seemed to loom portentously in the foreground.

"That's why I'm pounding my head over Hamlet and Ophelia this morning," he continued. "Because when people come to see the play, I want them transfixed by the soliloquies, yes, but I want them to taste the passion behind them. I want them to smell it. I want *Hamlet*, the love story, as well as *Hamlet*, the revenge play. I want the audience to know in their bones that Claudius lusted for Gertrude long before he killed Hamlet's father. I want them to know that Gertrude flirted shamelessly with Claudius before he killed the king, that she couldn't wait to bed him once her old king was dead. I want those 'incestuous sheets' to underscore the entire production, to permeate it. Hamlet knows about them because he sees how his mother looks at Claudius, and he understands them because of the way he feels for Ophelia."

I'd stopped taking notes. Malcolm noticed and I hastily bent to my task, the color rising in my cheeks.

"Think about what Hamlet says about his father, how he's a 'paragon and every virtue sits upon his brow.' And yet Gertrude goes berserk for Claudius. Why? Is she a cliché, the woman who loves an outlaw? Is she a strumpet, a classic bad girl who values hot sex more than she values dignity or class? Is there something Hamlet is completely missing? Was his father a cold and upright man, a man who ignored his wife? And then think about Elizabeth, think of the Virgin Queen in the audience, confronted by this other Queen who gave it all for love, who dies for love."

"How would you play Claudius?" It wasn't the question I intended to ask.

His face split in a wide grin. "I'd make him sexy as hell. Even Ophelia wouldn't be safe in my castle."

I swallowed, tried to get my breath. The sun danced on the waves and glittered in my eyes. I glanced down at my notes and changed the subject. "You moved here before Claire got sick, right?"

He stared out the window at the sea. "Yes, this house, the way it used to be, was our first home. Dad was getting old. The place was all but empty, run down. The Amphitheater hadn't been used in three, four years. I thought I'd retreat here, become my father, but then I had an idea for the movies, the Justice films, somehow I saw them taking place on this coast, right here. Because it wasn't used much for movies, because there was the hardship of winter, one more thing to fight against. It was far away from the craziness on the other coast. Claire loved it."

"But you broke up."

"We couldn't sustain it. That first-time thing; I think it was important for both of us."

"You couldn't sustain it for Jenna's sake?"

"There speaks the child of divorce."

"It's that obvious?"

"I speculate about people. Actors do. Directors do. I can't see you growing up in the bosom of a loving family."

I wanted to demand why almost as much as I wanted him to shut up.

"You bite your nails. You try to seem cold. You have no idea how attractive you are. You know you're clever, but you don't want anyone else to know."

"Jenna is your only child, isn't she?"

"Yes."

"You wanted her to grow up here, like you did?"

"Yes."

I sucked in a breath. This was disastrous. I was pummeling the man with questions he could answer in monosyllables. "Tell me something about her."

"Such as?"

I tried to smile. "Does she bite her nails?"

"Actresses tend to treat their bodies well unless they tip over the edge into anorexia. Jenna is spectacularly beautiful. I can say that because she looks like her mother, not me."

"Would you cast her as Ophelia?"

"Not in my production. I can't imagine listening to Hamlet yell at her, 'Be thou as chaste as ice, as pure as snow, thou shalt not escape calumny.' My impulse would be to keep her safe and a director can never keep his actors safe. Sometimes I wonder how Peter Hall feels when he sees his Rebecca in film and onstage, when she's half naked, seducing some man."

While he spoke, my eyes searched the photo wall. "Is that Jenna?"

He stood, removed the framed snapshot from its hook, and graciously handed it to me. "At the age of ten."

"My God."

"Does that look like any ten-year-old you've ever seen?"

"She's in costume."

"No one could keep her out of costume. She danced, she sang, she was a hell of a little actress."

The girl was long and lithe, dressed in a gypsy-like collection of leotards and filmy scarves. Carefree and joyful, she danced en pointe in the sand. Her blond hair caught the sunshine.

"Where was this taken?"

"Lord, let me see it. She looks even more like her mother now."

"Did you take this?"

He nodded.

"It's a lovely shot."

"You're a lovely girl to say so."

"Where is she now?"

"You are not to contact her."

"I know. I just wondered."

"I'm not sure whether she's in England or Australia at the moment. Her troupe travels, and yes, she is acting. Using a different name. Someday I'll probably agree with her, say it was for the best, that it allowed her to develop as an artist or some such claptrap."

"So it was her idea to see whether she could make it without your influence?"

He nodded. "Some children with famous parents do fine."

"I'm sure she will. Do you give her advice, the way your father—"

"My father was an autocrat. A dictator. Even after he died, he couldn't let go. Remember I mentioned his will? His Shakespearean will? He didn't rattle on about the used furniture or anything like that, but . . ."

It clicked in my head, almost audibly. Your scribbled note, 2nd BST BD, was no reference to a bedroom in a rented house. In his last will and testament, Shakespeare bequeathed his wife, Anne, his second-best bed. In a long and elaborate document, he'd granted her one scant sentence: "Item, I give unto my wife my second best bed with the furniture," and scholars had been speculating over what he'd meant by the phrase for four hundred years. The realization made me lose the thread of Malcolm's words.

He was saying, ". . . almost succeeded, inadvertently, in disinheriting his own much-beloved granddaughter."

"What? Who?"

"My dear father. With his utter stubbornness. He insisted on modeling his will after Shakespeare's. As he had modeled his life, you know? And he gave unto said son, heir of his body lawfully issuing, namely me, all his lands, tenements, and heriditaments whatsoever, to have and to hold, et cetera, during the term of my natural life, and then unto the first son of my body lawfully issuing, et cetera, hardly taking into account that an heir of my body might happen to be a child of the female persuasion. Thank the lord the lawyer who set up the trust intervened after Jenna was born."

"The land trust?" I remembered what the hairdresser had said, about his plan to set up a trust to lower his property taxes.

"You mean the conservation trust? No, no, that's something the board is looking into now, since local property taxes have gone berserk. God knows, the board wants me to do it, but Darren's keeping them away from me till I get this *Hamlet* off my plate. No, I'm talking about back then. My father called it a dynasty trust, but the lawyer used initials, a GST, some arcane lawyerly thing, a generation-skipping transfer, I think. Dad wanted to protect his theater, land, and fortune from the government, from the federal estate tax, so he effectively skipped a generation. This house is mine, but most of the land is technically Jenna's."

"Was your father—?"

"Sorry? Was Dad taken aback by the fact that he almost disinherited Jenna? Not he. No, he was quite convinced that my subsequent heirs would be male, and what was all the fuss about? Because even if I didn't have male children to rule the stage, Jenna would breed boys. Claire had no patience with the old dictator."

"Your actors say you're a dictator. Would you say you're like your father?"

"Christ, maybe that's true. Maybe it's the nature of the beast. Look, I have to get down to the Amphitheater. My assistant says I'm spending way too much time with you, and it's a fact, the time goes by very quickly."

"Can we meet again tomorrow?"

"I'm not sure. You'll have to check with Darren."

"Before you go, one more question."

"No. Honestly I don't have time." He leaned over and placed his index finger over my lips. "Enough."

His touch shocked me to the extent that I don't remember gathering my recorder and notebook, or following him down the hallway. I know he said something about the possibility of meeting for a drink later that evening. I know I refused. I could only imagine that he was trying to mock me, make fun of me. Then I found myself outside, gulping a lungful of salt air.

CHAPTER
twenty-nine

I could still feel the touch of his finger as a warm imprint on my lips. Was the invitation to have a drink some kind of test to determine whether every girl in the universe, no matter how unprepossessing, how plain, mousy, or ordinary, would succumb to his charm? As I drove I ran my fingers across my lips and caressed the lingering dent.

I might never see him again. He hadn't guaranteed another interview. I'd need to speak to his PA, and who knew whether Kalver would see fit to squeeze me into Malcolm's busy schedule? If Malcolm had time for a drink, couldn't he make time for an interview?

You must have gone for drinks with Malcolm, patronized some bar where he'd regaled you with the story of Ralph's Shakespearean will. You'd jotted a few notes, meaning to bring it up in a later interview or to instruct me to research the document. I was happy to know I was on the same trail you'd blazed before me.

I'd manage, even if the PA shut me out, even if Malcolm shut me out. I had the tapes, the films, the voice. My lip tingled where he'd touched it. I drove blindly and, instead of heading to the highway, I took the turn that led to the Old Barn, not that I needed or wanted anything at the barn, but because I knew I could sit there and ponder in the quiet oasis of the parking area.

Voices had been enough, Teddy. Transcribing, writing, hearing the clock strike the hours of each unremarkable day, had been enough. But now I felt empty, a shell of the person I'd been before meeting Garrett Malcolm. How could I return to my tiny apartment, to the quiet clock-ticking minutes of listening and writing, the drab view of the brick façade across the alleyway, after the glowing hearth of shared conversation with such a man? I debated entering the barn, inhaling the sawn-wood silence, reviewing the ranks of ordered gowns, the shelf of wigs.

Instead I reimagined the conservatory, the comfy chairs, the sun beating down through the glass ceiling, the shining windows, the faint aroma of pine needles and good whiskey. I shut my eyes, reached for my notebook, penned a quick list of the photos on the wall. I hadn't gotten the chance to ask about any of them except Jenna's, not the old ones that showed the Big House before it grew so large, or the framed genealogical chart that hung near the center, surrounded by a cluster of photos that looked like Malcolm, yet not like him, old-fashioned romantic poses that might have been publicity stills of Malcolm's father when he'd played Hamlet. Positioned next to these was a famous shot of Malcolm in his Broadway *Hamlet*. Photos of Claire were interspersed with pictures of other beautiful actresses Malcolm had directed. And then, the award photos: Malcolm in his tux, thanking the members of the Academy; Malcolm at the Directors Guild ceremony, a breathtaking beauty on each arm.

In a day or two, he wouldn't recall my name. I should have junked my prepared questions and used the wall as a lead-in. What could be more personal than the images a man chose to keep in the small private room where he worked?

I was surprised, considering his fatherly pride, that Malcolm didn't display a more recent photo of Jenna. How lovely she was and how lucky to grow up here, the exquisite image of her adored mother. But then, she hadn't grown up here, not really. She'd spent her childhood on the beach, but then she'd moved, sharing Claire's exile from the kingdom.

I recalled that gypsy shot of Jenna, saw again the wooden beams, the small structure behind the dancing girl. I was certain I'd seen it before, Teddy, but when and where? The answer, stuck in the basement of my mind, stubbornly refused to ascend. Possibly the same setting served as the backdrop for a scene in one of the Justice films.

Each had been shot locally, a revenue and recognition boost for the Cape. Tourists still made pilgrimage to Wellfleet's town center, scene of an intense chase sequence through Town Hall, an adjacent Episcopalian church, and a moss-covered cemetery. I opened the car door and swung my legs out. I could stroll the property, spot locations from the films, use that first-hand knowledge in the book.

"All my lands, tenements, and hereditaments whatsoever, to have and to hold." The language had rolled off Malcolm's tongue like thunder. Some said his magnificent voice resembled his father's, but I'd heard recordings and Ralph Malcolm's voice was heavier on the bass. What an inheritance Garrett Malcolm's father had given him. "Terrific times," his cousin James Foley said on tape. "Fed on hot and cold running Shakespeare," and even if the Amphitheater was a wreck and the house in disrepair, there was the land, the coastline, the view.

The memory of Foley's transcript brought me up short. What was wrong with me? If I were home, dealing only with words, I'd have made the connection immediately. Foley said he kept in touch with Brooklyn Pierce. That would explain how you'd made contact.

The sun, high in a cloudless sky, grappled with the cool ocean breeze and managed to turn the air surprisingly warm. The urge to stroll along the water's edge, to play hooky, in Malcolm's words, was strong. I told myself I'd get a better sense of the estate by walking it, experience the environs in which the master director had matured, the place where he chose to live and work, because the man who'd directed the Justice films could easily live in Paris or Hollywood or Manhattan, but had consciously selected this Cape Cod site over likelier locales.

Maybe I'd find it while pacing the grounds, that moment when I better understood his longings and his life. And even if the walk didn't lead to inspiration, I'd enjoy it. It would inoculate me against resisting the rest of the day's indoor work, bent over the keyboard.

I left my car out of sight of the main road and marched downhill toward the ocean. I told myself that when I finished this book, when it had been completed to acclaim, when my career as a solo writer was well and truly launched, I'd take a true vacation, here or maybe farther up the Cape in Truro. I'd buy beach shoes, venture unafraid onto pebbly beaches, swim through swelling waves. It seemed possible, frighteningly possible, as solid as the earth beneath my feet.

Why stop with the Cape? Authors routinely traveled to far-off destinations. You took Caroline to Portugal and Hawaii. You showed me photos of black sand beaches, beaches that made this one seem like a country cousin. Buenos Aires, Rio de Janeiro, Patagonia; the names breathed adventure.

This could be it, the book that unaccountably took off, sold an unimaginable number of copies. The industry was fickle, I knew, and based on self-fulfilling prophecy, you always said. If they paid a lot, they pushed a lot; they sold books they had a financial interest in selling. But every once in a while, a bolt struck out of the blue and a happy marriage of timeliness and content blew away the estimated royalties.

Me, a bona fide success. Me, traveling to exotic locales. The thought of either was almost as bizarre as the idea of going out for a drink with Garrett Malcolm. I crossed the sandy gravel and headed up a grassy hill. What would that be like, dating, having sex with a star, an acknowledged object of desire? What things he must know, what experiences he must have, what comparisons he might make.

I am a woman, Teddy.

I strolled on, unbuttoning and removing my jacket, first flinging it over my arm, then pausing to tie the sleeves firmly around my waist. The lawn gave way to sandy soil, grass-topped dunes, and finally the sand. At the ocean's edge, I turned toward the tip of the Cape, toward the Province Lands, and walked briskly for ten minutes, admiring the rocks and dunes, watching the long-legged seabirds hop, spotting the occasional fishing boat far out at sea.

The day was so glorious, the water so clear, I could see the waving stalks of seaweed to their liquid roots, and practically count the pebbles on the ocean floor. I took off my sneakers, almost giddy as I tied their laces together and swung them over my shoulder, walked barefoot along the coast, wading in the shallows. Such temptations rarely came my way in Boston. The desire to dip one's toes in the turbid Charles, even on the hottest summer day, is nonexistent.

The sand was warm and soft, decorated with a scattered pattern of canine and human prints. I wouldn't dally long. I'd watch the darting birds, smell the salt air, search for Justice locations, but mainly use the time to organize the book. I'd start with the first Academy Award evening. I had a terrific quote from the presenter, an apt and funny anecdote from a high-powered nominee. I framed and reframed the first paragraph, debated the merits of this opening sentence or that one. The sunlight shimmered on the waves, temporarily blinding me. I turned my head away from the dazzle of the ocean toward the dunes. That's when I saw the shack.

CHAPTER
thirty

Isolated, remote, weathered, and unexpectedly beautiful. Secretly beautiful because you had to be practically on top of the beach shack before you saw it. Quietly beautiful because of the way it blended with the shore and the sea and the sand, because it looked like it had always existed, not so much built as discovered.

A shingled box on high stilts, it resembled a cross between a lifeguard stand and a cottage, impossibly tiny and backed by an imposing dune. Squat, green-tinged utility poles, cross-braced by heavy three-by-sixes, bolted at the joins, made up the foundation. In a hurricane, waves could wash through the stilts.

Each of four small windows boasted its own tidy window box. A railed balcony faced the waves. An open staircase ran ten steps up to the door. Enchanted, I climbed the sandy path and circled the structure. On the dune side, a stubby propane tank sat next to a rusty grill. When I discovered an outdoor shower I was amazed such a rustic place could have running water. And not just water, but electricity. A meter hung from one of the poles and thick wires disappeared behind the dune. An iron smokestack poked from the peaked roof. The PA had mentioned only four houses on Malcolm's estate, but this would hardly qualify as a house.

I made my way slowly down to the shore again, zigzagging between clumps of beach grass, thirty, forty steps at the most, feeling like I'd wandered into a fairy tale, discovered a dwelling that might house a princess and her retinue of rowdy dwarves. At water's edge, I turned and peered at the shack in order to make sure it was still standing, visible and not some dreamlike apparition. And froze as though I, myself, had been placed under a spell. From this angle the building was eerily familiar. I'd seen it before, twice over, not only in the background of Jenna's gypsy photo, but as the backdrop for dozens of McKenna's scurrilous Web site shots.

My neck crawled and I pivoted, turning again to the ocean, seeking the hidden lens. Did the gossipmonger own a boat, lash a waterproof camera to a buoy, pay a fishing captain to spy on the place?

I clambered up the path, took the ten steep steps in a rush, and knocked at the worn, silvery door. Indignation played a major part—anyone inside ought to know the place was essentially under surveillance—but curiosity played a strong supporting role. Under the influence of McKenna's photos, my brain furnished the interior with fur rugs, hot tubs, sex toys. The desire to view the orgy den, the party place for the bronzed boys and beautiful girls, was powerful.

A dusty window to the right of the door provided nothing but the outline of a table. I knocked again, reached out a hand, turned the knob. Opening the unlocked door was reckless, foolish. I told myself it was about doing a comprehensive job on the book, following every lead, the way you did, but there was no sensible reason to trespass. I felt like I was moving in a kind of trance.

From the doorway I could see everything there was to see: a bed, a table, a living room, if the term meant that all living occurred in a single room. The bathroom was an uncurtained alcove with toilet and sink. A few dishes sat on open shelves next to a red fire extinguisher. No cupboard was big enough to hide a cat. The wide floorboards dipped in one corner. The bed, an old-fashioned iron bedstead, had a canopy covered in patterned curtains. A brown leather suitcase, open on the bed, looked as though someone had hastily removed articles from the lower depths without bothering to unpack the top layer. A can of shaving cream sat on the tiny sink, a safety razor nearby. A pleasant room, not a Dionysian hangout, nothing like Bluebeard's den.

The furnishings made an impression—they must have, because I can enumerate them—but the first thing that registered was the smell. Illness, not decomposition. I knew it was illness in a flash, just as I knew the sickness's name: alcohol poisoning. I never thought he was dead because, still as he lay on the floorboards, he snored. He was drunk, and it wasn't until I noted the striped shirt hanging over the ladder-backed chair that I connected the snoring drunk's body with the movie star, with the big-screen god, Brooklyn Pierce.

It felt like I'd entered not a fairy tale, but an hallucination. My mind refused to forge the link between handsome movie star and smelly drunk even though my eyes bore witness. The man I'd seen from a distance cresting the hill had been the exact image of the actor on the screen, perfect and ageless. The man who'd demanded the return of his tape had been less an exact image, worn around the edges. This man shared the superstar's long-limbed body, but his face seemed bloated and his swollen mouth curled in a disdainful pout. Shadows and deeply carved lines rimmed his eyes. It was as though I were seeing him through a distorted lens or a cruel fun-house mirror. A half-empty pack of cigarettes rested on his chest, a matchbook near his right hand.

He was Ben Justice, but not Ben Justice. That oppositional pull, a kind of disbelief, kept me from panicking. That and the smell. My childhood taught me bitter rules, and the rules took over.

Roll him on his side. I did this while mouthing words some foster mother must have required: *There, there, you're fine, don't worry about a thing.* Don't worry about the vomit or the puddle or the glass shards of the shattered bottle. If his eyelids had so much as flickered, I'd have fled. Drunks struck out with hostile fists. Disturbed, they attacked.

If it hadn't been the bloated shade of Ben Justice lying at my feet, or if I'd had less experience of drunks, I might have called 911. 911 would bring ambulances. Ambulances would bring attention, cameras. I listened to his stentorian breathing and opted for privacy. I'd find a blanket, cover him, and leave. I'd seen sufficient drunks to know he'd sleep it off.

Anger surged unexpectedly. Ben Justice, gallant and true, would never be found like this, sprawled stinking drunk on a bare floor. When Justice drank, he stayed cool and capable, ready to fight at a moment's notice. It was ridiculous, I knew, but I felt betrayed.

Look for the rest of the bottles. Spill their contents in the sink, but not every drop. Leave enough for one more drink, "hair of the dog." My heart pounded, but I knew my task wasn't finished. Clear up the broken glass. Look for the prescription vials, the drugs, dump those with the liquor, down the sink.

I didn't find any small brown vials, but the manuscript sat in plain view on the table.

It looked, in every detail, from thickness to deep green cover, like one of the manuscripts I'd seen on the corner of Malcolm's ornate desk in the Great Room. It held me there, motionless and gawking. That, and the almost naked body of a man once voted one of the handsomest in the world, clad in nothing more than plaid boxers that had ridden up the side of his right thigh. I averted my eyes, moved them to the fine golden hairs on his chest, thought again about finding some kind of blanket, but stayed rooted to the spot.

Staring at the manuscript, then at the unkempt star, I was aware on some subterranean level of Garrett Malcolm's treachery. Brooklyn Pierce wouldn't be staying here without Malcolm's permission, without his invitation. Which meant Malcolm had lied to me, touched his finger to my lips and lied.

Hamlet, Act One, scene 5: *Meet it is I set it down, That one may smile, and smile, and be a villain.*

If Pierce was not Malcolm's Prince of Denmark, what was he? Didn't I owe it to my readers—our readers—to find out?

Had you posited this very situation, given my fervent desire to know what Pierce had said on your missing tape, given even my consciousness of Malcolm's deceit, I'd have said that basic decency would have prevented me from snooping, violating a fellow human's privacy, touching, much less reading, that manuscript.

I pressed my lips together and attempted to slow my breath by forcing it through my nose. The possibility of hyperventilating, fainting in the middle of this impossible scene, terrified me. What a perfect blend: a snoring drunk, a panic-attack fainter, and somewhere out there, Glenn McKenna, gossipmonger, to photograph the whole graceless mess.

I stumbled, making such a clatter I feared Pierce's eyes would pop open. His harsh breathing kept up its inexorable rhythm; his chest rose and fell. He, at least, was breathing. The manuscript exerted an enormous pull, an intense and magnetic attraction. My hand reached out, snatched up the folder, and flipped quickly to the opening page.

The Black Stone
The Fourth Ben Justice Film
screenplay by Brooklyn Pierce

187

I turned the page. I turned many pages. I know I did, but my vision seemed oddly blurred, my breath a racing engine on a high-speed track, veering out of control. I knew the routine, knew I should sit, lower my head between my knees, but to sit here, on these floorboards, was impossible. Pierce moaned and moved, and I took off as though pursued by the spirits of drunken stepfathers.

CHAPTER
thirty-one

My toe caught on a riser near the bottom of the flight. I fell hard, then scrambled to my feet, hands stinging, and raced through beach grass onto the harsh-grained sand. My central nervous system ignited; badly wired impulses blinked on and off like tiny neon signs in a crazed video arcade. The clanging pulse of terror shrieked through my veins and demanded escape, but the faster my legs pumped, the slower my progress seemed and the more I flailed in the deepening sand. My knotted sneakers swung from my shoulder, pounding my chest and back with each propulsive step. Panic seized me, and none of my remedies were at hand. My Xanax was locked with my purse in the trunk of the car, along with my recorder and notebook. In my apartment, I'd have grabbed a paper bag from the drawer next to the sink, sunk to the floor, breathed into the bag. Here, the unfamiliar landscape, the terrible immensity of ocean, belonged to an alien planet that offered no relief.

Ten minutes, ten minutes, ten, ten, ten. The number became a refrain. *Ten, ten, ten.* Panic attacks last only ten minutes, most of them, but this one, I knew, I knew, I knew, was timeless, this one would be the last, the one that killed me, the one that drove me howling into the sea. I glanced behind me, slipped, and almost stumbled to my knees. Yes, I'd remembered to shut the beach shack's door. I'd left Pierce uncovered, but it was better that way. How shaming to wake tucked in like a drooling infant, to realize an unknown hand had covered your nakedness.

Clouds formed a layer over the sea, the sky darkened eerily, and I ran. It was like a scene in a horror movie; there should have been cameras arranged along the shoreline, a production assistant shouting the number of the take. I felt nauseated, dizzy, I couldn't swallow or breathe, and still I ran, ran as though old Hamlet's Ghost snapped at my heels, demanding that I swear, swear, swear my promise of revenge.

"O villain, villain, smiling damned villain." But wait: Couldn't Pierce be the villain of the piece instead of Malcolm? Why trust the word of an alcoholic? Maybe you hadn't interviewed Pierce after all; maybe there was no missing tape. Malcolm would still be a liar, yes, for not telling me that Pierce had taken up residence at the beach shack. But the omission could have been Pierce's idea, to keep secret his presence on the Cape. Malcolm might simply have kept his word to a guest. If I could believe that . . .

Maybe Pierce was at the shack as part of a detox program, here to kick his alcohol demon. Malcolm could be aiding a friend rather than trying to dupe me out of an interview. It wasn't that he didn't trust me. It wasn't that he was treating me with less respect than he'd treated you.

If Malcolm had invited you for a drink, you'd have accepted, no doubt about it. How bitterly I regretted my decision to refuse. Which foster mother had dictated the terms of my hasty retreat? The one who foretold I'd never be pretty enough to date, much less wed a man?

On ran my thoughts till they came up against Hamlet's dilemma: Was the Ghost a heavenly messenger sent to tell the truth, or a deceitful vision from hell? How do you interpret the evidence of your own eyes? Fact: Brooklyn Pierce lay drunk on the floor of the beach shack. Everything else was speculation. Except the manuscript, the new Ben Justice screenplay. Was that the secret of the tape, Teddy? Was that the revelation Pierce wanted to retract?

How far, how far, had I run? Should I turn away from the shore, strike across the dunes, up and over the gentle hills? Spiders crawled through my veins, numbing my legs. Where was the barn, the parking lot, the car?

"What in hell do you think you're doing?"

The voice came from behind me, but at first I didn't know if it was inside my head or outside it, real or imaginary, separate from or part of my terror.

"I said you could interview me, not spy on me. Where the hell have you been? What the hell do you think you're doing?"

With no breath I couldn't form any words, let alone the right ones.

Garrett Malcolm looked as full of wrath as any angry stepfather. I wanted to warn him—that Brooklyn Pierce was lying on the floor, drunk and vulnerable, that a man named Glenn McKenna had a nasty habit of photographing Brooklyn's refuge—but my tongue was a dead, twisted stump that had withered in my mouth.

"What are you holding? What have you got there?"

Not till he asked did I realize I had tucked the new Ben Justice manuscript under my arm, carried it away from the shack like a prize. In an instant, I felt my skin go clammy and cold. I would be accused of stealing. I hadn't stolen it, not really, not intentionally. I'd only wanted to keep it safe. Really I hadn't thought. I didn't know. I couldn't speak.

"Give it to me."

My arms were pegs glued to the sides of a wooden statue. I tried to move them, to give the towering, raging man what he wanted, whatever he wanted. He grabbed at me, at the manuscript, and I heard it, felt it rip, saw the pages spew onto the ground, scatter with the wind.

He swore at me. He stormed. Words were at the center of the cyclone, dimly heard and slowly perceived, heard as if from a great distance, and they said I was incompetent and a fool. They said the project was over, cancelled, that this was the end of the line.

CHAPTER
thirty-two

I don't know how I found the car or fumbled open the door or drove to the rented house. My face, unrecognizable in the rearview mirror, was pink and red and blotchy. I couldn't stop staring at my wrist, which was marked by a livid bracelet of white and a stinging scratch, fierce keepsakes of the struggle for the manuscript, shameful reminders of Malcolm's steel grip and my complete inability to defuse the situation, to defend myself, to state the facts. So totally focused was I on my wrist that I should have driven off an embankment or into a ditch. Even after the bracelet faded, I felt it like a burn, like a ring of flame, as though the outline of his thumb and fingers were tattooed on my skin. I could feel it, and I couldn't feel anything else. I couldn't hear. I saw only the road immediately ahead of me, as though I wore blinders, and the road was a path to ruin.

I floated out of the car, carefully locked the doors, outside of my own body, watching myself, and then I was inside the house, tossing clothes in the direction of my duffel. Gathering scattered papers, sorting them into haphazard piles, disconnecting my computer. My mind seemed to shift—in control, then out of control. I could imagine myself calmly finishing the book, turning it in to Jonathan, saying nothing about any problem, Malcolm saying nothing. I could see myself naked, surrounded by whispering strangers who muttered and stared and said that once I had been half of T. E. Blakemore, once I had owned a name, even if only half a name, but then I had done something so vile, so reprehensible, that no one hired me again. I saw myself as a bag lady, limping over a smelly sewer near the bus station, muttering to myself. As a suicide, hanging from a tree.

My cell phone rang and I started, then froze. I thought, *I should I answer it.* I thought, *Who would call me?*

Teddy, you called me. You were the only one. How I missed you. I could have gone home to you, confessed, and been forgiven. I could have crushed you in my arms and you would have Teddy-bear-hugged me in return and it would have been all right. You deserted me. You left when I still needed you.

The phone rang again and panic rose in my chest, surging, cresting and subsiding, breaking off pieces of me with its rise and fall. I felt as insubstantial as sea foam, battered and crushed. I sank to the floor and yanked the ringing phone from my pocket, and for a moment I thought it would have to be you.

"Hey." The voice was Jonathan's. I checked the screen. The number was Henniman's. I tried to speak, but my voice was lost in my throat.

"Em? Hey, it's Jonathan. We did a deal with the Literary Book Club. Marcy thought you might like to hear it from me. Hey, are you there?"

"Hi. Yes." I sounded like a mouse, a strangled mouse.

"It's not a great deal, okay? Not as much as the last one, but you know what's going on in the industry. Marcy's got the figures."

"Yes."

"So, you're good with the manuscript on the twenty-fifth? You can send a disc. That's better than paper. We're going to run with T. E. Blakemore on this one. Do you have a definite title yet?"

Tears started down my face. I whispered something about calling him back and punched the button to end the call. I pressed both hands to my eyes and thought, this can't be happening. I would have to call Marcy, tell her it was over. I would have to—

There was a sharp rap at the door and I realized I hadn't locked it just as the name "McKenna" solidified into a scary, threatening shape in my mind. Somehow he'd been watching, somehow he knew. He'd been in a boat with a camera trained on the beach shack. I anticipated the smelly gossipmonger charging into the room. He knew everything. He had photos of my wild rush down the staircase, my theft of the screenplay, video he'd splash across the Web site. Then the doorknob turned and Garrett Malcolm called my name.

And he was across the room before I could say a word and his long arms hauled me to my feet and I thought for a minute he was going to kill me and then I clung to him the way I used to cling to you, Teddy. And he killed me, Teddy. He killed me and gave me a new birth and I clung to him and he smothered me and we stumbled toward the door and closed it and locked it and pulled the shades.

We did all that, but our lips never parted. We never stopped kissing each other. We never stopped kissing as we stripped off layers of clothing, mine damp and sandy where I'd fallen to the ground. We never stopped kissing until we'd climbed the stairs and used the bed for what it was made for. He kept saying how sorry he was that he'd made me cry, that I was too young, too sweet, too innocent.

There must have been awkward intervals, even brutal ones. I'm usually shy about exposing my breasts, so far removed from centerfold proportions, but I don't remember a moment of hesitation.

Teddy, it was a hunger, a need. I could say I didn't know what came over me, what I was doing, but I did, and it was like a wave, a deluge, a tsunami after a roiling earthquake. It was a spreading fog, a haze, and its color was red, veering into violet. It was the ozone smell of a thunderstorm before lightning strikes, a mouthful of red wine. My hands grazed the electric hair on his chest and came alive, each separate finger thrilled by its discoveries. Rough sheets rubbed the satin of salty skin, and his eyes, oh, his eyes were the melted indigo of ice crocuses. And I was a dry spring flooded and refreshed, bubbling with life, spilling over with icy water and boiling water and all the currents of an unfathomable sea.

PART
two

Whoever turns biographer commits himself to lies, to conceal-
ment, to hypocrisy, to embellishments, and even to dissembling
his own lack of understanding. Biographical truth is not to be
had, and even if one had it, one could not use it.

Sigmund Freud,

in a letter to a friend

UMass Memorial Labs
UMass Medical Center, Inc.
365 Plantation Street
Worcester, MA 01605

DRUG SCREEN RESULT: TRACE OF HYDROXYZINE

CANNABINOID SCREEN: NEGATIVE

BLOOD ALCOHOL: .02

SPECIMEN IDENTIFICATION: THEODORE BLAKE

DATE SPECIMEN RECEIVED: 3/23

DATE TEST PERFORMED: 4/25

SPECIMEN SUBMITTED BY: L. Hirshoff, M.D., pathologist

TECHNOLOGIST: R. L. MacKenzie

Targeted Post-Mortem Profile

Amphetamines	Barbiturates	Benzodiazepines	Cannabinoids	Cocaine
Amphetamine	Amobarbitol	Alprazolam	Carboxy-THC	Benzoylecognine
Methamphetamine	Butabarbital	Chlordiazepoxide	THC	Parent Cocaine
MDMA	Butalbital	Clonazepam		
MDEA	Phenobarbital	Desmethyldiazepam		
MDA	Secobarbital	Diazepam		
Paramethoxyamphetamine	Talbutal	Flurazepam		
Phentermine		Lorazepam		
		Oxazepam		
		Temazepam		

Fentanyl & Analogues	Meperidine	Methadone	Opiates	Propoxyphene
Alfentanil	Meperidine	Methadone	Codeine	Propoxyphene
Fentanyl	Normeperidine	EDDP	Morphine	Norpropoxyphene
Sufentanil			Hydrocodone	
			Hydromorphone	
			Dihydrocodeine	
			Oxycodone	
			Oxymorphone	

Sedative Hypnotics	Tricyclic Antidepressants	Volatiles	Miscellaneous	
Carisoprodol/	Amitryptyline	Acetone	Acetaminophen	
Meprobamate	Clomipramine	Ethanol	Salicylate	
	Desipramine	Isopropanol		
	Desmethylclomipramine	Methanol		
	Desmethyldoxepin			
	Doxepin			
	Imipramin			

ALL ABOVE: UNDER REPORTING LIMIT

CHAPTER
thirty-three

Forgive me, Teddy, you've been largely absent from my thoughts for weeks, but I've been such a busy girl and I'm working so hard—honestly, I am—sprinting toward the finish line. Jonathan extended the deadline once Garrett put his foot down, which was so kind of him, of both of them, and I have been a trifle wicked, taking advantage of unseasonably warm weather, lying on the beach, soaking in the early spring sunshine when I should have been dutifully pecking at the keyboard.

God, Teddy, doesn't the previous graph read like a sweet little Catholic girl talking to her priest? "Father, forgive me, it has been two

201

weeks since my last confession, and during that time I have . . ." Enough of that. Let me state instead that the days have been incredibly sunny and the sky a cloudless robin's-egg blue. It would be utterly perfect if you were here.

But then if you were here, I wouldn't be.

Weighed in the balance, I know my exquisite happiness doesn't compensate for your death. I know you didn't willingly die for me. Who would sacrifice their only, their unique life for someone else's? I've read tales of loving parents tenderly laying down their lives for their children, fathers for daughters, mothers for sons, but I never met such parents.

My estate has changed: I've moved up in the world, ascended to the Big House. I have to pinch myself, to make sure I'm fully conscious, especially when I wake in my bedroom, my head cushioned by the coolness of an embroidered pillowcase, and lie quite still, looking out at a vast sweep of ocean instead of a cracked plaster wall.

It's not "my" bedroom; I'm aware of that. It's formally designated a "guest room," and I often speculate, late at night, concerning the identity of previous tenants. Was this once Claire Gregory's boudoir? It shares the same dramatic ocean view as the small office with the mechanical shades, although in some ways this view, elevated as it is on the second floor, is superior. Furnished for visiting royalty in pink and gold, the room has a huge brass bedstead and carpeting so thick it tickles my feet. I spend an immense amount of time here. There's an elegant writing desk, but I prefer writing in bed, nested in crisp percale and soft down, pounding diligently at my laptop, inhaling Garrett's piney scent.

While it lacks a connecting door to Garrett's bedroom, it opens off the same short corridor, so the two rooms form a kind of suite, each with its own bath. Jonathan is terribly impressed by my "access" to the subject. What would he say if he knew?

Teddy, I have qualms, a jittery feeling in my stomach that registers somewhere in between too much champagne and incipient nausea. All my dithering about whether knowing the subject would influence my writing, and now this. Occasionally I convince myself that it's helping me paint a fuller, truer portrait of the man, but I know I'm justifying behavior I would label unconscionable in anyone else. What can I say? It happened, and I'm not sorry it happened. It's transformational, this closeness, almost like he's my working partner now, my writing partner, like we're truly in this together. Oh, it would have been better if he'd waited, better if the book were already done and published. So we're keeping it quiet, as quiet and secret as mice. I'm completely invisible here, but then I'm used to being invisible.

How lovely to have secrets. It feels so powerful.

The sex, Teddy, the sex is wonderful, superb, beyond intense. How I live for the release, the afterglow. I love to come and come, and lose myself; how it quiets the nervous voices in my head. I pray it's as good for Garrett as it is for me, but how can I know? How can I know for sure? He's so worldly and experienced. His bath is a marble pleasure palace with a Jacuzzi big enough for an orgy and a steam shower stocked with scented massage oil. He does things to my body I've only read about in books, but I reciprocate enthusiastically. I am enthusiastic, but Teddy, oh Teddy, I am woefully inexperienced. There was only you, no one else, even after you stopped wanting to be with me. I never understood how you could be so cruel, but that's dirty water under the bridge now.

Once the cast and crew arrive, we'll need to exercise more discretion. But right now, at the planning stage, there aren't many people to fool.

The PA, Darren Kalver, we don't bother trying to fool him. Garrett treats him like a stick of furniture. As far as Kalver's concerned, I'm staying at the house to "facilitate further interviews." He's knows it's a lie, but it's his job to make Garrett look good. He doesn't want to lose his job, so he treats me the same way he always has.

We don't have to fool Brooklyn Pierce, because we don't see him. I don't see him at all. Garrett drops by the shack occasionally to monitor his progress. When he's like this, Garrett says, it's better to leave him in peace.

Pierce's drinking has been spiraling out of control for years. Remember how his agent kept claiming he was out of the country? Garrett says he's been through a revolving door of self-help and rehab programs. When he can't stick to a particular treatment plan anymore, when even Betty Ford boots him out, the beach shack is his last refuge. He holes up there alone, drinks and drinks, but eventually gets himself sober again. He claims he's going there "to write," but all he actually produces is a lot of half-page, half-baked "treatments," usually titled in the Ben Justice formula: *The Purple Bagatelle, The Scarlet Conundrum.* Garrett said his personal favorite was *The Periwinkle Paradox,* but I assume he was joking. If all you got from Pierce was a drunkard's scrambled ramblings, it makes sense that he'd want to retract them. And I suppose you might have destroyed the tape.

When I warned Garrett about McKenna's shack surveillance, he said he'd take measures to protect the privacy of the place. I didn't say I'd been in touch with McKenna, just mentioned that you'd shown me the man's Web site. I didn't want Garrett to think I'd been gathering gossip behind his back, not with everything so honest and open between us.

It's like a dream, this sweet new life. Sometimes I find myself thinking—only briefly, only tangentially—about a future beyond work, beyond writing, a future that might, that could involve this breathtaking house, meeting Jenna, being a mother, perhaps, to her and possibly to another. Garrett's not careful the way you were. Oh, don't get me wrong, he's never said anything about wanting another child, but he did want one once, and I know how much he loves Jenna. He's never asked whether I'm on the pill. And we talk about everything.

He talks, really. And I listen, rapt and attentive, more Desdemona than Ophelia now. Remember how Othello says "She loved me for the dangers I had pass'd, and I lov'd her that she did pity them"? He loves the way I listen.

He knows Cape Cod like a native, knows how and where the coastline has eroded, knows the names of seabirds and shorebirds and beach grasses. He once helped rescue a stranded pod of dolphins. When he told me exactly how it felt to rub water on their rubbery skins and hear their skittery noises, I could see it as clearly as a scene in one of his films. How much, how much you can know about another human being and still you've only scratched the surface of the surface.

We don't discuss our ages, or the way we fell into bed that first time, or the argument that preceded it. Of course, he's much older than I am. And he's been a bachelor far longer than he ever was a married man. But I don't spend my time dwelling on that. I'm too busy working. I'm helpful, very helpful in everything from assembling the director's book for *Hamlet* to pitching in and hemming a frock for a courtier.

Worker by day, muse by night, Teddy. An inspiration. Me.

CHAPTER
thirty-four

RE: Accident Reconstruction, misc.
SENT BY: rsnow@dennisportpd.org
SENT ON: April 5
SENT TO: Paul Jericho, Chief of Police

Paul,

Glad to be back at the desk. You get a copy of the tox screen? No easy out there. He wasn't driving drunk or impaired. The hydroxyzine is just over-the-counter allergy stuff and his wife says he took it all the time.

Spoke to Blake's associate, girl called Em Moore, who's finishing up that book they were working on. She wanted to know if we found a tape cassette at the scene or in the car. Little thing. Think I'll go around and check the wreck again. She was surprised Blake wasn't wearing his seat belt. Said he usually did.

Heard from Larry Hines over at ARU. Based on the skid marks in the diagram, he focused in on the brakes, took a chunk of brake hose in for analysis, but he's not sure there's enough of it left to tell whether it's damage from the fire or something else. Also, he mentioned a possible security problem at the lockup. Seems the seal was broken before he got there, tape sliced right through. I'll ask D'Arcy what's going on when I check on that cassette.

Sorry you had to deal with that McKenna guy. Rest assured, I had to listen to him, too. Kept talking and talking. Shirley reads all that gossip stuff and she says he's had a bee in his bonnet about Garrett Malcolm for years. I'll get over to the Malcolm place this week, find out what I can, but I think the road conditions justify a bigger sign and better lights and that's about it.

Good news is the brother of that woman lives in the house on Willow Crest, one who went on the damned cruise, he's due back today, so I'll be talking to him.

Russell Snow, Detective Grade One
Dennis Port Police Department
One Arrow Point Way
Dennis Port, MA 02639

CHAPTER
thirty-five

The Bloomie's bag possessed the same quality of fascination, exuded the same magnetic pull as Pandora's mythical box. If I left it sitting on top of the dresser, it caught my eye whenever I glanced up from the screen. When I shut it in a drawer, the drawer handle seemed to glow with an eerie inner light. I should have shredded the infernal thing and tossed the remnants into the trash, but I didn't, and after so many weeks, its attraction had increased until it seemed to shoot out diabolical rays.

Stop it, I lectured myself. Concentrate on forming sentences. Opening Pandora's box never helps.

Of course, I had already opened it once. Moreover, I'd found satisfaction therein. I'd successfully deciphered your shorthand jottings: JFLY meant James Foley, Malcolm's cousin. 2nd BST BD meant second-best bed, as in the item granted to wife Anne in William Shakespeare's final will and testament. I'd concluded that we'd traveled parallel tracks, Teddy, that each of us had been told about the Elizabethan oddity of old Ralph Malcolm's will.

I'd pondered the large figures and the meaning of HMB, but they continued to elude me. Caroline had displayed your check for a hundred and eighty thousand, but that was far less than the written numbers. None of our interview subjects had the initials HMB. The theater's board, the outfit Malcolm seemed forever to be dodging, was the Cranberry Hill Board, the CHB, not the HMB. Had the letters been HMB, in that order? Perhaps I needed to take another peek.

Aside from the notebook with its scribbled hints, what else resided in the depths of Caroline's bag? I recalled two business cards, one from a legal firm, the other from a Realtor. I tried to focus on the writing, but my mind was like a fly buzzing around the corners of the room, unable to light. My pace slowed to a painful crawl. The more I tried to concentrate the less I was able to, and as concentration waned, the pull of Pandora's Bloomingdale bag became a constant, irritating hum.

What foolishness. I opened the drawer in a rush, upended the bag on the bed, isolated the business cards. RUSSELL AMES AND HUBER, NEW YORK, and PICARIAN REALTY, EASTHAM, MA. I thumbed the heavy stock of the Realtor's card, ran a finger across the raised letters. Mr. Picarian hadn't printed his business cards on his inkjet home printer. The phone number had a 508 area code. I could lift the receiver, press a few buttons, and inquire whether a Mr. Blake had recently spoken to someone concerning local property values.

The telephone on the bedside table was a handset, one of many distributed throughout the various structures on the property, each linked to a central console located in the PA's office. I could use the land line, but not without the possibility of Darren Kalver interrupting or listening in. And I hated to use my cell. Cell numbers were routinely captured by other cell phones. Who knew where Picarian Realty's office phone actually rang?

I tried to reinvolve myself in Chapter Eighteen, but found myself staring at the rumpled bed instead, picturing Garrett's strong shoulders and slim hips, grinning foolishly at memories of the previous night's sexual adventures, wondering what he was working on this morning, and where. He had a flurry of activities to monitor, both at the Amphitheater and the Old Barn, not to mention several casting issues to settle.

It was a good thing we each had our own work. We didn't get in each other's way. We complemented each other. But for how long? My lips tightened as I tried to wrench my thoughts away from the shadowy future. The actresses were coming, arriving this week. The beautiful ones, graceful as butterflies, trained to charm.

The Realtor's address was temptingly close. I shoved my chair back, gathered my purse, and moved. Because I couldn't stand thinking about all the pretty girls waiting breathlessly for the chance to be Ophelia, the pros, the amateurs, the endless stream of ladies-in-waiting to enchant Garrett Malcolm. Anything was better than imagining that beckoning chorus line. I got in the car and drove.

Picarian Realty. A small, gray-shingled cottage with a large billboard. The sign featured the same script that flourished across the business card. I pulled into the gravel lot. Maybe you came here to do follow-up research. Maybe when I mentioned your name, the person behind the desk would snap to attention like a pointer sniffing the scent and reveal something that would illuminate your final days on the Cape.

Across the road stood an old windmill, a wooden structure lifted from a children's tale. As if to underline its picturesque quality, a bearded artist had established a work station slightly to the right from which he contemplated his palette, his canvas-topped easel, and the mill in turn. The wind was brisk, but the arms of the mill, the outspread wings, were bare, with no surface to catch the wind. I wondered whether the mill was undergoing preseason repairs, whether the artist would give it a great spread of canvas, like a sail, in his painting.

Picarian Realty's entrance was set at the top of three sagging wooden steps, a screen door that opened outward, a wooden door that opened inward. A sign in the dusty front window said OPEN. There was no doorbell, so I turned the knob and pushed.

"Yes, can I help you?" The man at the desk extinguished a cigarette as he spoke, hastily stubbing it out in an ashtray concealed by a drawer.

He had a fine voice, smooth but gravelly, and somehow familiar. Handsome in a blue button-down shirt and navy slacks, he seemed slightly older than Garrett, and when he turned to me, I suddenly felt as if all the sexual activity of the past weeks was tattooed on my face, that I smelled, reeked of intercourse, and that this was a man who would not only notice, but recognize the aroma.

"Is there something I can do for you?"

I studied my feet, hoping he'd mistake the color in my cheeks for sunburn. His question seemed laden with a variety of shaded meanings, and my prepared opening remarks, keyed as they were to an imaginary elderly and wizened Mr. Picarian, died on my lips.

"Are you looking for a house?" he said when I missed the beat again. "Jim Foley, by the way. At your service."

Foley. No wonder you'd kept the Picarian Realty card.

"Jim Foley," I repeated. "James Foley the actor?"

"My dear God," he said. "Good lord. I knew that if I waited long enough, a girl like you would walk through that door and recognize me. Who hired you?"

His timing was impeccable, his expression droll. I smiled in spite of myself.

"My ex-wife is not that cruel, not quite that cruel, so I'm betting on a drinking buddy," he continued. "Hank? Ernie, the bastard?"

"No, no, I have seen you act." My mind was spinning; I didn't know what to tell him, what to ask first. "I recognized your name, and your voice. You're Garrett Malcolm's cousin. I'm, uh, working on a book about him. You met my partner, Teddy Blake?"

"The Malcolm connection strikes again. Damn. I had a brief moment of hope."

"I'm sorry."

"Don't be. Then there'd be two of us at the pity party, and two's a crowd for that kind of thing. But I didn't know Teddy had a partner. Did they assign you to finish up the Malcolm book? Poor old Teddy."

"Mr. Foley—"

"Jamie. Call me Jamie, since you've seen me act." When he sat on one corner of the desk and arranged his lean face in a rakish smile, I saw a younger version of the man, the villain in *Red Shot*, looming up from under the bridge. He looked disconcertingly like his cousin, the same mouth, the same eyes.

"You were terrific in *Red Shot*," I said, "and I recognized your voice from the tape you did with Teddy."

"You're not going to use any of that, are you? I thought I was deep background."

"Your cousin doesn't want to focus on his childhood."

"Oh, it wasn't so bad. Nothing alcoholism or a lifetime of therapy couldn't overcome. Do you mind if I smoke?" He retrieved the cigarette from the ashtray and regarded its mashed end regretfully.

"It doesn't seem to have damaged him," I said. "His childhood."

"Don't let the actor in him fool you. I take it you haven't come to rent or buy a house?"

"No."

"Want me to open a window?" he said as he lit up. "Or we could go for a walk? I do quite a mean tour of Ye Olde Ancient Windmill."

"Can we talk here? I don't mind the smoke."

He nodded me into a straight-backed chair by the side of his desk. I wondered where Mr. Picarian was, or if a Mr. Picarian existed. The room was far from spacious, just the lone desk, a worn credenza, two filing cabinets, and a computer. I hadn't thought to bring the recorder, but I was able to pull a small notebook and a pen from my purse.

"I've got a lot of properties to rent," Foley said wistfully. "May's wide open and that's unusual this late in the year. Economy sucks and with gas prices high, people are going nowhere. Plus the kiddies are still in school in May. You could get a real deal."

We stared at each other in silence.

"You want me to talk about my cousin?"

"Yes."

"Everyone does."

"It annoys you."

"Just because he's famous and talented and I'm obscure, if not untalented? Just because he owns half the damned Cape and I own a teensy sliver grudgingly forked over by Uncle Ralph?"

"Like Shakespeare's second best bed."

His smile was a flash of white teeth. "So Teddy did take a gander at the will? There was a brief and glorious moment when it looked like I might come into a windfall, but the old man came to his senses. His lawyer did, anyway. Not that I'd have wanted to do Jenna out of the land, not like that, but I'd certainly be willing to do a deal, split the spoils. She can have plenty for the theater. I'll just take a bit of the seaside for a small resort hotel, maybe a few upscale condos. Think she'd go for that?"

"I haven't met her."

"And you won't. Not with cousin Garrett keeping her safely out of the country. A small chunk of Cranberry Hill and I wouldn't be slaving away at a desk on a day like this. Doesn't seem fair, but then 'Fair is a word for weaklings,' that's what Uncle Ralph used to say. 'Talent isn't fair, life isn't fair.'"

His face as well as his accent altered as he spoke and I understood that he was acting, doing Garrett Malcolm's father as the old autocrat.

"So I hear he's doing *Hamlet* again? The old revenge tragedy. What's he thinking? Modern dress? Rags? Leotards? Fire? Planning to outdo Branagh with fire and brimstone?"

"You should ask him."

"Yeah. Sure."

"Did Teddy tape you here?"

"We went to the Cove over on Twenty-eight. Nice quiet bar. Little early for that now."

"And I think you mentioned you were writing a screenplay? With Brooklyn Pierce?"

He glanced at me warily. "Did I? Well, let's just say we've talked about collaborating on a few things."

"And you asked Pierce to get in touch with Teddy. That was kind of you."

"Brookie's a decent guy for a superstar. Hasn't forgotten the debt he owes to Lady Luck. And he's got plenty of tales to tell about old Malcolm."

"Ralph Malcolm?"

"No. Dear Cousin Garrett. Only a tad older than I am, but I rub it in whenever I see him. And when I don't."

"What kind of tales?"

"The kind he won't repeat. Brookie doesn't leak other people's personal stuff. Or his own, for that matter. He's smart that way, gabs just enough to keep the press interested. It's a neat trick. Give 'em the shit they think they want, not the shit you know. Give 'em stuff you make up out of thin air. If you don't, they'll make it up themselves. Brookie does a good job."

"You've been friends a long time."

"Did Brookie talk to Teddy? Before he—you know? Before the accident?"

"I'm not sure."

"Brookie's been a true pal. Never high and mighty, just because he's good at what he does. No great family, no background, just a natural actor. He used to invite me out to his place in Brentwood. God, the parties he threw. He's been a good friend, to me and to my cousin. Garrett owes Brookie."

I kept my face carefully neutral and waited, pen and pad clutched tightly in my hands, wishing I'd brought the recorder, wishing I had your gift for inspiring confidences.

"Brookie deserves better than he gets from Garrett."

The second hand of my wristwatch swept several times around the compass as I waited, reluctant to break the intimate silence. Several times I thought he might speak, take the plunge. He seemed to want to unburden himself, but he kept his mouth shut and concentrated on his cigarette, watching smoke rise from the glowing tip and accumulate in the small room.

"But then Malcolms don't forgive or forget, do they?"

He stubbed out his cigarette and lit another one. The room grew stuffier by the second. I should have agreed when he'd suggested opening the window.

"What do you mean?" If I had been taping, the counter would have clicked through fifty digits before I finally spoke.

"Huh?" He did a lovely double take, a reaction that made me remember I was dealing with an actor.

"'Malcolms don't forgive or forget'?" I prompted.

"Oh, that. It's like I told Teddy. They never forgave my mother for marrying out of the profession."

"I thought you were talking about something else, about Brooklyn Pierce?"

"I don't talk about my friends. But hey, it's your job to ask. Like

215

selling and renting is mine. And I really ought to get back to it, writing keen little snippets about charming cottages on Salt Pond, only eleven K a week to you, ma'am, in high season."

"One more thing." I spoke even though I knew I'd been dismissed.

"Yeah?"

"You said Garrett was keeping Jenna out of the country?"

"You haven't heard that she's coming home, have you? To meet with the lawyers?"

"You mean with the theater board?"

"She can meet with them till hell freezes over. With the lawyers about the trust, the conservation trust. Garrett's mentioned that, I suppose."

"Yes, he has. And no, I don't think she's on her way home."

He seemed relieved. "Makes sense, doesn't it? Take those early pratfalls out of the limelight: a lot of pressure being the last of the Malcolm dynasty. I can't imagine my cousin wouldn't do whatever he thought best for her. I mean, he absolutely adores that girl." He rose as he spoke, ready to usher me out the door.

"Thanks for talking to me."

"No problem, and if you think of anything else, you know where to find me." He hesitated, biting his lower lip, an actorly moment: man considering whether or not to confide.

I waited, hoping he'd tell me more about Garrett and Brooklyn Pierce.

"Things working out all right for you?" His eyes, more gray than blue, were the same shape as Garrett's.

"What do you mean?" I asked.

"Garrett's not giving you any trouble, is he? I mean, he's going along with it, with you taking over for Teddy?"

"I'm good at my job."

"I'm sure you are, but just a cautionary word, okay? Don't let him bully you into anything."

I couldn't tell by his tone if he was mocking me or warning me, but I was washed by the same embarrassment and confusion I'd felt when I first entered the cottage, as though the intimacy of my relationship with Garrett was emblazoned on my forehead or written across my chest.

Determined to display my professionalism, I quickly asked another question. "Do you know anyone with the initials 'HMB'?"

He smiled and raised an eyebrow. "Is there a prize?"

I shrugged.

He opened the door, putting an end to the interview. "I guess the prize goes to the next contestant."

The artist, defeated by the breeze and the darkening clouds, was packing his canvas into the trunk of his pickup as I strolled past. I wondered what it was like to be James Foley, son of the famous Ella Malcolm, grandson of the great Harrison Malcolm, living on the same small peninsula as his cousin, a man who'd succeeded in the field for which they'd both been bred. Did Foley watch his cousin's movies on late-night TV or change the channel if one appeared onscreen? Had he come to terms with the limits of his own stage career or did he imagine he might be a star someday?

I was sure Garrett had told me it was Jenna who'd insisted on leaving the country. Foley must have gotten it wrong.

CHAPTER
thirty-six

Since I'd never before spent time as a guest in a big house, I had no way of knowing that as a guest I would wander the hallways, that rooms would call to me, murmur, *Come in, come in, look around* as I passed their narrow doorways. A strange curiosity possessed me, and I justified and fed it, assuring the nosy cat-pawed beast that we were searching for relevant information, clues that would yield a glimpse into the still and mysterious center of the hyphenate actor-director-producer Garrett Malcolm, who had grown up in this house or a smaller version thereof, who had lived here as a child, a newly married man, a father.

I should have quizzed James Foley concerning the Big House, its origin, history, and specifically its current worth. Maybe those huge figures on the pad of paper that resided in the Bloomie's bag, the numbers I'd automatically labeled lira, represented the value of this enormous hunk of rare oceanfront land on the expensive Cape Cod real estate market.

I wrote for hours at a stretch, head bent to the task, which was not unusual for me. What was unusual was the restless wandering, pacing corridors, climbing staircases, touching vases and lamps, shading my eyes and staring blindly out windows, even venturing up to the narrow rooftop balcony, the traditional ship captain's widow's walk, to contemplate the flat and endless sea.

Whenever I escaped outdoors to plod the sandy shoreline or clamber across the dunes, it generally signaled that I was finished writing for the day, although I kept an index card folded lengthwise and a pen or pencil shoved into my back pocket always, in case a felicitous turn of phrase or an apt revision should spring to mind. I had a firm grasp of the book's structure now. The entire first section was complete, and most of the second. The third and final meaty portion boasted a finished chapter here and there, with teetering walkways connecting them, transitions that needed fine-tuning.

Three days after visiting Picarian Realty, I was brooding over one of those creaky walkways, strolling idly down an unfamiliar corridor, fingers caressing a wall sconce here, a tasseled curtain there, when I came upon a room I'd never entered before, a small room, like an afterthought, and heard her voice. Startled, I lifted a hand to my mouth.

Caroline. Her tone and her piercing, drawling vowels were all but unmistakable. I thought I was having some sort of hallucination because it seemed impossible that she would be nearby, impossible and yet her voice cawed crow-like in my ears.

What was she doing within these walls? How dare she invade my space, my haven? Answers tumbled forth as quickly as questions.

Caroline was a fame junkie, a tracker of the rich and famous. She hounded you if we were writing about an attractive man, someone involved in the arts, a wealthy person who might buy a painting from her precious gallery or attend a gala opening where she could show off her catch. I should have expected she'd find a way to intrude on Garrett and demand his attention, playing the widow card for sympathy.

God, please, don't mention me, I willed Garrett, don't say a word. Because I could hear his voice as well, distinguish it in the burble of sound. I moved into the small room as though propelled and shut the door behind me, chasing the sound instead of recoiling from it, which didn't feel like the wrong thing to do. It was like listening to a recording, a logical extension of my daily work. The voices rose from the floor beneath. As I tiptoed into a corner near a painted bookshelf, I glanced out a window to fix my location by the view of the coastline, and determined that I must be above the great room, which seemed odd, this being such a tiny room. Here, in the very corner, the voices grew louder.

Garrett's tone was deep and reassuring, but a bubble of rage swelled in my throat. Why should the impeccable Caroline need reassurance? I imagined her perched on the sofa or in one of the leather chairs, silken legs tucked demurely beneath her, wearing a dress selected to display her lush cleavage, the proud figurehead of a sailing ship. I waited, still as a photograph, and the broadcast got clearer, as though I were fine-tuning a dial, homing in on a faint and distant radio signal.

The word "police" from Caroline rang crystal clear, followed by another blur of sound and the word "snow." If Caroline had driven as far as Dennis for an interview with Detective Snow, she might have continued on up the Cape, dropped in unexpectedly at Cranberry Hill. If Garrett's schedule had included an appointment with Caroline, he would have mentioned it, just as he would surely mention it tonight, maybe at dinner, confiding that she'd appeared out of the blue with some odd and inconvenient request.

For a while, strain as I might, I could make out only an indistinct word or occasional phrase, disjointed as the titles on the nearby bookshelves, where World War II memoirs mixed with car repair manuals and modern fiction squatted next to Shakespeare. Then either my ears adjusted to the distance or the station started broadcasting at a stronger frequency.

"You didn't notice a sudden change in him? Any sadness? Worry?"

"Nothing like that." Garrett's deep voice boomed. "I'm sorry."

"Oh, please don't be. I would have hated it if he'd been devastated. I mean, it's not as if we'd never disagreed before." The word might have been "argued" rather than "disagreed." Her voice was harder to make out. "The two of us have been married—we were married a very long time. People—lovers—say things they don't mean."

"Often."

A Caroline aria followed, an undifferentiated flow of grating sound. After a long silence, Garrett's voice again: "I really don't know what else to say."

I cupped my hands to my ears, closed my eyes, held my breath.

"Well, if you wouldn't mind calling, repeating what you told me, that Teddy wasn't depressed, they can settle this, stop this torture and harassment. Teddy would never do himself intentional harm. If I told him to leave, it wasn't the first time. Believe me, it wasn't. They seem to think he was a man without resources, which if you knew Teddy, is utterly unbelievable."

Her voice crescendoed on the last two words and I nodded my head in agreement. The entire scene was utterly unbelievable, unless you knew Caroline and took her personal quirks into account. In which case there were two interpretations.

One: She'd discovered some life insurance policy that contained a clause precluding suicide. If Snow had so much as hinted at the possibility of suicide, she'd instinctively begin assembling a defense.

Two: She wanted something from Garrett, his attention, his

validation, his deference, his admiration. She was a mantrap and always would be a mantrap. Hadn't she and Garrett met before, Teddy? You'd mentioned something about a dinner during which she'd monopolized the conversation.

"If there's any way I can help, you'll let me know, won't you, Mal? Have you selected the photos? Teddy always asked my advice because of my background. I'd be delighted to work with you."

"No photos in this one. We already agreed on that."

"None? But that will be so disappointing to your fans."

"Simpering" was the word that described her tone and manner, simpering and seductive. I pictured her in the midnight-blue velvet gown she wore the night you accepted your award. I felt hot and cold at the same time, rooted to the spot while film looped my brain: a continuous image of me racing downstairs, screaming, "Leave him alone, leave him alone, he's mine." The room was small, tight, and snug, with walls that pressed too closely. The books, with their yellowed pages and mouse-gnawed covers, reeked of age and mustiness. The air seeped out underneath the door. I needed to escape, to move, to run, but the ill-timed squeak of a floorboard would betray my presence. The room below went silent. What if they were ascending the stairs?

My feet miraculously freed themselves from the sticky gum that fastened them to the floor, and I took refuge in my bedroom, sitting at the dressing table, peering into my own gray eyes in the mirror, despairing at their drab and colorless shade.

CHAPTER
thirty-seven

Later that week, the weather turned for the worse, wind rising from the northeast, sky darkening to a sheet of dull gray metal. I assured Garrett the change would be good for my work, diminish the temptation to stroll the shoreline, but that proved false. The ocean's attraction increased with the wind's velocity; its storm-tossed surface summoned me to watch spellbound as waves smashed and broke against the rocks, rushing beyond the high tide mark to deposit seadrift treasure. Measuring spray against a seawall could absorb entire daydream-filled afternoons.

I did work: There were moments at the keyboard when power

pulsed through my fingers like electric current, when I held the charged reins firmly in my grip. But then the power would sputter and short out. I needed you, Teddy, standing sternly at my side, reviewing, admiring a paragraph, reassuring me that a chapter was sufficiently polished, finished. Alone and unsure, I rewrote passage after passage, fine-tuning, nit-picking, seeking that old enemy, Perfection. I was such a good little girl, wanted to be such a good little girl.

Or was I such a bad little girl? The bedroom acrobatics Garrett and I got up to every night and most mornings were wrong, outside the code, and unlikely to end in orange blossoms, rice-tossing, and long-term bliss. I held that thought far away and stared instead at the stormy ocean, exulted in the foam-topped waves.

It seemed to me that buyers would form a line, pay any premium for the died-and-gone-to-heaven views that presented themselves from each promontory, cove, and beach. The property taxes alone must be staggering.

No wonder Garrett was considering a conservation land trust to lower the property tax. Since most of the land was unspoiled and empty, with only a small portion devoted, one way or another, to the theater, such a trust seemed a good arrangement. With a conservation trust, the estate would be taxed far more leniently on condition that no one would subdivide or develop the property.

I wondered what the estate had been worth in Ralph Malcolm's day, whether the old man had been tempted to cash in and sell off a few acres to an eager developer. I wondered where James Foley's small slice of land was located, whether it possessed an ocean view, a house the size of the tiny beach shack or something larger, more on the order of the Red House or the Old Barn. I wondered whether Foley, the real estate broker, disapproved of prohibiting development on such a large tract of land.

The rain beat down on my hair and face, but I felt strangely at home, comfortable on the windy beach. Who had the old man's lawyer been, and how had he convinced Ralph Malcolm to ease his male chauvinism and allow the fortunate Jenna to inherit? Thoughts of Malcolm's will flowed seamlessly as the tide into thoughts of your will, Teddy. Garrett had said not a single word about Caroline's visit. I took it for granted that I was your literary executor, but was that true? I checked my cell phone. The service was uneven, but I was considering phoning Marcy to discover what she knew about the business of literary inheritance, when my cell buzzed so violently I almost dropped it in the sand.

"Em? Is that you? Can you hear me?"

"Jonathan?" It would be bad news, bad news to counter the good, the lovely book club offer he'd relayed in his previous call. Now there would be a delay, some unforeseen obstacle, or worse, a talk show, an appearance you'd scheduled that couldn't be postponed.

"Can you hear?" His tone was filled with suppressed excitement.

"Yes. How are you? What is it?"

"You know who Amory Russell is, don't you?" he said. "Can you hear me?"

"Yes."

"God, you're so young. You probably only know his son, the start-up media guy, Evan Russell?"

"I've heard of him."

"But did you know Teddy was after him? Amory Russell? Did you have any idea? No, don't tell me, because if you knew about this and didn't tell me, I might get angry and I'm so thrilled, yes, I'd have to say thrilled. This could be incredible. Are you there?"

"Yes."

"The next book. The new book. I mean, you know the Garrett Malcolm book is the last one in this contract. Teddy hinted that he had a big one up his sleeve, but I never thought he'd land a whale like Amory Russell."

"The lawyer."

"God, yes. Lawyer with a capital L. The Henry-Rothschild divorce? The Jenson thing, that Ponzi scheme that lost billions? Teddy had nerve, I'll say that. Everybody's been after Russell's story, but most of us, myself included, thought the old bastard would go to his grave without spilling a single rotten bean. Look, I can't promise you'll handle it, not on your own, but I need to know whether you think you're up to it. Now that you've done some interviewing? Maybe there's someone else you want to partner with? I've never had any trouble with your writing."

"Jonathan, I don't know what to say."

Say thank you, a voice roared in my head. Say thank you, and hang up, get off the phone.

Amory Russell. The lawyer's card in the Bloomie's bag. The Russell in Russell, Ames, and Huber was Amory Russell. And Jonathan wanted to know if I was up to interviewing the great man.

CHAPTER
thirty-eight

Time expanded and contracted, widening and narrowing, elongating and compressing like an old-time squeezebox accordion. Hours with Garrett, in my bed or his, passed in lightning flashes of sensation. Minutes of close manuscript study stretched into hours as I agonized over an adverb or pondered shifting a sentence, even an entire paragraph from one chapter to the next.

Garrett was so sweet, so considerate and kind. His thoughtfulness threw me off balance, teetering between joy and despair, made me debate my precise location on the unimportant-to-important person scale. Over and over I replayed his comments concerning actresses he'd bedded, parsing exactly what he'd meant when he'd declared sex "another way of getting to know" a person. I wondered whether I'd turn up as a character in one of his movies someday, went so far as to cast my role, choosing among upcoming character actresses, wondering whether I'd turn out secretly beautiful, shedding hair clips and eyeglasses as character actresses so often did at the end. Or if the actress playing my role would perish, walk into the ocean with stones weighting her pockets.

That kind of thinking drove me outdoors earlier than usual the next morning, determined to take a brisk walk as a remedy. I'd discovered a magical alchemy between walks along the seashore and writing, a sort of cross-fertilization. If I didn't consciously think about work, if I packed it away and exercised legs rather than brain, answers to tangled problems often came scurrying sideways, like crabs scuttling across the sand.

Afraid the muckraker McKenna might catch me in his lens, I scrupulously avoided the shoreline near the beach shack. I indulged in a brief fantasy and imagined the scruffy man behind bars, but even if Garrett had heeded my warning and alerted the police, I doubted he'd gotten the gossipmonger arrested. It wasn't hard to imagine what McKenna would do if he knew about Brooklyn Pierce, how he'd run with the tale of his drunkenness, destroy the man's dignity.

I had no wish to compromise Pierce's dignity. I simply yearned to solve not only the case of the missing microcassette, but the puzzle of the relationship between the movie star and the director. Initially, I'd assumed dislike, an enmity that precluded a fourth Ben Justice film. But if Pierce could take refuge in Garrett's beach shack whenever he needed it, that bespoke a friendship, a kind of sponsorship.

My feet pounded the sandy turf. Garrett could have tired of the Justice series. The memory of Claire Gregory's perfection in *Red Shot* could have rendered thoughts of another sequel unbearable. A redtailed hawk flew low over a spit of land, veered, and rose into the sun.

I would never jeopardize Garrett's memories of Claire. When he looked at me he'd see no scrap of resemblance; I was unthreatening, a safe, plain woman: That was my charm, my only charm. But the actresses were coming soon. The girl who played Ophelia had the face of a tombstone angel, a body like Venus rising from the sea. Who did I think I was, who did I imagine I'd become? In which fairy tale does the handsome Prince's kiss transform a serving drab into a royal beauty?

The scalding tones of yet another stepmother rang in my ears. If I wasn't good enough for my own mother to keep, who would want me, who could ever want me? Would I never stop whipping myself with that particular scourge? No wonder the power shorted out when I needed it most. No wonder the words wouldn't flow.

Two TV stars, one rising, one fading, still sparred for the role of Hamlet. Each was book ready, prepared to perform at a finger-snap, and each would cheerfully chew cement for the chance to work with Garrett Malcolm. Just as a multitude of potential Gertrudes and Ophelias would do anything to grace his bed.

I crested a hill. My steps had taken me overland to the beach shack, but I hung back, intimidated by the fear of McKenna's hidden cameras. From this angle the place was more outline than building, a high peaked roof pierced by a smokestack. Over the wash of waves, I heard the distinct sound of a door opening and my heart lifted. If I happened to see Brooklyn Pierce out for a walk, that would be different. Then, I'd pounce.

Footsteps clattered down the stairs, then ceased, drowned by the pulse of the waves or the sound-deadening sand. I took shelter behind a dune and waited. The red-tailed hawk circled overhead, but no actor ambled along the shore toward the Amphitheater.

The second noise was speech, not distinct words, but chatter. I should have turned smartly and retreated, but I edged closer to the lip of the dune, protected from view by its precipitous rise, and crouched to peer through the woody stems of bayberry bushes.

Two men fought the wind, spreading a striped blanket on the sand. One kicked off his flip-flops. I assumed Pierce's companion was Garrett at first, and anger flared because Garrett had carefully outlined his agenda, so much work we'd be unable to lunch together and all of it at the Amphitheater.

The men wore low-slung bathing trunks, one bold plaid, the other Hawaiian floral. Brooklyn Pierce, in the floral trunks, seemed to have regained his golden glow. His companion patted him on the shoulder, turning slightly and revealing more of his profile.

Not Garrett, but cousin James Foley, the family resemblance stronger here than in the stuffy realty office. My anger died, replaced by the interviewer's lust for answered questions. My eyes sought a path down to the beach. I could casually happen on the scene, enter stage right, inquire about the screenplay collaboration James had claimed. And if Pierce asked about the missing tape, I could say it had gotten lost; no, better, destroyed in the car crash.

An outburst of laughter drew my focus to the sand. The men were racing into the icy surf, shedding their trunks as they ran, tossing them aside, and whooping as they plunged naked into the foam. It was a flash, a moment engraved in memory: the twin dimples in the very small of Pierce's back, the shoulders and pale flanks, the golden hair. I watched, and after that I could no more have appeared on the beach than I could have sprouted pin feathers.

I found myself marching across the hills back to the Big House, pointing straight for the small office with the mechanical shades where I stopped directly in front of the wall of framed pictures and confronted the framed Malcolm genealogy. I ran my index finger over the glass, tracing elaborate curlicues. So many famous actors, but the family had run to daughters in Ralph's generation. A girl, Jennifer, who had died as a child, that's where Jenna's name must come from, then Ella, who bore James Foley. Ralph's third sister, Lydia, a much-married actress who had enjoyed a Broadway vogue as a grande dame, had died childless.

Harrison Malcolm, Garrett's grandfather and a renowned actor, had not been a wealthy man. Academically rather than commercially minded, he'd run Cranberry Hill as a sort of run-down theater school on a chunk of land too stony for crops and ill-placed for cranberries. Harrison begat Jennifer, Ella, Ralph, and Lydia, all gone now. I reviewed the chart.

Ralph, the commercially minded one, had enlarged the estate, buying more and more land from his neighbors. He'd taken advantage of the natural rock bowl to create the Amphitheater. Legitimate stage had been his passion, but he'd done movies for money late in life, when his hawk nose and plummy vowels made him a natural villain.

Garrett didn't want his bloodlines or childhood to dominate the book. His work was the focus, his films and plays. But I couldn't help speculating about the family in whose house I lived. Had Harrison willed Cranberry Hill exclusively to his son, Ralph, trusting their husbands to provide for his daughters? The tradition of leaving the land to the eldest male might run in the family. Primogeniture as well as love for the Bard of Avon might have figured in Ralph's will.

Bereft of ornamentation, the family tree tapered rather than widened. James Foley had mentioned an ex-wife. I found her name, Katherine, but either she and Jamie had no children, or the chart had been framed prior to their birth. I reviewed and deconstructed the scene at the beach, trying to decide whether it was evidence of a homoerotic, a homosexual, relationship. Had I witnessed caresses or high-spirited locker-room play? Had I miscontrued, misunderstood? If I'd viewed the same scene in a movie, unguided by focus, angle, film score, its meaning would have been ambiguous, a matter of interpretation.

Was Brooklyn Pierce one of the reasons Jamie's marriage had ended?

Part of the reason he'd received so little land? I doubted it; actors of all people were tolerant. But Ralph had wanted a troupe of actor-sons.

James Foley had mentioned how close he'd come to inheriting all the land. I wished I could see the exact terms, the precise wording of the Shakespearean will written by Ralph Malcolm.

I touched Jenna's name on the chart. Lucky, lucky Jenna, sole fruit of the illustrious tree. With so much at stake, there would be contingencies, in case something happened to lucky Jenna. James Foley must be listed as a fallback, an alternative. If the lawyer who'd set up the generation-skipping trust hadn't insisted on a change in language, Jenna, not a "Sonne of my Body," but a daughter, could have been disinherited. I considered the lawyer's business card in the Bloomie's bag. Amory Russell's firm was located in New York. I doubted they concerned themselves with Massachusetts estate law, and Jonathan seemed certain that you'd spoken to Russell about ghosting his biography.

Back in my pink and gold room, I replayed the tape in which Garrett talked about his father. I could almost hear the quotation marks when he spoke of "Ralph's Shakespearean Will." I smiled at the portentous quality of the rolled r's, the invisible caps, the implied italics as he intoned Ralph's reluctant change from "Sonnes of My Body Lawfully Issuing" to "Heirs of My Body, et cetera," and then it came to me. *Heirs of My Body.* Would you have made a note of that, and if you had, would you have used shorthand, so that the note read: HMB?

JFLY: James Foley. 2nd BST BD: Second-Best Bed. HMB: Heirs of My Body. I was following your path, but I wasn't yet sure where the path led.

CHAPTER
thirty-nine

The more I considered it, the likelier it seemed: There would have come a night when you worked late, sipped wine over dinner, chatted long after the meal. Garrett would have offered a fat Cohiba cigar from the box on the side table, and you'd have downed a snifter of brandy while you smoked. It would have been the most natural thing in the world for Garrett to say the hell with it, don't drive tonight, there's plenty of space in the house.

I couldn't imagine you sleeping in gold and pink splendor, but bedrooms lined the corridors. In any one of them, you might have left behind a tell-tale sign. You might have carelessly mislaid the micro-cassette Brooklyn Pierce had begged me to return.

I'd wandered the Big House before, enjoying its rambling spacious-ness, but I hadn't searched it. I'd fingered ornaments because their textures seemed to demand a caress, but I'd drawn the line at grubbing in cabinet corners while keeping furtive watch for housekeepers and maintenance staff. Now, successfully avoiding all onlookers, I investi-gated six different bedrooms before taking a break during which I peered out a low window and took note of the car parked below.

Beige and gold, the cruiser crouched like a waiting lion in the drive-way. The shield emblazoned on the hood displayed the palindrome-like initials of the Dennis Port Police Department.

Quickly descending a flight of stairs, I crossed hallways and shot down corridors like a bullet with barely a thought for my trajectory till I arrived in the corner of the tiny room over the Great Room, marvel-ing at my speed and lack of hesitation, thinking that if my heart would stop pounding in my ears, I'd make a better eavesdropper. Detective Snow's voice was less distinct than Caroline's. His words slid into one another, eliding into a strange foreign-sounding tongue. I shifted my position, inched slightly to the left, nearer the bookshelf, seeking the sweet spot, straining with concentration until the rumbling noises sorted themselves into words and sentences.

Garrett, calm and bell-like, resonant: "Sorry, I don't remember. That would be Wednesday night?"

A noise from Snow, a grunt of assent.

"I don't believe I saw him after our Tuesday session, but my assis-tant keeps my schedule if you want to check."

"You didn't meet with him later, for dinner or drinks? He wasn't staying here? On the property?"

"No."

"It's just his neighbors aren't sure whether or not his car was parked at the house Tuesday night."

"I'm sorry, but I'm afraid I can't help you."

I missed a sentence or two after that, caught only a word here, a word there. Had the speakers moved to another location? Should I risk moving? Just as I started to take the first of three prospective steps toward the window, a complete sentence rang out.

"Was Blake working on anything else while he was here?"

A murmur from Garrett, no specific words, but a tone of demurral, disavowal. *I wouldn't know, I don't know*, something in that vein.

"He didn't speak to you about any other project? Some kind of exposé?"

The next thing I heard was a rumbling squawk as though a chair were being pushed back. I imagined Detective Snow lurching unsteadily to his feet, his complexion gray and sickly.

Garrett: "Is it important? Where Teddy was on Wednesday night?"

In the burst of speech that followed, the only words I caught were "wondering why," "that stretch of road," "deserted," and "that's all." Then Garrett chimed in with something that sounded vaguely cheerful. Snow's response included "follow up," and "routine."

The clack of footsteps signaled the end of the interview, so I turned to leave the room. Remembering too well the wild panic the enclosed space had engendered when I'd eavesdropped on Garrett and Caroline, I'd left the door ajar. Darren Kalver stood like a pale scarecrow in the shadows and a faint smile played on his lips.

"Quite a view from that window," he said when he caught my eye.

I had no idea how long he'd been standing there, no idea how he could have approached so silently.

"Yes, it's lovely." My face set into a sculpted mask as I waited for him to move aside so I could scuttle past. He planted himself in the doorway, watching me with speculative eyes.

Weeks ago, Teddy, I might have melted into tears at his gaze or run off like a mouse caught eating the cheese. But I was Garrett's favorite now. A new and steely confidence ran in my veins, and I could stare down the likes of a personal assistant. The deadlock was broken by a burst of classical piano that I didn't recognize as the ringtone of his cell until he swooped it from a pocket and tucked it to his ear.

"Cranberry Hill Theater. Garrett Malcolm's office. How may I help you?"

He rolled his pale-lashed eyes when he heard the response. "Wayne, I'm so sorry. Yes, it was a terrible mix-up and I'm so sorry. I know. I know. Yes, you had every reason to expect the meeting as scheduled. I absolutely sympathize, and I know you need to get the documents ready, but he's rehearsing full time, and you know how he gets."

Kalver backed out of the doorway and shot me a look that said, *Go away and stop listening.* When I didn't, he pivoted and lowered his voice. "Wayne, you know I'm in your corner. No, look, I did not cancel on you. I don't know what happened and I promise I'll try to wedge you in, but I think you should be prepared to wait till after we open. I know. I'm really sorry."

He shoved the phone angrily into his pocket. His tone changed from sugary syrup to steel as he pointed a finger at my face. "You haven't been playing private secretary, have you?"

"What do you mean?"

"They blame me. And they ought to blame you."

His pale flap of hair was ridiculous and his accusation so transparently unfair, I decided not to dignify it with a response.

"He's got important decisions to make, about the future of this theater. They want to cross the t's on the trust, but Mal postpones every damn meeting. All he wants to do is direct and act. Artists!" He uttered the word like a curse.

"Is that the conservation trust?" For a moment I thought anger would overcome his customary discretion, but he recalled his position too quickly. And mine. And sought to reestablish the balance of power.

"What are you doing up here?" he demanded.

I kept to the offensive. "When can I interview you about your boss?"

"I'm a confidential assistant. I think that precludes interviews."

"And how did you get your job?"

"I applied for it."

"Does the board have any say in the selection of plays?"

"The Cranberry Hill Board? Are you kidding? If they did, we'd do nonstop musicals. Malcolm keeps all the power. And if you'd let him get out of bed occasionally, he might exercise it."

I tried to summon a withering response. Failed, edged past him, and walked steadily down the hall to the bedroom, my bedroom. I was still there, hands poised at the keyboard, when Garrett cracked the door to tell me dinner would be late. I smiled and thanked him. And waited, but he didn't mention Kalver catching me in the act of eavesdropping. Nor did he mention Snow's visit.

I considered bringing it up during pre-dinner drinks, but Kalver was telling some pointless story about last year's production of *Love's Labor's Lost.* I thought about it during the soup course, but the stage manager and the lighting designer were reminiscing about *Hamlet*s they'd enjoyed in England and Australia, and *Hamlet*s they'd despised in Spain and Germany, and could even the best translation of Shakespeare ever be said to truly work? I speculated about it during the entire endless meal, about casually announcing that I'd noticed a police cruiser parked in the driveway and had someone neglected to pay a traffic fine? The crème brûleé was tasteless in my mouth, the coffee bitter. Garrett said nothing, I said nothing, and our silence sprouted and grew like ivy creeping up a stout brick wall.

CHAPTER
forty

With the extended deadline looming, the next morning I forced myself back to the text and attacked the twenty-ninth chapter with something approaching gusto. I had the facts, the hard, round beads of information that, correctly strung, would inform the chapter, but the rhythm of Garrett's thoughts and actions on the occasion of his second Academy Award nomination proved stubbornly elusive and I knew I couldn't seek guidance or clarification from the source, who'd be a bear all day, dodging between Amphitheater and Old Barn, conferring with the lighting designer, haranguing the carpenters; strictly off limits. I started over, butchered a sentence, mangled a paragraph, and found myself debating between a trip to a Chatham boutique and a return to the Cape Cod Mall. Really, my boudoir apparel was a constant joke: nudity or nothing. I didn't own so much as a nightgown worthy of the name. I craved silk, something skimpy and erotic like the blue gown I wore our first time, the one currently encased in plastic in my bottom dresser drawer in Boston. I hungered for another brightly colored bra, a racy thong, a trousseau of foamy lingerie.

God, do you remember, Teddy, how shy I was, how frightened, how many months it took to lure me to your bed? How I hid in the closet to disrobe and ran to the bathroom afterward, carefully closing the door? How tortured I was then, how whipsawed I felt, how ignorant I remained in spite of modern advertising and skimpy clothes and archly knowing TV shows. In and out of schools and institutions, with different families in far-flung towns, I'd missed it all, the lectures on menstruation, the talks on sexuality. Everyone I knew seemed to know everything I didn't know, and no one shared because I didn't know to ask.

How ashamed I was of my scrawny naked body. But I learned how to use it, didn't I?

It was more pleasant to contemplate nightgowns than brood over Garrett's continuing silence about Caroline's visit and Snow's queries. A shopping trip wouldn't take longer than an hour. To assuage any lingering guilt, I grabbed the recorder and plunked it on the passenger seat of the Focus, promised myself I'd listen to Garrett's voice all the way there and back as well. If I listened with half my mind while letting the rest wander through lacey groves of lingerie, the click might come, the small sideways glimmer that would illuminate Chapter Twenty-nine.

As I pulled out of the winding driveway and slowed to turn onto the two-lane road that led to the highway, two things happened at once. I spotted the navy blue van parked on the verge and a man stepped directly in front of the car.

I hadn't been speeding. The sharpness of the turn dictated caution, but the sudden and unexpected need to halt drove my foot and the brake peddle to the floor. Casually, Glenn McKenna put a hand on the hood.

In a fit of fury, I lowered the window. "Are you insane? Get out of the way."

"Hey, you trying to avoid me?"

I pressed my lips together to keep them from shaking with the same tremor that possessed my hands on the steering wheel.

"Where are you heading? Up cape or down?"

"What does it—?"

"Wait till I get in the van, then follow me."

"I don't think we have anything to—"

"I can't talk here. Your pal, Malcolm, took out a restraining order on me. You have anything to do with that?"

"I didn't know he—"

"We need to talk."

Leaning over, he rapped the windshield with his fist. It wasn't exactly a threatening gesture, but it frightened me. Feeling numb, with relief at not knocking the man down, but with dread as well, I waited obediently while he clambered into the van. When he pulled onto the road, I followed as instructed, and when the van took a left at Route 6, I did the same, telling myself I was headed in that direction anyway, assuring myself that I'd keep going straight after he turned off. I would ignore him. Everything was perfect now and any discussion with McKenna would only mess it up.

As I drove, a fog stole over my soul, a return to the passive old days, to before, when every action and activity was limited, dictated by a demanding foster mother or a strict stepfather, by some outside voice that controlled, condoled, consoled. It was as though you were leading me on, Teddy, as though you were telling me what to do, and when and how to do it.

The van veered left and so did I, the steering wheel rotating inexorably. If I slowed, the van slowed; an invisible tow-rope might have linked the two vehicles. We headed briefly southeast on Cable Road, then the pavement curved east toward the Atlantic, threading between dense patches of silvery pines and low thickets of yew.

Beyond the small parking lot at the end of the road, sea met sky in banded shades of gray. The blue van waited there, but McKenna was already skulking across the road. As I tracked his scarecrow figure through the scattered pines, the lighthouse caught my eye and held it captive.

It dominated the promontory and diminished the lightkeeper's house below. Halfway up the tower changed color, from arctic white to deep red. The turret was iron-black so the structure seemed to have three tiers like an absurdly elongated wedding cake. With a cheerful blue sky as backdrop, the effect would have been overly pretty, lifted from a picture postcard. In the dour gray light, the tower looked grim, austere, and powerful as a castle keep.

McKenna, dwarfed by the lighthouse, lurched uphill, backpack sitting between his shoulders like a hump. His hair was stringy and greasy. Unless he owned multiple pairs of similarly ripped jeans, he hadn't changed clothes since our sunset meeting at First Encounter Beach. I had no idea whether lighthouses enclosed public rooms, but I was determined not to follow him indoors. The wind snatched my voice and carried it out to sea, but he must have heard my protest because he pivoted on the steep path, paused, and attempted to light a cigarette while I fought the wind on the incline.

"Totally different view of the ocean, huh?" As I approached, he waved his cigarette in the direction of the waves. "Like a big bathtub, the bay side of the Cape, but this side is wild water, nothing out there but pirate wrecks and sharks all the way to Spain. Closed the Chatham beaches yesterday, you hear about it? Great white shark, cruising for seals. Come summer, it'll be cruising for tourists." He paused for a quick drag on the cigarette. I opened my mouth to speak, but he didn't let me get a word in.

"Fraternizing with the enemy, huh? Teddy never moved into the house." He turned and attacked the path, leaving me to scramble behind. At the lighthouse door, he tried the handle, rattling it while I wondered what he meant by "fraternizing," what he knew, what he surmised.

"I used to come here when I was a kid," he shouted over a gust that shook the nearby shrubbery. "Back then, you could walk in, climb up top. Nauset Light used to be part of the double beacon at Chatham, but they disassembled it and moved it here years ago, when the government decommissioned the twin lights. Used to stand over there, across the road. Had to move it again, back from the edge, in 'ninety-eight, so it wouldn't fall off the cliff. Erosion."

"I'm not in the market for another history lesson. It's too cold."

"Okay, so Coast Guard Beach is right down the shore there. You didn't come meet me. I thought we had an agreement."

"There was no reason to—"

"What did you think of my stuff?"

"I do my own research."

"If we move down this way, the house will shelter us. Or we could sit in the van."

"I'm not getting in your van." The thought of the enclosed space nauseated me. Anger, simmering underneath the passive fog, started to churn and bubble. No matter what agreement the two of you had reached, I hadn't been part of it. I hadn't received any benefit. The man wasn't even good at what he did. If he'd been any good, he'd have known Brooklyn Pierce was hiding at the beach shack, right under his celebrity-sniffing nose.

"Fine." He scuttled swiftly to the flattest part of the hill as sun broke through the clouds. Like spokes of a giant fan, the rays lit patches of cream-topped waves far out at sea, turning them to molten gold. If I'd seen the same thing in a movie, I'd have dismissed the director as a hopeless romantic.

The wind slapped my face and made it real. "Look, whatever deal you made with Teddy, consider it off. I do my own research and my own writing."

"Under a pseudonym."

"A combination, Teddy's name and mine. Blakemore."

"You didn't get it, then?"

"Get what?"

"You didn't understand my notes. Because you don't have the sources I've got."

"I don't need them. Not for the kind of books I write."

He scanned the horizon warily. "Do you know about Snow?"

I considered snow in April. It's not unheard of in New England. Then "Detective" popped into my head like a tardy translation on the screen of a foreign film.

"He talked with Malcolm, right? At Cranberry Hill, a few days ago? Did Malcolm call his lawyer? Later, after Snow left?"

"Why should he?" On film, the view would have been breathtaking. On the windy hill, the sea was immense and terrifying, the line between water and sky blurred and indistinct.

"Because it's become a criminal investigation."

Suicide, I thought. Suicide must be a criminal act in Massachusetts. What did it matter, anyway, one way or another, because you didn't commit—

"Teddy was murdered."

Murdered. The word clanged off the shadowy horizon line, echoed and reverberated. Oh, Teddy, time murders us all, in dribs and drabs, slowly, with the inevitability of the waves. Even if no sharks lurk beneath the surface, the waves tumble us, roll over us, and pull us under. The gossipmonger's lips formed soundless words and the sandy path swam up to meet my eyes. It tilted, revolving and spinning like a roulette wheel, and I remember thinking that some angry father would blast McKenna with a shotgun, murder Glenn McKenna, murder him, not you.

CHAPTER
forty-one

Y*ou fainted once.* Jonathan's voice blasted my ears, querulous and accusatory. Until he pointed the words and pulled the trigger, I hadn't realized you'd told our editor about the night I fainted, Teddy.

It must have been three years ago. Yes, in the spring, in the McAfee Ballroom at the university, such an austere place in my experience that I hadn't imagined it housed a ballroom till you proudly displayed the invitation and announced that you would be receiving the Bessemer Award for your essay on teaching. The one I wrote—edited, you said—but truly, I wrote that essay. The image of the ceremony flickered like an old newsreel: You, resplendent in your tuxedo, Caroline, in midnight blue, beaming on your arm, and I was a tiny ant crawling in your wake, wearing a pathetically prim trouser suit, and never in that sprawling acceptance speech did you mention me. My speech again, of course, but I actually believed you might glance over it in advance, augment it with a few of your own stray thoughts, such as gratitude to the one who'd made the award possible. You thanked your department chair and the members of the committee. By the time you acknowledged dear Caroline, I was having trouble breathing. The ballroom was too warm, too moist, too heavily scented with perfume and sweat. Applause sprang up, scattered at first, then a wall of noise as deafening as the roar of a thousand lions and all the air got sucked from the room.

"You okay?" This voice came from a distance, issued from a far-off void. The buffeting wind had ceased, gusts mysteriously becalmed. I was enclosed, shuttered, and it was darker than it should have been. Windows, I thought, tinted windows.

"Teddy?" Desolation washed through me like a wave. Turning my head, I caught a glimpse of a tiny plastic tree dangling from a rearview mirror. I was in McKenna's van and the tree accounted for part of the smell, unwashed laundry and rotted food the remainder. Breath caught in my throat and choked me. "Let me out. Open the door."

"Calm down. It's okay. You passed out or something."

"Stop the van. Open the door."

"Relax, it's not moving."

"Please, please, I'm going to throw up."

The darkness parted with a metallic creak, and I rolled to my feet, lurching toward the light, vaulting through the rear doors as they separated. I stumbled on the rough pavement, but hands caught me before I fell to my knees.

"Take it easy."

"Let go of me."

"There's a bench. Come on; sit down."

As soon as the wooden slats pushed against the backs of my legs, as

245

soon as I sat, I felt stronger, just like the last time. Once they'd carried me outdoors, once I was able to sit, I'd been fine, humiliated at my weakness, now as then.

My lungs did their work, pumping air like a bellows. The bench overlooked the same stretch of shoreline as the lighthouse, but from a lower vantage point. The key factors, rather than sky and waves, were sand and rocks. A wavery green line of seaweed marked the high tide.

McKenna sat beside me, so close our knees kissed. He must have dragged or carried me across the road to the van. My skin prickled beneath my clothes, and I took a quick inventory; my jacket was still zipped to my chin. The man started rattling on in his mile-a-minute monotone, saying he wasn't really concerned about a written credit on this book, that it was the next one he was thinking about, the new book, as though the two of you had signed a long-term agreement.

"Wait, wait; you said police, Snow, about a—" The remembered word caught in my throat. "Teddy's death was an accident."

"Snow doesn't think so." McKenna smiled crookedly, excited to be the bearer of bad news, pleased, as well he might be. Now he could slap it across his Web site: "Celebrity Biographer Murdered," followed by a string of question marks and exclamation points. He could use your death to sell real estate ads.

"You put Snow up to it," I said. "You filled his head with—"

"He found his witness."

It was like I'd never heard the word before, could barely recall what message the two syllables of "witness" conveyed. My lungs might be pumping, but my mind was whirling in mist, confused, blinking on and off like a warning beacon.

"Witness finally came home. Jerk went off on some cruise," McKenna said. "If Snow hadn't been stuck in the hospital, they'd have gotten to him before he left, but you'll see, the circus is really gonna come to town now."

"Someone else in the car? Another driver?" I was fixated on the word "witness," but not so much so that "circus" didn't register. The bastard was enjoying himself, reveling in a what promised to be a dream-come-true story, tailor-made for his Web site.

"Somebody saw something, that's all. Guy in a house on a hill. You know the place it happened? Down by the Harwich border? Tricky piece of road, pond on one side, reservoir on the other, steep embankments? They've had smash-ups there before. There's an old graveyard at the top of the hill?"

You liked old graveyards, I thought. McKenna peered at me strangely; I might have said it out loud.

"Guy staying up there, little house behind the graveyard. Visiting his sister, some old coot watching from a window, worried teenagers could be drinking and making out, hooking up, you know the type. Hoping to watch. Saw Blake's car parked up there. Saw two people, one looking at the gravestones, the other just a shadow, lurking around the car."

"Is this a witness you found?" The words burst from my lips as though escaping. *Is this a witness you coached and paid?* That's what I wanted to ask, wanted to demand. The police were humoring him, I decided, and I should humor him, too. I would smile and nod, stand up, walk to my car. The wind grabbed his hair and blew it into a frizzled mane.

"If you think there's anything Garrett Malcolm wouldn't do to protect himself," he said, "you're nuts."

"If you think Garrett killed Teddy, you're the one who's crazy,"

"Garrett, huh?" His eyes lit with satisfaction.

I forced my teeth together. It had happened before, this post-faint chattiness, this garble of words rising unchecked to the surface. I knew it was better to keep silent; anything was better than charging ahead full steam, assuring this madman that you'd never print anything a subject

247

didn't want to reveal. If McKenna had seemed rational, I might have asked why Garrett would cooperate with a biographer if he were hiding some diabolical secret.

"Some people think money buys everything." McKenna answered the thought as though reading my mind, and once again I wondered if I might have unwittingly spoken out loud. "Who makes out like a bandit if Teddy's dead? That's the kind of question cops ask."

"Caroline." Too late, I pressed my lips shut.

"Teddy's wife? You figure she tooled all the way up here and gimmicked his brakes? She a mechanic?"

"Gimmicked his brakes?"

"He wasn't drunk or drugged or anything. No heart attack. But the Accident Reconstruction Unit found something funny with the brake line. Snow knows what he's doing, all right; he just got sideswiped, delayed, getting sick and all. Look, I don't give this number out, my cell, but you call and I'll get there twenty-four/seven. Bring a videocam, bring the cops." Shoving his face too close to mine, he slipped a piece of paper into my trembling hand, all the while warning me to watch myself with Garrett Malcolm, to be careful, on guard.

"You're wrong," I said.

"Listen, you gotta watch your back. I mean, where's that tape, the one you thought I had? You find it? You know who it was he interviewed? What do you bet Teddy got the goods on Malcolm, nailed the bastard?"

A red Mazda pulled into the parking lot and ejected a trio of early tourists. McKenna shot me a sideways glance, the same squirrelly look he'd displayed at First Encounter Beach, the glance that said, *I'm a secret agent and my cover just got blown.* Quickly, he reached into the frayed pocket of his jeans and yanked out a battered envelope.

"Here," he said, lowering his voice. "I'm pretty sure this helped get Teddy killed."

I recoiled. "Shouldn't you give it to the police?"

"Don't get me wrong. This isn't everything, not by a long shot. It's part of a bigger picture, but I can't talk now." His sweeping glance encompassed the red car and the wandering tourists. "It could make a book with real consequences, a once-in-a-lifetime story, and they're all in it, the politicians, the landowners, the government, I wouldn't be surprised. I mean, they own the rest of the land, don't they?"

Hands in his pockets, head ducked low, he retreated to the van and gunned the engine while the tourists posed for cell phone photos with the lighthouse in the background.

CHAPTER
forty-two

A criminal investigation into your death. A need to watch my back. I shifted my eyes from the trio of harmless tourists and stared blankly at the crumpled envelope that McKenna, with the grim élan of a cold war spy, had shoved into my unresponsive hands. Chilled to the bone, bleached and bloodless as a rock, I felt my lower jaw tremble. How could even a madman abandon me on a windblown bench in the raw April cold? I hardly knew, but I was intensely relieved when the navy van disappeared in a spurt of gravel and shells. As the tourists investigated the lighthouse, calling to each other in high-pitched tones, I stumbled toward the Focus.

A criminal investigation into your death. I unlocked the car, ducked inside, started the engine, and turned on the heater. Prying open the envelope, I withdrew a single snapshot, smoothed its curling edges, and ran a finger across the central image. If this photo had gotten you killed, it should have been the death of me, the death of McKenna as well, since both of us had already screened it on his preview Web site.

McKenna had to be playing some kind of game. The conviction grew and strengthened with the stream of warm air from the vents. He knew I was staying at the Big House, assumed I'd developed a rapport with Garrett. He was jealous and vindictive as well as crazy.

I grabbed the purse I'd stashed under the seat. As I pushed the photo into the outside pocket, I noticed the lighted screen of my cell: a missed phone call, a voice message. When I entered my password, Detective Snow's rumbling voice filled the car, asking me to call, repeating his number twice in a stern monotone. The horizon line seemed to tilt, and I thought I might faint again.

McKenna hadn't lied: Snow wanted to talk again. Something must have changed. His visit to Garrett, which I'd filed under routine, might not be routine after all. Garrett's silence on the subject, which I'd attributed to his harried director's schedule, now seemed sinister.

Snow was investigating your death. How quiet it seemed. The tourists on the hill were distant stick figures, distorted by the windshield glass. Were they calling to each other or was that the keening cry of the swooping gulls, snatching at seaweed?

I followed the flight of a gull, skimming, sinking, then rising on an invisible current. Did the gull notice the car? Sense my gaze? If I left the tepid warmth and threw myself off the cliff, how would that final unconsciousness differ from the fleeting unconsciousness of a fainting spell? What would fill the void?

For in that sleep of death what dreams may come,

When we have shuffled off this mortal coil,

Must give us pause.

Hamlet, Act Three, scene 1. How could anyone make sense of it, Teddy, the massive significance and utter insignificance of a single life, a single death? And not end up barking mad, howling at the tide, taking ship for England in the company of Rosencrantz and Guildenstern? I plucked the photograph from the envelope again and carefully centered it at the hub of the steering wheel so the horn wouldn't sound and alarm the tourists or the gulls.

A younger Garrett Malcolm gazed at me steadily from the lower-right-hand corner of the unposed shot, his left arm outstretched, hand tugged by the hand of the cut-off figure of the dark-haired woman. I stared at the image until it blurred, recalling the caption as it appeared on the Web site: 939495. I let my eyes close, but the image stayed, as though the picture had burned into my retinas.

Waves crashed against the rocks and the wind tried to penetrate the crack at the top of the window. I considered other images—on McKenna's Web site, the girls frolicking in the waves, then the framed photos on the wall behind Malcolm's Oscar-laden desk. When I got as far as the photo of young Jenna Malcolm dancing in the sand in front of the beach shack, my lips tightened. What if I ignored the figures in the foreground?

Where had I seen that low, flat building, that diamond-shaped sign? The letters were unfocused and illegible, but the conjunction of shapes, the curbed sidewalk, the narrow driveway brought a glimmer of recollection. That sign, or a similar sign, fronted the women's clinic situated next to the hair salon, and the couple could have been headed for the entrance.

CHAPTER
forty-three

No lingerie shops lined this drab street in this drab town. Hours earlier, I might have called the narrow lane charming, the small shops with shingled exteriors and hand-painted signs quaint. But color had been washed from the day, the sky, so vivid over the ocean, had dulled to gray, and I had no eyes for dainty window displays. The aperture had closed, the lens narrowed, and I was left with tunnel vision as I studied the small figures in the foreground of the print.

Garrett was ten years younger, probably more, possibly twenty, so that he would have been perhaps twenty-five, a year younger than I am, a young man still. There are long years in which men change very little. The lines at the corners of his eyes cut deeper now; the shadows beneath them had darkened.

McKenna's mind was as twisted as a nest of snakes, but one of those serpents had dug a fang into my veins and injected pure poison. The gossipmonger believed Garrett had done something to harm you, Teddy, believed you'd discovered some dire secret in the director's past.

A picketing protester tried to catch my eye, but I ignored him and concentrated on the photo. The hairdresser at the beauty salon next door said that local girls who got in trouble with baseball players or actors came here for relief. "In trouble" as in pregnant, "relief" as in abortion. This could be a photo of Garrett escorting a local girl, some underage girl he'd impregnated, to the clinic. The hairdresser said the actors joked about a local "directory" of female "talent."

I concentrated on the female. She didn't look like a teen. She seemed older, but it was hard to say why, hard to peg her age. Women too, have those years, twenties to thirties, even forties, when the facial muscles hold fast and makeup aids the youthful illusion. Little of her face was visible, just the corner of an eye, the shadow of a cheekbone. She was defined by her hair, that dark flying wedge.

I stood on the pavement near the hair salon, careful to keep my distance from the few picketers who kept vigil across the street from the entrance to the women's clinic, glancing down at the photo, up at the clinic, easing myself into the exact position where the photographer once stood.

Garrett was easy to identify, but I was sleeping with him; I knew his every pore. I'd studied photos of the man in his teens and twenties. McKenna had picked him out as well, but McKenna, too, was a specialist who recognized his celebrities. Garrett's fame was a fairly recent by-product of his success. His renown as a film actor, dependent on a variety of chameleon-like roles, had been less than his glory as a director.

Until recently, Garrett had been a man who walked under the radar, but in the photo, he wore a trench coat with the collar turned up. Since he had made an effort at disguise, the woman might have tried to alter her appearance also. There were costumes at Cranberry Hill, rods laden with them, neat rows of wigs on the shelf in the Old Barn. I shifted my grip on the snapshot so that my thumbnail covered the wedge of dark hair.

"Age cannot wither her, nor custom stale her infinite variety." Not *Hamlet*, but still Shakespeare: *Antony and Cleopatra,* Act Two, scene 2. If Claire Gregory had ever played Cleopatra, I might have recognized her sooner in her dark blunt-cut wig.

A man in a trench coat, a woman in a wig. Garrett and Claire. In disguise.

I stared down at the photo, up at the clinic, and experienced a strange dissonance, a sense of disconnectedness. It was the same clinic, but not the same clinic. The sign was the same, the sidewalk the same, the building to the left that housed the hairdresser the same, but the clinic building itself was set closer to the sidewalk. As though wandering in a hypnotic trance, I perambulated toward the door.

A gray-haired, gray-faced man intercepted me. "Don't kill your baby."

"Get your hands off me."

"You don't have to go through with it."

I brushed him aside and rushed through the door. Disinfectant and air freshener battled for dominance in the refrigerated chill. Someone had made an attempt at a homey touch, scattering throw pillows across mismatched chairs and a low sofa, but the waiting room still screamed doctor's office. Magazines studded a circular coffee table. A water cooler burbled in an alcove. A sign read OUR SERVICES and listed them in alphabetical order: abortion, body image, men's sexual health, morning-after pill, sex and sexuality, sexually transmitted diseases, women's health.

"Your name?" A snub-nosed young woman shifted her gaze from her laptop screen.

"I'm not here to see anyone. I—is there another clinic that looks almost the same as this one?"

The woman assumed a defensive posture, straightening her back and pursing her lips, making me wonder whether the picketers ever sent anyone—say, a young woman with questions—inside for the express purpose of annoying her while she worked, or if working in an atmosphere of constant, muted, daily threat, disconcerted her.

"I'm sorry, are you looking for another address?" She stayed barely polite, her tone caustic.

"Is there another branch, another clinic with the same sign?"

"No, miss, but we might be able to help you here." Her smile, when it came, was surprisingly warm. It seemed she had decided I was too young and naïve, too scared to mention the reason I might wish to see a doctor. I hesitated. I didn't want to show her the photo. Garrett Malcolm was definitely recognizable now.

"She might mean the old building."

I turned my head and caught the glance of a second receptionist, this one plump and motherly, her right hand raised to fit a sheaf of medical records into a bookcase that stretched across the rear wall.

"The old building," I repeated.

She offered a wide smile with a dimple at one corner. "Yes, this isn't our original space here. When they rebuilt, they made a few changes."

"Remodeled?"

"Not intentionally. The old clinic burned to the ground."

"Fire-bombed," the younger receptionist chimed in, "and they still let those picketers stand there every day, harassing us and bothering our clients."

"No one ever proved it was arson," the motherly woman said mildly.

"But it burned?" I said. "When?"

"A long time ago." This from the young one, a dismissive snort.

"When dinosaurs ruled the earth." The older woman raised an eyebrow. "And, yes, I was working here at the time."

"Was anyone hurt?"

"Oh, no, nothing like that. It happened late at night, thank God, must be fifteen years ago. Back when we kept paper records. Nothing on line, so the whole thing was a nightmare."

I turned away, took a step or two, and sank into a sagging armchair. Claire might have undergone an abortion prior to Jenna's birth, but she would never have considered aborting Jenna, the long-awaited child. Unless Garrett, worried about his father's bias toward boys, compelled her to come, forced her to find out the sex of the unborn child.

That didn't work; the baby girl hadn't been aborted. But the clinic, the clinic in the photo, had burned to the ground. Surely McKenna wasn't accusing Garrett of burning down a clinic. The director certainly had a thing about fire; Darren Kalver pointed out the fire extinguishers in the barn on my first visit, cautioned me against smoking, mentioned a fire that occurred when Garrett was young. And he used fire with great effectiveness in his films. But to base an accusation of arson on such sketchy ground was as bad, worse than having O'Toole, the fool of a district attorney, accuse Garrett of being involved in Helga Forester's death just because he hadn't volunteered to step up and swab his cheek.

"Miss, are you sure we can't help you? Doctor Gerson will be free in fifteen minutes."

Garrett got in trouble with the DA because he refused to give a DNA sample. When other men in Truro and Wellfleet and Eastham volunteered to help with the Forester investigation, Garrett refused.

The clinic burned. The records burned.

I stared up at the motherly face of the older receptionist. "My brother—that is, my boyfriend—" I lowered my eyes to my lap. "Um, do you think, uh, can you give me a rundown of the services you provide, um, for men?"

"Birth control, infertility, testicular cancer, and UTIs. That's urinary tract infections."

When I wrote, when I organized my writing, I thought of facts as beads, each a hard, round object, each complete in and of itself. Facts, like beads, need to be strung on thread of a certain length and composition, arranged in a particular order.

"Do you want to make an appointment for him?" the younger woman said impatiently.

Facts, like beads, can be manipulated, restrung, crafted into kaleidoscopic patterns. A dangling necklace of facts can be broken, with each isolated bead taking on a new and separate significance.

"Miss?"

"Uh, no, uh, that is—um, I'll have to talk it over with him. Thank you. Thank you for your help."

CHAPTER
forty-four

Tape 063
Sybilla Jackson
3/15/10

Teddy Blake: *Good morning, I have—*

Sybilla Jackson: I can't believe Garrett actually wants me to talk, but then he knows I'm not the type to harbor a grudge. Still, I find myself surprised he didn't send me the finished script, tell me exactly what I could and couldn't say. Such a control freak, really, who could live with him?

TB: *You did.*

SJ: Yes, for three years, almost four, wasn't it? But we were apart so much of the time. I was traveling nonstop, making big money then, absolutely in demand, Rio one week, Milan the next, with a layover in Paris for a runway show. Those were my best years, really, and Garrett was such a lovely man for putting up with the hullaballoo. He wasn't so much the big director then, but he was already leaving acting behind, turning the tables, which was so clever of him because he was a good actor, but he wasn't going to be a star, just a flash in the pan, and then a has-been in a year or two, you know the kind. It's a dog-eat-dog thing, acting, not that it's any worse than modeling. In my business, you're lucky if you get to be the flavor of the month. Actors have a teensy bit more time to develop a career. A model simply has a look, and if it's your time, it's your time.

TB: *He started writing screenplays when the two of you were together.*

SJ: We didn't talk about work, really, we went to parties, and I went even if he refused to go. He had a bit of a dreary streak, to tell the truth. I always wanted to run out and play, and he was sometimes just a tiny bit stick-in-the-muddish, something about that dour New England background, that stuck-up theatrical family. He was overinvolved in his career. You tell him I said that. I know it all paid off, all that dreary work, but I certainly didn't want to be stuck slaving with the ants when the grasshoppers were hosting a blowout.

TB: *Did he drink a lot then?*

SJ: Well, listen to you! Who said he ever drank a lot? I'm not talking about drugs and drink, dear, you always get in trouble for doing that, and I am the very soul of discretion. Except when I'm drinking, I suppose, but you've caught me cold stone sober. This isn't exactly a party we're having here.

TB: *Touché, and speaking of parties, you went to the Academy Awards with Malcolm when he won for the first time, didn't you?*

SJ: God, do you remember my dress?

TB: *Tell me about it.*

SJ: Well, everybody wanted to dress me that year, because they all knew I'd be on the red carpet, front and center, and the competition was brutal. Malcolm felt quite overlooked in the brouhaha. Dior was phoning every day—Galliano, you know—and after Dior, then Versace. Both Armani and Marchesa were in the final four, and I desperately didn't want to offend anyone because gowns were my absolute bread-and-butter then, because they wanted younger and younger talent for bathing suits, and makeup ads were going entirely celebrity, which was—and is—infuriating. I wanted to go with something risqué, cut down to here and up to there, and then, well, then Malcolm and I had a terrible fight and I thought the whole thing might turn to ashes and fall apart. I was devastated.

TB: *Did you argue often?*

SJ: Hardly at all. What's the point, but I was so upset. It turned out to be nothing but a particularly ill-timed pregnancy scare. Nerves, you know, and I just wasn't eating enough. And I wound up wearing Versace, and that gown became an international hit. Everyone copied it. You remember? A deep tangerine color, one shoulder, and slit to the top of the thigh?

TB: *Did you ever consider marriage, the two of you?*

SJ: Oh, if I'd gotten pregnant, he'd have married me in a flash. That was the deal. And I tried. I mean, I wasn't opposed to the idea, but nothing ever happened. Beyond that scare. I remember I was angry with him at the time. I figured he'd gotten himself fixed. But then didn't Claire go and prove me wrong?

CHAPTER
forty-five

RE: D'Arcy's Garage
SENT BY: rsnow@dennisportpd.org
SENT ON: April 17
SENT TO: Paul Jericho, Chief of Police

Paul,

Stopped by D'Arcy's, and guess who's working for him? Remember that kid, Gary Blessing, with the scarred face? We used to have him and his dad in regular before you were made Chief. Kid would never talk, even though we figured his old man was beating him pretty bad. D'Arcy hired him five months ago, followed all the rules, ran a CORI on him. Kid's got no police record, but his dad's over in Plymouth, beat up a girlfriend evidently didn't know about the code of silence.

Talked to Gary and he's still real good at keeping his mouth shut. He was there, he had access to the lockup key, and he knew the wreck was in there. There's no tape in the wreck now, and if Gary took it, I'd say there's not much chance we'll find out about it.

I might have him come down the station, see if that makes his tongue any looser, but I'd hate to get him fired over something might not be his fault. D'Arcy says he's a real good mechanic.

Verizon records came in: Nothing out of the ordinary except a call to a legal firm in New York. Followed up and got to talk to Amory Russell, that lawyer guy everybody quotes, but turns out he's a friend of Blake's. I wonder about that tape.

Russell Snow, Detective Grade One
Dennis Port Police Department
One Arrow Point Way
Dennis Port, MA 02639

CHAPTER
forty-six

Fire extinguishers bloomed like scarlet flowers on the kitchen counter at the Big House and in the foyer of the Red House, which was filling rapidly with actors and stagehands, gaining in population nightly. Backstage at the Amphitheater, rows of extinguishers sat next to trunks filled with *Hamlet* props, plastic sacks of stage blood, and baskets of silk flowers. NO SMOKING signs took on a new prominence. Riggers were careful to move at least fifty feet from the stage before lighting up, gathering behind a sheltering dune and hurriedly snuffing out butts when the stage manager approached.

The sun warmed the stone benches in the bowl-shaped auditorium, where I huddled in the spot designated Seat P-17, a forty-eight-dollar ticket in season. Carpenters, riggers, and most stagehands were banned from the Amphitheater today. The actors had come hither, hardly "the best actors in all the world," but a cast of Garrett's choosing. The major stars were not yet present. The younger of the two potential Hamlets had joyfully accepted the role, but was tied up on the set of his TV show till the beginning of next week. Queen Gertrude was finishing the run of an Oscar Wilde in Stratford, Ontario, but Polonius had arrived last night, joining us for a jovial dinner during which he'd prattled on in the same manner as his character, pontificating on wine and food and Shakespeare, doing everything but launching into "To thine own self be true, and it must follow, as the night the day, thou canst not then be false to any man."

Later, in bed, Garrett and I giggled and debated whether the man was still auditioning or had ventured so far inside the school of Method Acting that he couldn't control his Polonius-like tendencies offstage. Garrett seemed splendidly untroubled, undisturbed by Caroline's visit or Snow's interrogation, undeterred by the absence of his Hamlet. With his film background, he assured me, he was used to shooting scenes out of order on a variety of sets, filming all the scenes set in one particular location, then all the scenes in another, sacrificing linear flow for considerations of time and money.

This morning he'd overseen swordfight choreography, critiquing slow-motion thrusts and feints, gradually increasing their speed till the sharp clang of metal blades rang crisply in my ears. Then he'd worked briefly with Fortinbras's army, marching them down the aisles of the bowl. Under his guidance, twelve eager-to-please locals cast flip-flops aside, threw shoulders back, and paraded as though on royal review.

On to Act III, scene 3. *A room in the Castle.* Rosencrantz and Guildenstern, well-cast, neither twins nor brothers, but alike as bookends in height and girth, detailed the plan to escort mad Hamlet safely overseas to England. Puffed with self-importance, Polonius scurried onstage and revealed his intent to hide behind the arras. I'd forgotten how many of *Hamlet's* scenes involved eavesdropping.

I was engaged in that same activity, eavesdropping myself, since Garrett kept a closed set. When I'd mentioned auditing a rehearsal, he'd curtly replied that since he was working, I should also work. And I should have; I agreed. I would have been hard at work, writing, except that my mind was clouded with fire, obsessed with images of fire extinguishers and smoky pictures of burning buildings.

O, my offense is rank, it smells to heaven;
It hath the primal eldest curse upon't,
A brother's murder!

The rhythmic pulse of Shakespeare's verse delivered by a master raked my attention to the stage. Compared to this, Rosencrantz and Guildenstern, even Polonius, had tossed off their lines like waiters relaying orders to the kitchen staff.

What if this cursed hand
Were thicker than itself with brother's blood,
Is there not rain enough in the sweet heavens
To wash it white as snow?

Garrett wasn't filling in for Claudius the same way his PA was filling in for Hamlet, droning speeches to help the lighting tech number his cues. My God, Garrett was going to play Claudius; the role as he'd envisioned it, Claudius the King Slayer, a strong and determined foil for a strong and active Hamlet, was too alluring for the actor to resist. He'd already conceded that he might take on the part of the Ghost. I'd heard him do the Ghost at a table-reading, pitching his voice sepulchrally high. The Perfect Ghost, I'd named him, and we'd laughed because I, too, was a ghost. A matched pair, we could share the spirit role, I as his ghost writer, he as the Ghost of Hamlet's father. Shakespeare himself is said to have played the Ghost.

Burbage to Burton to Branagh, theatrical history is studded with stellar Hamlets. There are fewer renowned Claudiuses, but Claudius is often double-cast as the Ghost since they never appear onstage together and the eerily lit Ghost wears full armor. Garrett Malcolm playing Claudius would generate as much buzz as the TV-star Hamlet. Draw a crowd. And he hadn't told me. Another secret, another fact he'd failed to mention.

The guilt-ridden King dropped to his knees mid-sentence to pray for his blackened soul. The ragtag army, slumped in the first row, ceased their whispering and shuffling. The stage manager sank onto a bench transfixed. Kalver, onstage as Hamlet's stand-in, froze in place and listened, cues and script forgotten.

My words fly up my thoughts remain below:
Words without thoughts never to heaven go.

At the soliloquy's end, the silence grew, expanding like a bubble till one of the soldiers broke it with a flutter of applause. Others took up the cue and a wave of approval and admiration surged from the wings as well as the seats. Garrett Malcolm, actor, briefly reveled in the acclaim, but Garrett Malcolm, director, swiftly regained control and summoned the stage manager.

"Henry, get this down," he said. "And Darren, take notes. Where's the pyro guy? He ought to be here. Tell him I want fire during this speech, small flames at the base of the column first, like a grate, but with a hint of hell, an echo of what we'll see during the Ghost scenes. He can use the flame projector, focus it in tight. I don't want anything gimmicky, no flash powder, no flame pots. I want flickering and slowly growing flames, a projection on the column, but low, as though it were a fireplace. The flames of hell glimmering through the whole damn speech."

He glanced at the house as though searching for the pyro guy, and I willed myself invisible, molded my body to the hard stone bench, so unyielding compared to the velvet seats in Garrett's private screening room. It was the contrast that made me recall what I'd seen so vividly—the contrast, and the talk of fire and flames.

I'd discovered the screening room in the basement during one of my perambulations, a recently renovated space with three rows of six chairs, each so comfortable I'd been afraid I might inadvertently cat-nap. I'd secured Garrett's permission to watch *French Kiss* and *Twisted Silk*, review two of his early acting roles. I wanted to make sure I nailed every detail, dotted every "i"—that's what I'd told him, but you'd have said I was procrastinating, Teddy, snatching at any pretense to delay, indulging my desire to remain enshrined as biographer, guest, and lover.

I'd watched scenes from the two films in quick succession, admiring Garrett's boyish face and agile body. He'd had facility and charm, but little depth. He'd grown heavier as a man, weightier as an actor; the seeds of Claudius might have been planted in the teenager, but they'd been dormant. I'd fed the disc of *Blue Flame*, the first Ben Justice film, into the maw of the machine even though I knew the film by heart.

Onstage, Garrett gestured at the stage manager and lectured the now-present and attentive pyrotechnics expert. They lowered a rail and adjusted a Klieg light. But all I saw were scenes from *Blue Flame*.

Hooded terrorists scaled a wall at a military installation, detonated a blast, burst through a doorway. Face blackened, Ben Justice elbowed his way across an obstacle course. Terrorists broke into the safe room. Justice biked the spindly bridge, legs churning faster than a Tour de France contender. Credits flashed over the opening action montage, and the body of the film began with fire, the first of a series of small-town fires of apparently accidental origin.

The direction was bold and assured and the action flowed seamlessly, the terrorist scenes moving with the clockwork precision of a good caper film. Ben Justice was a measured, nuanced presence. Brooklyn Pierce, young as he was, under Garrett's direction, told us everything we needed to know with a flicker of his eyes. Suspension of disbelief had settled over me like a wooly blanket, descending naturally despite the number of times I'd watched the film. Dramatic scenes rang vivid and true. Comic scenes defused the tension just when it grew too taut to bear.

After the ending, after the final credit and the music, I'd watched the second arson scene again, in slow motion, recalling Sylvie Duchaine's interview, her praise of Garrett's filmmaking skill, his grasp of detail, his expertise in starting fires.

Onstage, Garrett spoke to the pyro expert. "Work closely with sound on this. I want tight coordination. I want the sound strong, but not overpowering. The crackle of flames has to lap at the edges of Claudius's speech. Okay?"

The idea for a new chapter sprang into my brain as I considered his use of fire and conflagration, not just in *Blue Flame*, but in other films, and coupled it with his delight in the pyrotechnic possibilities of this new *Hamlet*. The man reveled in fire, with its antithetical powers of purification and destruction, used it to underline the thematic concerns of his work.

His fascination with fire could have been born during that early fire on the estate, the one the PA had mentioned. Garrett might not want to concentrate on his early years, but early years affect us out of all proportion, no matter what success might follow. I wondered if his cousin James Foley had been living at Cranberry Hill during the fire and, if he had, whether he'd talk about it. I yanked the ever-present three-by-five card out of my back pocket and started making notes, focusing on that early fire, until the memory of McKenna's photograph interfered, blocking my vision, and making me ponder the fire at the clinic instead.

CHAPTER
forty-seven

The Dennis Port Police Station hadn't changed, but it no longer emitted the genial aura of a general store. Its gray-shingled exterior was stern rather than warm under a glowering sky. I mounted the steps with trepidation to be greeted in the lobby by a no-nonsense officer who guided me to a different room than the small office in which I'd previously met with Detective Snow. There I waited, simmering like a kettle on a hot stove.

Aside from the rectangular table, the room was furnished with seven mismatched chairs. Along the outside wall, three casement windows were hung with dusty blinds. Two gray interior walls were completely bare and a third featured a large, unframed mirror and a clock that ticked off eighteen slow minutes before Detective Snow shoved open the door and made a show of apologizing for his lateness. By that time, my hands were damp.

Detective Snow was regaining his health, that was clear. He hadn't gained weight; if anything, he'd grown leaner. But his manner was different, sharper, keener; he was like a hound on the scent. With the return of his vitality he'd become a stronger presence, his most recent phone call a summons rather than a suggestion.

He sat on the opposite side of the coffee-stained conference table. He spoke slowly but firmly. He intended to interview me. Formally. On the record. He touched a button and a tape recorder hummed faintly, the scratchy sound as irritating as a rash. If I hadn't been terrified, I might have appreciated the irony.

"How well did you know Garrett Malcolm before you began writing this book?"

I cleared my throat. "I didn't know him at all. I knew of him, I knew about him, but we'd never met."

Snow said nothing and I said nothing. If this were a Garrett Malcolm film, this was where he'd cut to a room behind the mirror, show the other detectives eating and cursing as they evaluated my reactions.

"And you've been staying at Cranberry Hill for how long?"

"He's very kindly allowing me the use of a guest room until I finish working on the manuscript." I kept my eyes on the wooden veneer of the table.

"Did Malcolm know Blake before they started the book?"

"Not as far as I know. They may have met. I think Mister Malcolm requested T. E. Blakemore."

"By Blakemore, you mean Mister Blake?"

"I meant both of us; we're—we were a team." Now that I'd imagined the mirror as two-way glass, I couldn't get rid of the sensation of being watched, studied like a moth under a microscope.

"But you'd never met Mister Malcolm before." I should never have said "Mister," given Garrett the respectful, distant title. Snow was using it to bait me, emphasizing the word.

"That's what I said."

We regarded each other in wary silence. The recorder whirred, and I imagined its counter ticking off the seconds while I wondered whether the detective had even considered ordering Garrett Malcolm to the station for questioning before making his pilgrimage to Cranberry Hill.

"Where were you the night your—what? teammate, coauthor—died?"

The question caught me off guard: I was prepared to feint and parry concerning my relationship with Garrett. How I wished I could tell Snow I'd been in bed with Garrett Malcolm the night you died, clear both of us in one fell swoop, wipe the suspicion off his narrow face and replace it with a new and different emotion. I wondered whether he'd believe me if I claimed the famous director as my lover.

"I was at home," I said, "in Boston."

"Alone?"

"Yes."

"You didn't see anyone who might vouch for you? A neighbor?"

"No."

Silence. During which I inhaled and exhaled and considered what I'd ask if this were my interview, if Snow were the subject of my next book.

"Is there anything unflattering in this book you're writing, anything Malcolm might object to?"

"No."

"What about your research? Did Blake uncover anything unpleasant? I know he spoke to a man named Glenn McKenna—"

"McKenna approached him, not the other way around."

"With?"

"Gossip, nothing but gossip, as far as I know."

"And what about James Foley?"

"He's Malcolm's cousin."

"They don't get along. So why would Blake want to talk to him?"

"He and Malcolm were close as children. We interview as many sources as possible. It's standard operating procedure."

In the ensuing silence, I consciously relaxed my fingers, knuckle by knuckle, and prepared for the next onslaught

"Did you take care of Blake's car?"

"What do you mean by 'take care of'?"

"Take it in for service, gas it up, drive it?"

"No."

"But you do that for Melody Farragut?"

"Melody? Yes. I take care of her van."

"And why would your roommate contact us and mention your access to her vehicle?"

"She's not my roommate."

"Your neighbor. Why would she call me?"

"Did she?"

"The question is why."

I pictured uniformed men behind the mirror taking notes and muttering as I considered my reply. "Has there been press coverage in Boston? In *The Globe* or *The Herald,* that she might have seen?"

When he said nothing, I summoned a smile. "I would assume jealousy or boredom, a little bit of a desire to be a drama queen."

"Do you happen to recall the odometer reading on her van? From the last time you had it serviced?"

"I hope you're joking."

"When was the last time you used her van?"

"I'm sorry, but I don't remember. Either the mileage or the last time I did the grocery shopping. She might remember, because she's the one who always gives me the key. Did she mention that?"

"How would you characterize your partner's relationship with Garrett Malcolm?"

"I never saw them together."

"Did Blake talk about Malcolm?"

"He talked to him, with him, interviewed him, asked him questions, the way you're asking me questions. I transcribed the tapes and worked from there."

"Would you say they had a cordial relationship?"

"Absolutely. Very warm. Cordial, certainly."

"Thank you."

That was it? Awkwardly, I gathered my belongings, my purse and umbrella, pondering questions he'd left unasked, debating questions I wanted to pose.

"Garrett Malcolm is a wonderful man. He has been incredibly kind to me and I can't imagine him being any less kind to Teddy."

"Thank you," he said again, gravely.

"You didn't find that tape I was looking for?"

"No. I asked around. I thought one of the guys works over at the garage might have seen it, but no."

"Have you ruled out the possibility of an accident?"

"We haven't ruled out anything."

I wanted to demand why McKenna had it in for Garrett Malcolm, ask if the police had suspected, if not charged, anyone in the long-ago clinic fire. But I felt short of breath, winded, as though I'd run a marathon, and for the moment, it was all I could do to get up and leave without taking a parting glance at the mirror.

CHAPTER
forty-eight

That there were detectives lurking behind a two-way mirror was improbable, fanciful, the stuff of films, the stuff of craziness. The constant eavesdropping in *Hamlet* coupled with my guilt at listening in on Garrett's conversations was weighing on my mind, causing a bizarre paranoid delusion which might be related to a panic attack. I shook a Xanax, a small round antidote, into the palm of my hand, but decided to wait till I got home to swallow it.

I was nervous when I left the parking lot, anxious as I drove, shoulders hunched, hands clutching the wheel. I considered pulling over, phoning Melody Downstairs to inquire whether she'd actually called

Detective Snow, but I decided against that as well. We didn't have that kind of relationship, didn't enjoy much of a relationship at all. She was a stuck-at-home, stay-at-home victim while I was a woman temporarily trapped in an inadequate and subpar dwelling. She would always live on Bay State Road, but Bay State Road was a way station, a blip on the radar for me. I hadn't realized how much the apartment cramped my style, how little air permeated its tight walls, how colorless its surroundings were. I was far more at home at Cranberry Hill.

I was at home in my work, so it was work I turned to as a Xanax alternative. At a red light on Route 6A, I grabbed the first tape that came to hand and stuffed it quickly into the recorder on the seat beside me. Casually, I pressed the play button, expecting the sweet velvet of your voice, Teddy. Instead, I found myself confronted by my own. My groping hand had selected the tape of my first, no my second, session with Garrett and my own voice, familiar and yet different, grated harshly, my tone reedy and hollow, my esses sibilant enough to be called a lisp.

I hit the fast-forward button reflexively, then changed my mind and forced myself to listen as the scene swam slowly into focus. I remembered how frightened and eager I'd been, how overwhelmed by the lofty dimensions of the Great Room, with its spectacular painting of Claire Gregory and panoramic bay of windows.

Garrett's taped voice: "Do you mind waiting on the patio? If it's too cold—"

My taped voice replied, "It's fine."

The French doors clicked as I left the Great Room, but the tape kept rolling. Inexperienced, I'd forgotten to stop it. I'd ignored the machine perched on the little side table, and Garrett must have forgotten about it, too.

I heard him lift the receiver and say a smooth hello.

"Yes, delighted to hear from you." His tone said he was anything but delighted. Such a well-trained voice. "No, not yet. Don't trouble yourself about it. I can act without Jenna. Of course I can. Don't be a fool."

After a long pause, the quality of Garrett's voice changed, tightened. "I didn't say I didn't like it, I only asked whether it was his screenplay or yours." Angrily, he bit the end off each word.

The taped silence was punctuated by an occasional grunt, a few muttered noises indicating reluctant agreement. Then Garrett spoke again: "I wouldn't say inspired, I'd say far-fetched and ridiculous. I'd go so far as to call it sci-fi."

My hands gripped the steering wheel during another long stretch of silence. The engine purred and the wheels bumped along the pot-holed roadway.

"Look, this isn't a good time. I've got somebody here, a girl. No, not a tart, and not an actress either; just some homely little dull-as-dirt girl, but I can't get rid of her. Have to humor the damned publisher or I'll wind up with a lawsuit on my plate."

Dead air was followed by laughter, the kind of raucous boys-will-be-boys laughter that set my teeth on edge.

"Hey, cuz, give me a day or two to charm the pants off her first. No, really, I didn't mean it like that. Oh, come on, it wouldn't be worth it. Well, if you're going to issue a direct challenge, I'll add her to the directory. You want her when I'm done?"

Another long pause. Another comment made, no doubt.

"Oh, please, I'm more than willing to share. She's earnest and drab as a pigeon. Yes, Teddy Blake's little girl Friday. Makes you wonder how he managed. Right. Look, we'll hash it out later, talk it over, work something out."

On it went, on it played, a one-sided conversation from hell. I clung to the wheel and Garrett's voice filled the car, squeezing out the air till I could barely breathe. Garrett and the unheard listener on the phone discussed me, dissected me, and stuck their fingers in the bloody ooze of my entrails.

While I, all unaware, had stared eagerly over the smooth and beautiful sea, contemplating from the terrace my new, spring-blossoming career. I was a fool, worse than a fool, ten times a fool.

"Well, don't worry about me," Garrett said. "It'll make a change till the actresses turn up. Yeah, we signed some beauties. Fast and easy."

Hamlet plays the fool, but it's a feigned madness, north-northwest: when the wind is southerly, he can tell a hawk from a handsaw. Hamlet only feigns insanity; ironically, it is Ophelia who truly runs mad.

I scrabbled at the recorder with clumsy fingers, snapped it off. But I couldn't help it, couldn't help myself. As I pulled into the estate, neared the soaring roof of the Old Barn and turned into the broad driveway of the Big House, I pressed rewind. And listened again, each word a fatal hammer blow resounding in my skull.

I swallowed one Xanax; then another, to no effect. The words stayed etched by acid in the circuitry of my brain. A shiver shook my body, and no wonder: The engine ran, but I hadn't turned on the heater and I had no idea what time it was, how long I'd sat motionless as a stone. My toes ached with cold. I stared through the windshield and recalled the invisible glass tunnel I'd constructed on my purposeful stroll down Fifth Avenue so long ago. I felt hemmed by the same tunnel now, a wall of glass that shut me out, exiled me forever.

The Prince of Denmark only pretends, pretends ignorance, pretends to turn a blind eye to the ghostly apparition of his poisoned father, pretends he doesn't know his stepfather murdered the sleeping king, his mother betrayed his father. But I'd believed Garrett implicitly, believed in the promise of his bed.

I sat in the car and replayed the tape again. I patted my eyes with a tissue, tried to pull myself together.

"'. . . whether it was his screenplay or yours.'"

There was a pile of screenplays on the corner of Garret's desk. The corner of Mister Malcolm's desk. A little snooping might be in order.

Hamlet snoops: He overhears; he lays traps; he pries. And what is it he says?

Act One, scene 2. *A room in the Castle*, the end of the first major soliloquy: "But break, my heart; for I must hold my tongue."

CHAPTER
forty-nine

The Black Stone
The Fourth Ben Justice Film
Treatment by Brooklyn Pierce

It's 1995. During the filming of a taut action thriller set in and around Cape Cod, on the Massachusetts coast, MARKHAM, the film's director, and CLAUDIA, star of the movie, also husband and wife, argue between scenes.

CLAUDIA flirts with her young and inexperienced costar BRADLEY. MARKHAM objects to her behavior during the twosome's steamy love scenes and tries in vain to tone them down. CLAUDIA seems to enjoy taunting her older husband.

BRADLEY, after rehearsal, comes across the distraught CLAUDIA, in a cove off a secluded beach. She confesses that all is not right with her marriage, that she believes her marital problems could be cured by bearing a child. CLAUDIA and BRADLEY start by rehearsing one of their movie scenes, but end up making love.

CLAUDIA, serenely pregnant, is gruffly congratulated by her father-in-law, the famous and wealthy RAYMOND MARKHAM, who lectures her on the importance of having a large family with many male heirs, so that the family's eminence and property will stay secure.

RAYMOND and MARKHAM argue over the older man's will, the younger man insisting that the older man's obstinacy could leave the estate to his cousin JEREMY.

It wasn't *Hamlet* or *Macbeth,* not even a minor or disputed work, a *Love's Labor's Lost.* Hurriedly I scanned the six-page document, reading Malcolm for Markham, substituting Claire for Claudia, just as Pierce would have intended the reader to do. It wasn't *Lear,* but like *Lear,* it concerned wills and inheritance and the stubborn pride of old men. Unlike Shakespeare's plays, it wasn't written with performance in mind. Other than his presence in the subtitle, Ben Justice didn't participate, didn't enter a single scene. The treatment, as written, was nothing more than a thinly veiled attempt at blackmail.

Possibly true; possibly untrue. Facts are like beads. They are what they are, elemental, hard, and unchanging, but they can be strung in a variety of configurations, by any number of hands, linked by thin chain, knotted silk, twisted rope. This sequenced chain was long and circumstantial. I sat at Malcolm's desk in the Great Room, a single beam from my flashlight illuminating the manuscript, and told the accumulated beads like a rosary:

—At the still center of the photograph-covered wall of the small office, in the place of honor, hung a framed family tree, the genealogical chart of the Malcolm dynasty.

—Garrett Malcolm was an only child.

—Malcolm's cousin James Foley, reminiscing about their shared boyhood, mentioned that the two boys were so close they caught each other's diseases. "Mumps. I got a mild case, but he didn't get them at all, not till way later, and then he got them bad."

—Malcolm's father, Ralph, proud of his lineage, eager for grandchildren, delighted in Jenna and proclaimed that the "line was extended" when he recognized her acting talent.

—Malcolm fought the divorce from Claire and then suddenly, overnight, gave up and relinquished his demand for custody of Jenna.

—Malcolm, even when suspected of a hideous crime, refused to give local authorities a DNA sample.

McKenna had given me the photo: Malcolm and Claire, in '93, '94, or '95, according to his Web site notation, a legitimately married couple with apparently nothing to hide, disguised as they headed for the clinic door—he in a trench coat, she in a wig. Had they made an appointment to find out why she hadn't gotten pregnant yet? Discovered what I thought they'd discovered, that Malcolm, who'd been shattered when Sybilla Jackson's pregnancy scare proved only a scare, that Malcolm, who'd never inquired whether or not I used birth control, that Malcolm, illustrious heir to acting royalty, had no hope of fathering a child?

The clinic's records were destroyed. No one had been arrested or charged for the clinic fire. Claire Gregory was dead, ashes scattered to the wind off the California coast. The only sure proof would be DNA, the DNA Malcolm so jealously guarded, his own DNA and Jenna's. And Jenna was conveniently kept far from home; she'd been out of the country for years.

What if Jenna were not Malcolm's child, not the heralded HMB, the Heir of my Body, the heiress of Cranberry Hill? If you'd discovered that, Teddy, what might you have done with the information? More to the point, who would you have told? If not me?

Not McKenna. If McKenna had known, the world would have known. He'd have plastered it all over his gossip site. He'd have sold it to Gawker, to any site that would post it. He'd be pontificating on celebrity immorality via cable TV and talk radio.

I gathered the pages, straightened their edges, and replaced them on the desktop. Then, my hands under my chin, I blew out a long breath that warmed my chilled fingers. If I'd been onstage, it might have looked like I was praying.

CHAPTER
fifty

Y ou seem preoccupied this morning."
      The pink and gold wallpaper faded to gray, like an empty
sky after the last vanishing trace of sunset. Malcolm shifted beneath
the comforter and yanked at the back of my right knee so that my leg
came to rest against his hardening penis.

"Is it the book? Because we can cancel the whole deal. I really don't
care, one way or the other."

"I do." I wrestled with the top edge of the sheet, trying to slip it out
from under my back so I could sit up.

"Come on, relax."

He kneaded my spine with one hand, cupped my rump in the other and roughly hauled me on top to straddle him. I participated in the action, but with markedly less enthusiasm than previously displayed. I'm not sure he noticed, one way or the other.

I was brushing the tangles out of my hair when the phone rang. He picked it up eagerly, then grimaced and held it out to me.

"Who is it?"

"I'm not your secretary."

"The police?"

"It's your editor, dammit. Are you going to take it?"

I couldn't very well refuse since he hadn't bothered to cover the mouthpiece. There was a time to hold my tongue, yes, but also a time to speak. I reached out my hand, grasped the phone, and willed cheerfulness into my voice.

"Jonathan, how lovely to hear from you. No, no, I did mean to call," I said. "Yes, I did call him. Right away. And I'm so sorry, but you must have misunderstood. Amory Russell is definitely not planning any kind of memoir. Yes, Teddy did call him, but with a legal question, that's all. They were old friends. Nothing important. No. Absolutely. Yes, I'm sorry, too. It would have been a terrific project. No, we'll never know. Yes, I'm almost done, just the finishing touches now."

As I hung up, Malcolm said, "What was that about, pet?"

How I used to relish his casual endearments, the way he called me "pet," "angel," "darling." Now I could only imagine he'd forgotten my name. I watched as he buttoned one of his crisp blue Turnbull & Asser shirts. "Nothing. Will you be busy all day?"

"And all night, too. Don't pout. The lighting designer's an ass, so I don't know when or if I'll get back. We might wind up eating sandwiches on stage."

We, I thought. Meaning he and which of the wanton actresses? Which new addition to the directory? Ophelia, perhaps? An eager extra? A serving wench?

"Well, don't worry about me; I've got plenty to do," I said. "Tell me, do you remember the fire?"

"What are you babbling about? What fire?"

"The fire here on the estate. When you were a kid."

"Vaguely. Lots of fuss."

"Did they ever find out what caused it?"

"I have no idea."

"Your cousin, James, he wouldn't know, would he?"

"Listen, I have no idea what you're talking about. I've got other things on my mind."

I smiled. "Of course you do. Sorry. So is it okay if I work in the Great Room today? Or the little office? Since you won't be here?"

"You are hereby granted the freedom of the castle."

"My lord." I bent my knee in an awkward curtsey. "And it's okay if I scan your photo wall?"

"As long as you know I'm not sticking a bunch of photos in my book."

I didn't flinch when he said "my book," but as soon as he'd dressed and gone, I did likewise and hurriedly made my way downstairs into the room with the mechanized shades, more interested in the old-fashioned leather-bound calendar on his desk than the photos of his triumphs. I traced the list of dates marked "Teddy" or simply "T." A blank square marked the date of your death. No alibi. I took stock of the bottles of booze on the bookshelf.

Seated at Malcolm's writing table in the Great Room, I reviewed pages, editing in a blaze of concentrated energy, ignoring the PA when he inquired if I wanted food, ignoring even the bleat of my cell phone. My string of beads was practically completed. If I could have discovered exactly which beads Detective Snow possessed without answering any more of his questions or trading any of my beads for his, I might have returned his calls.

When I finally typed THE END and lifted my head, the light was almost gone from the sky. Ignoring the gaudy sunset, I appropriated a dark green binder, arranged and inserted pages, closed the metal clasps, and inserted the manuscript carefully into the pile of screenplays on the corner of Malcolm's desk where it blended into its surroundings, fell into place like the missing piece of a jigsaw.

A time to hold my tongue, a time to speak, and a time to act.

Hamlet, Act III, scene 2.

'Tis now the very witching time of night,
When churchyards yawn and hell itself breathes out
Contagion to this world: now could I drink hot blood,
And do such bitter business as the day
Would quake to look on.

CHAPTER
fifty-one

Ghosts are silent; ghosts are quick. I stole lightly across the undulating hills, a flashlight my guide over choppy clumps of crabgrass and sandy turf. The gravel parking lot slowed my stride to cautious tiptoed steps. In the vast and deserted Old Barn, I borrowed a floppy hat and a trench coat from the costume rack, spent time trying on wigs, rejecting the dark blunt-cut Claire had worn for her clinic appointment, choosing soft blond locks instead. Appearance duly altered, I set out across the hills. Because the shoreline approach would definitely be under surveillance now, with McKenna alerted recently and anonymously, via his gossip Web site, to the likelihood that Brooklyn Pierce was staying at the beach shack.

Fact: Claire and Pierce costarred in *Red Shot*, and Claire must have gotten pregnant during the shoot. I matched the rhythm of my thoughts to my steps. Fact: Malcolm never worked with Brooklyn Pierce again. Fact: The successful Ben Justice franchise came to a screeching halt at the apex of its popularity. Fact: When Pierce drank and had nowhere else to go, Malcolm took him in, gave him shelter. Pierce might or might not have a sexual thing going with James Foley. It wouldn't rule Pierce out as Jenna's father; his affairs with assorted actresses and models were notorious.

The wind swept the dunes and rustled through the beach grass, murmuring my name. A slender fingernail of moon ducked behind the fleeting clouds, then reappeared, silvering the waves.

The descent from the high dunes to the beach was precarious in the darkness. Flashlight extinguished, muscles tensed, wary of falling, I wound up crawling backward down the slope, twining my hands into the tall beach grass. The sand, when I finally reached it, felt gritty and cool. I felt my way up the steps with little difficulty. The trivial lock would have been no challenge, but I chose not to tamper with it. I knocked instead, waited, then knocked louder. Malcolm had assured me Pierce had moved on, but I took that for what it was worth.

" *'Doubt truth to be a liar.'* " He'd quoted Hamlet's love poem and stared into my eyes. *"But never doubt I love."*

"My lord, I have remembrances of yours,
That I have long longed to redeliver."

So speaks Ophelia. Act Three, scene 1.

But Hamlet denies her. *"I never gave you aught."*

"What? Huh? Who is it?" A lamp flared in the window.

In the doorway, sheltered from wind and cameras, I peeled off the blond wig and stowed it in my bag. Knocked again, louder.

Feet lurched unevenly to the door and hands cracked it open. Brooklyn Pierce blinked red-veined eyes and expelled foul breath into the salty air. I'd prepared a tale about returning the missing tape, asking more questions.

"Hey, great, Jamie send you over? What's your name, baby? Hey, c'mon in and have a drink."

"Hey." I didn't need a tale because the movie star, reeling drunk, supplied his own backstory. Because he didn't recognize me, and why on earth had I expected that he would? I ducked my head so he wouldn't see the angry flush rise in my cheeks.

"C'mon in, honey. Jamie's the man, a fuckin' prince." His words were slurred. He leered at me, hands poised to grab, but then he halted abruptly, perhaps questioning my mousy, wig-mashed hair, lack of bosom, and blotchy, flushed face.

"What the fuck's Jamie playing at?" he muttered.

He was no treat, either. I'd admired his naked body when he ran into the waves, but that was a long-distance, panning shot. In close-up, it was hard to believe this drunken wreck had ever been a movie star.

"I don't know anything about Jamie," I said. "They sent me down from the Big House. To clean up." The pungent stink of vomit hung in the air, and the role of maid suited me better than interviewer or author. Maid became me better than lover, fiancée, or hooker hired by a pal for an hour's entertainment. If I hadn't been the victim of temporary blindness, a kind of self-regarding insanity, I'd have appreciated my true worth sooner. I stepped briskly through the portal.

"Clean up? This late?" He rubbed his red eyes, sniffed, and shook his head like a weary dog.

"If that's okay?"

Puzzled, he retreated before my energetic onslaught. "What the hell kinda hours you work?"

I shrugged as I flipped on the overhead light. "Sorry if I'm bothering you. I can come back some other time."

Blinking, he gazed at the disordered room, sink mounded in filthy dishes, floor littered with greasy take-out wrappers. After the fresh air he'd inhaled at the door, the indoor fug would be newly offensive.

He ran a hand through his hair and yawned. "I suppose it's okay. Long as you don't use any damned machines, nothing makes a damned noise. You got a mop? I think there's one in the closet. A couple things might've got busted." He leaned against a wall, yawned again, then slumped into a chair.

Since I was the maid, he didn't comment when I donned plastic gloves. I doubt he noticed them as I diligently emptied the ashtrays and swept the wooden floorboards, leaving his empty bottles in situ, adding my own touches as I progressed, setting the stage, dressing the set. As I placed the lighter from Malcolm's desk drawer next to Pierce's packet of Camels, I could almost see the movie and hear the tape recording in my head, Teddy, and the two combined to form an instructional video. I could hear your patient voice and Sylvie Duchaine's accented, enthusiastic response:

TB: *Remember the arson sequence in* Blue Flame?

SD: . . . he'd had such fun learning about fire that he thought the audience would like an education, a break in the middle of a tight action film for a little schooling on arson methods. He totally obsessed about the fire-starters, the alarm clocks the terrorists rigged to delay ignition. I used a few quick cuts, close-ups, the wooden floorboards, the damaged propane tank, the flaring lighter. He played with the sound, too, the long hiss of the escaping gas, the striking of the lighter.

If Pierce hadn't been so drunk, I might have inquired about you, for curiosity's sake. Asked if you'd known his favorite liquor, encouraged his confidences with a bottle or two, bribing an alcoholic with his poison of choice. You were such a naughty boy, Teddy.

I'd taken a bottle from the shelf in Malcolm's office, Johnny Walker Black, expensive stuff, but I hadn't found anything cheaper. By now, Pierce was snoring and that became the soundtrack as I pried open the Scotch and splashed a few shots across the floorboards. I refilled the actor's half-empty glass, added crushed Xanax, and placed it near his outstretched hand, so he wouldn't need to move if he woke and wanted refreshment. I downed a shot of my own, unadulterated, for courage. The alarm clock came from the office, too, the wire from a shelf in the Old Barn, the fuse cord from the backstage pyrotechnic box. As the warmth of the liquor hit my gut, I carefully unwound the cord. There was enough to easily reach the propane tank and the old grill stored under the shack. I used the movie star's own cell phone to text McKenna at the number he'd given me in case of emergency, twenty-four/seven.

The Ghost made her preparations, fully awake, alive, and yet in a kind of trance, almost a dream state. The sequence of events seemed predetermined, inevitable, done, the metal jaws of the trap already snapped shut. I had thought the waiting time would be the hardest, but it wasn't because I knew he would come. One of my stepfathers, a stern and bitter man, made me watch while he baited mousetraps with treats, peanut butter, cheese, and chewing gum, made me watch while the mice came to the traps. He called it an experiment, but I saw his eyes when the traps did their job, and they were shining.

When McKenna came, we sat on the moonlit steps and I filled his ears till his eyes shone as well, till they glittered. Filled his ears with tittle-tattle that he accepted uncritically, every dubious morsel lapped up as eagerly as a dog laps blood. I filled his ears with gossip and his mouth with whiskey, and I kept one eye on my watch. He didn't seem to notice the bitterness of the drink, and the Ghost thought only of fire. Fire, the cleanser; fire, the eraser; fire, the god, and it seemed good, the anticipated unleashing of inferno. By the time McKenna, at the Ghost's urging, at *my* urging, climbed the stairs, his steps were heavy and his eyes half-closed.

They were sleeping fitfully, snoring in their chairs, mouths agape, when I left a few minutes later.

Malcolm was sleeping, too, later that night when the fire broke out.

CHAPTER
fifty-two

Tape 128
Brooklyn Pierce
April 4, 2010

Teddy Blake: *Go on, Brook. Hey, don't fall asleep on me, buddy. You were telling me a story.*

Brooklyn Pierce: Yeah, right, a story. But come on, don't you think I'd have done a good one? One for the ages? Like Burton and Branagh?

TB: *No hope of Hamlet, huh?*

BP: No hope. Pour me another one, okay? A stiff one. I'm gonna quit tomorrow. Cold turkey, I swear, that's the only way to go.

TB: *And nothing doing with a Ben Justice revival?*

BP: I told you the damned story, what he sees when he looks at me. Didn't I already tell you? Talk, talk, talk, talk, talk.

TB: *But that's all there is? Christ, then he doesn't know. You said you don't even know whether—*

BP: Not for sure and, hey, I don't wanna know. Jamie's the one wants to make trouble, test everybody's DNA, but what the hell? I don't want screen credit, you know what I mean? Christ, I shouldn't let Jamie talk me into this kinda shit. Is your glass empty? Fill it up. C'mon, I'm not drinking alone.

TB: *You're just an agreeable guy.*

BP: Right, that's me, whatever, I roll with it.

TB: *But you did do it, you and Claire?*

BP: Hey, man, I rolled with it. I mean, we coulda done the turkey-baster thing, but we figured we're grown-ups and Mal's puttin' it to her, too. I mean, they didn't quit screwing, so Jenna could be his kid, for all I know. It's not like docs are never wrong.

TB: *And with the screenplay, you weren't worried about the legality, about the police?*

BP: I let Jamie do the worrying. And he said first off, Mal would never call the cops on us. Hell, call the cops, he might as well call *People* magazine—

TB: *But when did you tell Jamie? If he'd known when the old man was alive—*

BP: Christ, I don't remember, musta been pretty recent. This visit. I don't remember telling him, honest, but I must've, huh? I oughta lay off this stuff, quit it cold. Anyhow, what was I saying? Yeah, yeah, second thing: We can't get in legal trouble 'cause none of it's fuckin' true. I mean, hey, it's a screenplay, piece of fiction, made-up shit. Right? Claire didn't come on to me like that, like in what we wrote. Asked me, as a friend, as a favor. Christ, I musta been pissed.

TB: *Drunk?*

BP: Pissed off, angry, and hell, drinking again, too. Telling Jamie. I mean, I didn't think screwing Claire would fuck up my life, you know? I was so young, and she was so damn beautiful. I guess I wasn't thinking at all much, but I figured we'd still work together, Malcolm and me, but it was like, after that, every time he looked at me, you know, he musta sensed it. He's lookin' at me, but he's seeing a man who fucked his wife and I blame Claire, which is shitty 'cause she's gone. But she had no business telling, threatening him when she left. Mal was always gonna get screen credit for Jenna. That was the deal.

BP: *And the property passed to her.*

TB: But that's got nothing to do with it, never did. No, really, Mal loves her, and I barely know her. I mean, I went to parties with her when she was on the Coast. Jamie wanted me to come on to her, marry

297

her, you know? Get the land back for him. That was a little too weird for me, I'm telling you. Plus, she was practically jailbait and when Mal found out she dated me, he damn near threw her out of the country.

TB: *So she doesn't know?*

BP: Jamie says Mal owes him for what old Ralph did, cutting him out of the will 'cause he caught him one time with a boy, and for what Mal did, passing Jenna off as his own, said it was some kinda fraud. That's what Jamie says, and he's my friend. Mal shoulda given Jamie a big chunk of land, bought him off a long time ago. Jamie's always after him, picking and picking. You know how Malcolm wants to fix it so nobody can ever build?

TB: *Lower his taxes, right?*

BP: Jamie's about given up with Mal, but Jenna might listen. Jamie wants Mal to quit what he's doing with that conservation shit, 'cause if he does that, Jamie will never be able to talk Jenna into giving him a hunk of land, or even selling it cheap. Mal's a fucking artist, busy playing with his doll-actors. He's not an adult, he's still a fucking child-genius-director, too busy doing holy theater, too damned holy to cast a movie star as Hamlet.

TB: *Has Jamie ever canceled a board meeting?*

BP: He does a great Mal imitation. And Jamie's got this local guy, writes a gossip blog or something. Jamie plants shit with him alla time, keeps the townies fired up against the theater. Stall, stall, stall.

TB: *Right. And then you handed him the keys to the kingdom.*

BP: Mal hasn't exactly helped my career, you know what I mean? Everybody figures there's a reason he won't work with me, like I'm unreliable or something. And I wasn't, not back then. Shit, I was somebody. I was box office gold. God, if he'd just give it to me, I know I could do it. Goddamn, but I want that part.

TB: *"They all want to play Hamlet."*

BP: Don't go making fun of me.

TB: *No, I wasn't. I wouldn't.*

BP: He won't give it to me. Christ, I shouldn't be talking to you. I screw everything up, don't I? Sometimes I wish I was fuckin' dead, wish I had the guts to swim out into the ocean, just swim out till I can't move my arms anymore, just let go and drown. "'Tis a consummation devoutly to be wished." See? I could do it; I know I could.

TB: *You'd be great.*

BP: Don't fuckin' make fun of me. What the hell do you want anyway? I shouldn't be talking to you, either. I yak it up when I drink. Am I talking too much?

TB: *So there's nothing to that thing about Mal setting the clinic on fire?*

BP: Hell, no, just Jamie's idea of a good climax for the screenplay, see? You're not taping anymore, right? Hey, is that bottle empty?

TB: *No, no. Here you go.*

BP: And why shouldn't I help Jamie out? Jamie's gonna get land for his hotel now, get this place, too, so maybe he'll be satisfied, but I don't care. Fill my glass up, okay?

TB: *Don't tell me you're not going to get anything out of the deal?*

BP: Money is all. I'm gonna get some money, Jamie says, but I don't care. Because that's not what I want.

TB: *What do you want, Brook?*

BP: Besides another drink? Hell, I want to be seventeen again. I want to play Ben Justice again. I want to play Hamlet. And don't you even say it. You know what? I don't like your fucking attitude. I'm changing my mind about this, okay? This isn't something I ought to be doing. I want that tape. C'mon, give it to me.

TB: *Hey, you can trust me. You know you can trust me. This is all off the record.*

PB: You promise? You fucking promise?

TB: *Cross my heart.*

CHAPTER
fifty-three

Sound engineer: I'll give you a ten-count. Remember to look directly at Camera Three. Okay, we're going live: ten, nine, eight, seven, six, five . . .

Music up and Voiceover: *And now, welcome back to the Angela Rivers Show.*

Angela Rivers: *I'd like to welcome our next guest, Em Moore, the woman behind* The Blue Flame: Garrett Malcolm and the American

Cinema. *C'mon, people, put your hands together and clap. Em—can I call you Em? Your book couldn't be more timely. I understand the publisher pushed up the publication date, rushed it into print. You were actually finishing up the book the night the beach shack burned? Have we got a visual on that? Yes, this was taken the next morning after the fire, filmed by a news photographer from a boat off the Cape Cod coast.*

Em Moore: The ruins were still smoldering. Even though it was so close to the water, there was nothing anyone could do.

AR: *The shack actually exploded.*

EM: At first, I thought it was a beach fire, a campfire on the beach that had gotten out of control. But it was too big and it kept growing. The sky turned red. It was like an early sunrise, but it was much too early for the sun. I called 911.

AR: *And you ran down to the shack in time to see Malcolm try to break in.*

EM: The structure was engulfed in flames. He was incredibly brave.

AR: *Did you realize anyone was inside?*

EM: He did. He knew Brooklyn Pierce was staying there.

AR: *You're seeing film of the floral tributes left on the gate of Brooklyn Pierce's apartment building in L.A. Police had to erect a barrier to keep fans at a distance.*

EM: The outpouring of grief has been amazing.

AR: *Yes, it has. And no one else had any idea Pierce was staying on the Cape? Besides Garrett Malcolm?*

EM:. Well, Glenn McKenna, the gossip columnist, must have known.

AR: *That's the man who ran the Cape Cod Truthtelling Web site. His was the second body found at the shack. Hold on, I think we've got a few visuals from the Web site. Joey, can you run those, please? The site was taken down by law enforcement personnel shortly after McKenna's death.*

EM: Yes.

AR: *So were you surprised when Malcolm was arrested? Shocked?*

EM: I'm sure the police will find they've made a mistake. The case against him is entirely circumstantial.

AR: *He took out a restraining order against McKenna.*

EM: Yes, but that's hardly—

AR: *And the method the arsonist used, wasn't it exactly the method detailed in Malcolm's film,* Blue Flame?

EM: Millions of people world-wide have seen that film. Glenn McKenna could certainly have seen the film.

AR: *So you're making the case for murder-suicide, that McKenna set off his own funeral pyre? And decided to take Brooklyn Pierce along for the ride?*

EM: I didn't say that.

AR: *Didn't the police find a screenplay Brooklyn Pierce had written? Isn't it true that the screenplay gives a motive for the crime?*

EM: If it did, wouldn't Malcolm have destroyed it?

AR: *There's been a lot of speculation about what's in that screenplay.*

EM: It's a Ben Justice script, I know that. Titled *The Black Stone.*

AR: *You've seen it then?*

EM: A short excerpt. Of an earlier version.

AR: *Brooklyn Pierce had never written a screenplay. His agent says he didn't know anything about a screenplay.*

EM: Pierce had every reason to want to play Ben Justice again. It was his most successful role. Maybe he thought he understood the character better than anyone, that he had an inside track with the director. A lot of actors turn to screenwriting as they get older. Look at Garrett Malcolm.

AR: *You must have heard the rumors? That Pierce wasn't so much submitting the script to Cranberry Hill Productions as he was giving Malcolm the chance to pay him not to show it to anyone else? TMZ and several other sites have speculated that the manuscript outlines a story in which a man, a movie star, comes forward to the media with evidence that he is the biological father of another man's child. That the other man is a successful director with one daughter . . .*

EM: There are always rumors.

AR: *One site says that characters in the film are identified only by initials, that the woman who has the affair with the actor while married to the director is identified as CG. Garrett Malcolm was married to Claire Gregory.*

EM: I don't think that's true, and even if it is, they're just initials.

AR: *But isn't it true there's a lot at stake here? A considerable amount of property was deeded to Malcolm's daughter on the assumption that she was his biological heir.*

EM: There will be a trial. I don't think it's fair to assume—

AR: *But if Malcolm refused to pay, and Pierce was actually meeting with a man who ran a celebrity gossip site? Don't you think the fire was just a bit too convenient?*

EM: Garrett Malcolm was very kind to me during the time I was writing *Blue Flame*. I hope this terrible event doesn't cloud the way people remember him as an artist. I'm sure that in the long run he'll be found innocent.

AR: *And meanwhile, your book has found a very receptive audience, here and overseas, and I understand there's an incredible amount of interest in Hollywood. Are you going to write the screenplay?*

EM: Angela, I really haven't thought about it. I don't have any experience writing for the screen.

CHAPTER
fifty-four

Y ou would have been proud of me, Teddy.

Everyone applauded. Jonathan beamed and patted my arm. Marcy showered me with air kisses and asked how it felt to be a celebrity. There was champagne in the green room, and by the time I left, I had a bit of a buzz on. I know you always longed to do *The Angela Rivers Show,* but she didn't ask about you, Teddy, didn't so much as mention your name. It was as though you'd never existed.

Marcy's driver dropped me at Penn Station. The train was running twenty-seven minutes late, so I settled into a metal chair in the waiting area. A long-faced woman in the next row of seats hauled her laptop out of her luggage and set to work with a sigh. A man complained about Amtrak, always late, always crowded, at megaphone volume via cell phone. A teenage boy, slim in frayed jeans and gray hoodie, slouched by. He reminded me of the mechanic with the scarred face who worked at the Dennis garage.

How much?

That's all he said. Before I even got the question out of my mouth. *Did you happen to find—?*

Underweight and pimply, he made a cup of his outstretched hand. He couldn't have been more than seventeen. There was a line of grease under his ragged fingernails. His other hand rested too casually in his pocket and we both knew what we were talking about, and we both knew we weren't going to bargain now or talk later.

I never took it, he said. *Understand? I never went in there.*

Facts are like beads, Teddy, precious and rare gems.

I handled the televised interview like a pro. I let Angela Rivers make the case against Malcolm, Teddy, and is it any stranger than the truth? I mean, let's look at the truth, the bald and naked truth.

The loudspeaker interrupted my thoughts: The Boston-bound train was ready to board on track 2B. I slipped on my new leather jacket and headed for the escalator. A man ran the wheel of his suitcase across the toe of my high-heeled pump. It didn't hurt, but it left a scuff mark, and I glared at him as I settled into a seat in the quiet car.

Let's examine the truth, Teddy, but first let's evaluate your source: a drunken actor down on his luck, rejected for the role of his dreams, a self-confessed party, along with a passed-over, hate-filled cousin, to blackmail. Did you believe his story? *In vino veritas*, you might have reckoned, but I don't think you cared one way or the other. It was a tale that would sell, and it might have been true.

As for proof, when I searched the Big House for Pierce's screenplay, I failed to find it. I was forced to replace it with my own treatment, based on my own excellent, if speculative, research. As for proof, the missing tape, number 128, is gone forever, drowned by a Ghost in the ocean near the beach shack. No transcription was made; no copy exists. My memory alone holds it, so does it really matter what's true and what's not true, concerning Claire and Malcolm? Pierce and Foley? Jenna?

I doubt Foley will race to his cousin's rescue. Not when he has so much to gain by keeping silent.

Let's look at the truth that matters, Teddy, the underlying truth: How you underestimated and devalued me. How you used me and dismissed me, how you buttoned my soul into a plain brown wrapper and discarded it in the trash. How I accepted your rejection of me as a woman, your indifference, and your cruel disregard. And then let's look at how you dismissed me twice over. It was wrong, Teddy, wrong to disrespect and belittle me as a colleague, too, to devalue the one thing I had left, my work, to think you could toss my life, my hard-won valuable life, out the window like some used and crumpled tissue.

You didn't have the balls to jettison me face to face. A phone call, Teddy, a piddling phone call: You were returning the advance to Jonathan with your regrets, sending a check for a hundred and eighty thousand, the full amount, and I could reimburse you for my share. Didn't I know there was a clause that said you could opt out of the partnership whenever you wanted? Sorry and all, but Caroline was divorcing you, and you needed time to sort things out.

Did you think I'd sympathize?

I borrowed Melody's van instead. I was parked in the road near the rental house, with the lights out, pondering the next act, choosing the words I could best employ to convince you to change your mind when you came out and got in the Explorer. I followed you to the graveyard when you made your midnight pilgrimage to Ralph Malcolm's grave. You were surprised to see me, but you stubbornly refused to change your mind. You didn't owe me anything, not even an explanation. If I wanted to sue you, fine. You'd describe me to the press as a "jilted lover," "your assistant," "a typist."

You stayed in the graveyard, poking your stupid flashlight at the stones of the dead while I stumbled blindly downhill toward Melody's van, and as I skidded on the steep, gravel walkway my hand tightened on the file in my purse. I could never have used it, my bastard file, on your soft flesh, not then, even though you were ten times, twenty times a bastard. But when my knees gave out near your car, when I fell near the wheels of your Explorer and they were turned to counter the steep incline, exposing the tender brake line, something happened.

Something snapped. And I'm sorry, Teddy, I'm so sorry.

It wasn't me, Teddy. It wasn't me. Oh, Teddy, believe me. It must have been the ghost who did it, jabbed the slender line with the tool at hand. Jabbed it in anger, Teddy, struck out in rage. I believed you'd buckle your seat belt. I had a vision of myself in white, a forgiving, ministering angel who'd nurse you back to strength and health. You would have fallen in love with me all over again. We would have finished this book together, started in fresh on the next, made another baby to make up for the one we lost.

The ghost says it never happened, but in my mind's eye, it's palpable, real, the cold cubicle and the blue-patterned wallpaper, and I clutch the thin blanket and hear the noise again, the whirring gulp the machine made as the blue-garbed strangers with shielded faces made it go away, the growing thing that had stopped growing, as if it sensed your lack of love. You should have loved me, Teddy, not blamed me. You should never have named my disaster your good luck. I would have cared for her. I would have loved her. I would never have let her pass into the hands of strangers who might neglect and abuse her.

Teddy, you should have loved me, not died and left me to blunder into a full-blown, five-act drama, blind as an ingénue who knows only her own twelve lines, never having read the whole play. I see it now: Caroline was divorcing you, or so you thought, and to hell with any academic ideals. Better to ferret out gossip, go for the cash, seek the highest bidder. I actually thought you'd asked your old friend Amory Russell's legal opinion of Ralph Malcolm's will. I'd forgotten his son was Evan, *that* Evan, the multimedia gossip king.

He must have offered you more than Henniman's could: first serial rights and foreign rights, fistfuls of silver, buckets of lira and pesos, for the unauthorized bio of Garrett Malcolm, the one that spilled the juicy secrets. But what about me, Teddy? Me? Your student, your lover, your clever chameleon? *Who is not and will not be Ophelia, doomed to drown in the weedy river.*

Let the truth drown instead.

"Excuse me?"

"Yes?"

"Sorry, but didn't I just see you on *Angela Rivers*?" The man who'd run his luggage wheels over my toe was standing in the aisle, swaying with the motion of the train. "You were terrific."

I murmured a thank-you, but he kept on talking.

"Are you planning to do any Boston media? I'm asking because I work for a radio station, a small one, FM. You probably wouldn't want to—"

People in the surrounding rows were looking at us with arched and disapproving eyebrows.

"Sorry," I said, raising a finger to my lips. It was the quiet car, after all. I shook my head and the man subsided into his seat.

Hamlet, Act Five, scene 2.

The rest is silence.